PERENNIAL

PERENNIAL

RYAN POTTER

SKYSCAPE

Published by Skyscape, Seattle

www.apub.com

Amazon, the Amazon logo, and Skyscape are trademarks of Amazon.com, Inc., or its affiliates.

ISBN-13: 9781477818183
ISBN-10: 1477818189

Library of Congress Control Number: 2013919371

Printed in the United States of America

PROLOGUE

Dream Guy

He first appears late at night in a dream. Except "appears" is the wrong word. In the beginning there is no physical presence. That takes time. That takes trust. It's simply a feeling, innocent and unlike anything I've ever felt before, an awareness of a male presence my age.

Soft and cloudy white light as far as I can see. I feel like I'm floating through a sea of illuminated cotton. Part of me wonders if I've died in my sleep.

Moving forward through the warm light now, getting closer to his presence. It's attractive in a way that suddenly worries me, and panic sets in when I look down and don't see my body. Like the presence, I'm here, but not physically. Rather, I'm a human soul encapsulated within an orb of light.

Danger and uncertainty now trump curiosity. I want out. Please let me awaken and get ready for my school day. Nothing good can come from this experience. Somehow I know this. Somehow I know he has intentions that threaten everything I've worked so hard to achieve.

But he won't let go. He's like an otherworldly magnet, an opposite force drawing me closer. It's as if he has some invisible leash around me, and he's using it to pull me toward him. I fight the feelings and sensations rushing through me in the moments before he communicates. I want nothing to do with him, yet I want everything to do with him. I try screaming myself awake but no sound comes out.

What does he look like? Why is he here? What does he want? And most importantly, why me? Why Alix Keener?

A flaring blast of white light blinds me. I'm moving faster now, on a direct course with him. A sense of helplessness forces me to stop resisting. This is about as far from my comfort zone as I can get. I'm a puppet in this world. I have no control here. I'm forced to give in and see it through. Events in my life have made me strong and independent, so I despise playing such a passive role.

Anger. Fear. Frustration. And yes, attraction—I can't deny that. An attraction to something or somebody I haven't even seen, a fact that only fuels my anger.

He knows all of this. I can feel it.

Stop. There it is. A sudden stop and a clearing through the cloudy light. It's still bright, white, and warm, but a crisp clarity surrounds me now. Silence. I'm hovering. We're closer now. He's right here. I can't see him, but I feel him—stronger, more intense. It's like I'm underwater with my eyes closed as he swims around me without physically touching me.

And that's when the messaging begins.

A frustrating series of inaudible voices inside my head. The water analogy again—it's like I'm trying to understand a group of people speaking to me underwater. The garbled chorus quickly narrows to one voice, still indecipherable, and I sense him struggling to adapt to our surroundings in order to communicate with me. This is new for him as well, I realize. He's never attempted this sort of thing, and before I know what I'm doing, I find myself mentally encouraging him to message me something I can actually understand. I've rationalized this strange dream as a learning experience, meaning I need more details if I expect to interpret it upon awakening.

There's not much time left. Finally, his long strings of meaningless and gurgled sounds tighten and transform into an understandable but fragmentary chain of words and phrases. What I hear sends terror snaking through me:

Face.
Suffering.
Violent.
Aruna.
Impenetrable.
Timing.
Oval City.
Help me, Alix.
Perennial is all around you.

The encounter ends with the slightest invisible touch, barely perceptible, a simple brush of what feels like a warm fingertip against the right side of my face. I should be furious with such an advance, but what actually enrages me is the fact that I'm receptive to it, closing my eyes and, deep down, not wanting it to end.

Another brilliant explosion of white light, this time followed by a deafening blast of what sounds like one of those firework test booms you hear before the real show begins.

"Stay away from me!"

I'm shouting the four words as I finally awaken sitting bolt upright in bed, body and pajamas damp with sweat, chest rising and falling rapidly as I try to catch my breath. It's quiet and semidark in here. Why is my right hand balled into a tight fist?

I glance at the clock on the bedside table. The blue digits are blurry smudges. My glasses. I unclench my fist and reach for the same thick, black, chunky frames I've had since freshman year. It's 2:30 a.m. Good. Still more than three hours of sleep before my first day as a senior.

I take a deep breath and stare across the room, lowering my gaze to an area where the wood floor meets the wall opposite me. Something isn't right there. Small, glistening objects reflect the dull and annoying yellow light slicing in from the streetlight across from our front yard. I roll out of bed, stumble toward the door, and flick on the bedroom light, shielding my eyes from the sudden brightness.

The remains of my water glass lie in several jagged pieces along the base of the far wall. The knifelike shards look like abstract ice cubes resting in the spilled puddle of water. The booming sound just before I awoke. That must have been the glass shattering against the wall after I threw it. I've had my share of nightmares, but I've never done anything like this before.

"Good riddance, Dream Guy," I say, shaking my head and raking a hand through my short, spiky hair as I cross the room to retrieve the broken glass. "Good riddance forever."

But the fear returns as I remember his final two sentences:

Help me, Alix.
Perennial is all around you.

I don't even notice the glass shard cut my fingertip. The sharp pain of the slice makes me wince. I instinctively draw the wounded index finger toward my glasses for a better view. The cut is harm-less—just a dash of crimson spreading slowly from what amounts to nothing more than a scrape—but for some reason the blood makes me remember his touch.

I place my finger between my lips and press the tip of my tongue over the cut. The blood tastes tinny. I close my eyes and admit to myself that all the "good riddances" in the world won't hide the fact that there's a part of me—an unknown part I fear—that longs to have contact with Dream Guy again.

CHAPTER 1

Tuesday, September 4

My father is a police officer, and I've long been a master at reading his moods. One look at Clint Keener's face as he steps through the door after work tells me how his day or night went. I always think about what I'm going to say before I speak to him—especially at night. Although he doesn't drink much, he becomes silent and distant when he's had too much alcohol. I suppose we all have demons and fight them in our own ways, but Dad loves me and wants the best for me.

Mornings are the best time to be around him, and today is no different. I'm sitting at the new, white kitchen table, studying my class schedule, finishing a banana protein shake and a fried egg topped with Trader Joe's kimchi. Dad enters from the spacious living room full of new furniture and heads straight for the coffee beans and fancy high-end grinder he recently bought.

"Good Lord, Alix," he says, eyeing the brownish-red kimchi and scrunching his nose as he passes. "What died on your egg?"

"Very funny," I say. "Nothing died. It's vegetarian kimchi. I saw it on TV and decided to try it. It's really good. Want some?"

"If I can't spell it, I don't eat it, so no," he says, scooping the dark, shiny beans into the grinder. "You definitely have your mother's taste buds. She liked taking me to hole-in-the-wall Asian restaurants in and around Detroit when we first started dating. I finally had to break it to her that I'm a lot happier in a Burger King than I am in a Vietnamese diner."

He looks at me and winks and smiles as the hum of the grinder fills the house. Dad rarely talks about work and never talks about his time as a marine during the 1991 Gulf War. I respect this and never ask about either topic, knowing from my own research and from Mom that it's often difficult for cops and combat veterans to discuss their experiences.

Still, there are things I know about his law-enforcement life, mainly through observation. For example, I know he's been doing undercover work the past six months or so. His long hair and almost-mountain-man-like beard make that clear. Mom hated it when Dad worked undercover. She used to joke that it was in his best interest to work a regular patrol shift because she refused to kiss him until he shaved and got a decent haircut.

"Are you used to the house yet?" He empties the ground beans into a paper filter as he waits for water in the electric kettle to boil. Dad might not be a food snob, but he sure is a coffee geek, and I love smelling the different aromas from the beans that fill the house every morning.

"It's a big house," I say. "But yeah, I guess I'm good with it."

"It's big but we deserve it," he says. "Your mother would say the same. How'd you sleep?"

"Not great. Bad dream." I pause. "Well, bad in parts."

He gives me a concerned look, walks over, and sits across from me. "Look, Alix. I know it's only been a year, and I know I've made some bad decisions, but we needed to move away. You said so yourself. We talked long and hard about this, and you said you didn't mind spending your senior year in a new school. I couldn't take it in that house or that city anymore. Everywhere I looked, everywhere I went, everybody I saw—it all reminded me of her. It was torture." He massages his temples with his fingertips. "I know people say I'm running from reality, but this seemed like the right thing to do. If you've changed your mind, I'm sorry. I can't change the past, but I can give us a fresh start without forgetting about the past."

"Dad, relax," I say. "I'm fine. The dream wasn't about Mom."

He closes his eyes and shakes his head. "Right," he says, eyes opening. "Sorry about that. I'm just trying to do the right things for you." He exhales deeply. "For us."

"I know," I say. "But try not to worry about me so much."

"Easier said than done," he says. "Care to tell me about the dream?"

"It was nothing," I say, pocketing my schedule and checking my phone for texts. As usual there are none. I take the last bite of my breakfast, gather my dishes, and head for the dishwasher.

Dad follows and says, "How does it feel to be a senior?"

"I'm relieved but annoyed," I say. "I'm more comfortable around adults. You know that." I close the dishwasher and grab my car keys from the hook in the side foyer. "I wish I could just skip the next nine months. I mean, U of M's basically already said yes."

"I love your confidence, Alix, but don't get cocky." Dad pours boiling water over the ground beans and into the pot. "All I ask is that you do what you've always done: stay focused and keep your nose clean. And it's okay to have friends as long as they're not boys."

"God," I say, rolling my eyes, "you're such a cop."

"Exactly."

A series of three loud beeps we both know well. It's his work phone and the most annoying ringtone ever created. I'm about to leave, but Dad raises an index finger, says, "Wait. Hang on a sec," and takes the call.

This isn't unusual. He answers work calls in front of me often, and if it's private he simply goes into his office. So over the next minute, as I watch his face grow increasingly concerned, I wonder why he's staying within earshot of me as he says things like, "Okay . . . I'm not sure . . . the last name again . . . I'll be there as soon as I can," and so on.

He ends the call and studies me—Dad thinking hard about something.

"What is it?" I say. "What's happened?"

"You said you have some sort of advanced history class, right?"

"It's called Independent Study in American History," I say, nodding. "I had to take a test to get into it, remember? It counts for college credit and is one of the best classes at Beaconsfield High."

"Who's the teacher?"

"Why?" I say, squinting. "Does it matter?"

"Who's the *teacher*, Alix?" he says, all serious and cop-like now. "And yes, it does matter."

"It's Mr. Watkins," I say without having to check my schedule. "Marc Watkins. He teaches history and chemistry. I end my day with him. Sixth hour. I researched him before picking the class. He went to U of M and is an incredible teacher. His reviews online are amazing."

Dad glances down for a moment before meeting my gaze. "I'm not supposed to tell you this yet, but there's something you need to know." He clears his throat. "Honey, I'm afraid Mr. Watkins won't be your teacher."

"What?" I say, swallowing hard. "Why not? Did he do something wrong?"

"That's a good question," he says. "I don't know the answer yet."

"Then what's the problem?"

Dad mulls it over for a few seconds and says, "The problem is he's dead, Alix. Murdered. They found his body yesterday. Multiple gunshot wounds." He pauses. "I'm sorry."

"What?" I say, covering my ears and fighting back a wave of nausea. "Jesus, Dad, why are you even telling me this? It's the first day of school!"

Despite the initial shock, I lower my hands and try not to overreact, telling myself to breathe calmly and deeply. I pride myself on the self-discipline Mom and Dad taught me from a young age, so I tend to hate myself when I allow drama or gossip to get the best of me. Dad doesn't like me this way either, so he doesn't say another word until he thinks I can handle it.

"That's better," he finally says. "And you asked another good question. I'm telling you because I'd rather you hear the truth from me than some rumor at school. The family's been notified, and they're releasing his name today. I'm sure it'll be in the news before noon, but don't say anything until it's public. Got it?"

I nod.

"Are you okay?"

There's a long silence.

"Yeah, I guess," I say. "It's just creepy. I never met the guy, but like I said, the students who posted reviews adore—*adored*—him." I adjust my glasses and scratch my head. "What a freaky way to start my senior year."

"I know," he says. "This might sound strange, but try to have a good day, okay?" He pauses. "I love you, Alix."

"Love you too, Dad."

I'm halfway out the side door when he says, "Hey, what happened to your finger?"

"Huh?" I turn in the open doorway. "What are you talking about?"

"The cut on your right index finger. It wasn't there yesterday."

"Oh that," I say, raising the wounded digit I'd nearly forgotten about. "It's nothing. I broke a glass in my room and nicked it. It's like a centimeter long. How'd you even notice?"

"Because I'm a cop," he says. "And your dad."

He forces a smile and takes his first sip of steamy black coffee as I leave the house.

CHAPTER 2

Driving to school in the black Ford Explorer Sport that Dad bought me, I'm trying to push away the troubling news about Mr. Watkins, so I think about Mom instead.

She was the best. Martha Keener taught middle school science for twenty years. Then, on a beautiful Friday afternoon just over a year ago, a pathetic excuse for a man consumed a massive amount of alcohol at a bar and decided to drive. Mom was coming home from work when the drunken asshole blacked out at the wheel on a busy four-lane road and crossed over into oncoming traffic at more than sixty miles per hour. His SUV slammed head-on into Mom's aging two-door compact, killing her instantly and injuring four other motorists in nearby vehicles. Mom was the only fatality.

The medical people assured us that she didn't suffer, a fact that did little to help me at the time but has brought some comfort since. As for the drunken asshole, he survived with only minor injuries. He's currently in prison and will be for at least twenty years. Personally, I wish he were dead. I think Dad feels the same. Maybe one day we'll both let go of the anger, but right now that's a long ways off.

Mom's death made us rich. There was a hefty life-insurance policy and other investments involved. I don't know how much money we have, but obviously Dad and I would rather be broke and hungry with Mom alive than millionaires with her dead. I miss her so much. I miss talking with her. I miss watching her and Dad. They were such a perfect couple. She was such a perfect mom.

Dad didn't buy anything with the money for several months. I think he felt guilty about having sudden wealth due to the loss of his wife. He finally started purchasing things around the time he went back undercover. What I've noticed is that each of the three big-ticket items he's bought has some connection to Mom. We haven't discussed this, but I'm sure he's aware of the link. The Cadillac Coupe for him because Mom loved fast Cadillacs. The new Ford Explorer for me because he thinks I'm safer in an SUV than Mom was in the old two-door. Most recently, the stately white 1920s colonial in Beaconsfield, Michigan, the wealthy community we now call home. Mom and Dad dreamed of buying and renovating an old home during retirement. Well, Dad now has the house, and he's five years away from retirement and a full pension, so it won't be long before he has all the time in the world to renovate. With the money, he considered retiring early but admitted he wasn't ready to stop working yet.

Beaconsfield. Twenty minutes northwest of Detroit but it might as well be another planet. Everybody has money here. It's a far cry from Wayne, the blue-collar city I called home until a month ago. Beaconsfield houses are huge and old. The people wear expensive clothing and drive pricey cars. I get the sense they're competing with each other and enjoy displaying their wealth in public. I don't fit in here, but I'm not complaining. I picked Beaconsfield because of the high school, which consistently ranks among the best academic public high schools in the nation. As for private schools, they weren't an option. Mom was a staunch proponent of public education and would surely come back from the dead and haunt me if I spent even one day in a private school.

I'm lost in thought and don't see the man until it's almost too late. He's just suddenly standing there, ten feet away in the middle of the wide neighborhood street. My eyes bulge like baseballs. I hit the brakes hard. The tires squawk, and my seat belt locks.

The Explorer stops barely three feet from him, but it's not a "man." He looks more like a teenager, although the glare of the bright morning sun through the canopy of mature, leafy green trees makes it difficult to see many details. My heart races and feels like it's in my throat. I adjust my glasses and swear at myself for daydreaming at the wheel. Then again, somebody needs to teach this kid how to cross the street safely.

As he rounds the front of the Explorer and approaches my window, I decide he looks anywhere between seventeen and twenty-one. He's incredibly beautiful too, tall and slender with long, wavy black hair. He reminds me of somebody, but I can't quite put my finger on it—a famous musician or actor maybe. I check my rearview mirror and am relieved not to see any approaching vehicles. There's no traffic in front of me either, and I don't see any nosy neighbors watching from their lush green lawns.

Everything Dad has taught me over the years tells me to hit the gas and not say a word to this stranger, but the sight of the retro yellow Beaconsfield High logo on the backpack slung over his right shoulder and the same logo on the left breast of his black hoodie convinces me this guy is harmless.

After a quick, paranoid double check for any sign of my dad, I power down my window and prepare to apologize, but the boy with the rock-star black hair and aqua-green eyes that look like tropical lagoons beats me to it.

"I'm really sorry about that," he says, adjusting his backpack. "I didn't even see you coming."

"Likewise," I say, finding it hard to maintain eye contact with him. "No worries, but we're lucky nobody got hurt."

"True." He looks beyond me toward the passenger seat, where my own plain black backpack rests. "Beaconsfield?"

"Yes," I say, obsessively checking my mirrors. "And I'm guessing from your backpack and hoodie you go there too."

"It's my first day," he says. "My parents work in China right now, so I'm staying with my grandparents for senior year." He nods toward his backpack and hoodie and smiles. "They bought me a lot of Beaconsfield gear. They went to school there ages ago and love it when I wear this stuff." He pauses. "So, what year are you?"

"A senior as well," I say. "Actually, this is my first year at Beaconsfield too. My dad and I moved here about a month ago."

"Cool," he says, shrugging and glancing up and down the street. "What a coincidence. The first year for both of us, and we're both seniors."

"I was just thinking the same thing."

We exchange a quick smile, and I pray to God I don't look as awkward as I feel.

"Guess I'll see you around," he says. "My name's Lewis, by the way. Lewis Wilde."

"Lewis Wilde," I say. "Got it. I'm Alix. Alix Keener."

There's a silence, during which a look of surprise crosses his smooth, pale face.

"Wait," he says. "Keener. You live in that big white house on Maple Grove, don't you? Your dad's the cop, right?"

"Yup," I say, raising my eyebrows. I'm not surprised he knows. Mom's story was huge in the state and local media. Dad still gets occasional calls and e-mails from reporters and journalists. "Word travels fast around here," I add.

"Everything travels fast in Beaconsfield, Alix," he says. "Get used to it."

We stare at each other for a moment, but something doesn't feel right, so I look away and gaze into the rearview mirror, almost thankful to see a car finally approaching in the distance.

"Good to meet you, Lewis," I say, shifting to drive. "Be a little more careful the next time you cross the street."

"Will do," he says. "Hey, Alix, can I ask you something?"

"Make it quick," I say. "There's a car coming."

He spots the car behind me, leans toward the open window, and in almost a whisper says, "What do you know about that house you moved into?"

"What are you talking about?" I grip the steering wheel hard. "Jesus. I thought you were going to ask me for a ride to school or something."

"You don't know what happened, do you?"

"No. I guess not," I say, shooting him a glare. "Good-bye, Lewis. Have a nice day."

He takes a few steps back and calmly says, "I'm sorry about your mom. I mean it."

I don't know what to say, so what I do is shake my head, power up the window, and drive off, but when I realize I should at least thank him for his words about Mom, I pull over curbside and wait for the car to pass, which it quickly does.

When I check my mirrors, Lewis Wilde is nowhere in sight.

CHAPTER 3

Beaconsfield High School is a beautiful and enormous ivy-covered brick building that dates to the early 1900s. Everything about the place, from the finely manicured, sprawling grounds, to the modern technology that dominates the interior, reflects the wealth and attitude of the community. I was expecting my share of glares and comments from my fellow female students, but what I experience goes beyond any worst-case scenario I imagined.

On my appearance: "Oh my God, those baggy jeans. They're so Wayne." "She has money now. It's okay to quit the resale shops." "She must be gay with such a butch haircut." About my life: "My parents said her dad is the first cop to ever live in Beaconsfield." "It's sad about her mom, but why did they move here? It must be like Mars for them." "I hear she's supersmart but superdifficult. Just stay away from her."

I developed a tough skin when I was bullied in middle school. It was then that I first realized I was more comfortable alone than around kids my age. When it comes to my education, I'm a firm believer in the "If you want things done right, do them yourself" philosophy. Thanks to Mom and Dad's guidance, I have a specific career path I won't let anybody steer me away from. Yes, I'm confident, but I'm not mean. The problem is my peers often interpret my confidence for arrogance and decide I must be a bitch.

Whatever.

My point is that bullying is nothing new for me, and so although some of the girls at Beaconsfield bombard me with stinging verbal put-downs from day one, I force myself to hold my head high and stare right through anybody who says something mean. That's another thing I learned from Dad. He calls it The Look. Dad believes that a menacing stare is a powerful conflict-resolution tool. You'd be surprised how well it works. For example, every mean girl I give The Look to today breaks eye contact before I do, which tells me two things: First, they don't want any real conflict with me. Second, like most bullies, they're engaging in petty behavior to mask their own problems.

Dad was right about Mr. Watkins. His death goes public shortly before lunch, but it's too soon for authorities to reveal its violent nature, so rumors about what happened swarm through Beaconsfield High like maggots on spoiled meat. Carjacking gone bad. He was with a prostitute who happened to be a serial killer. Heart attack while driving. Severely depressed and shot himself. The list goes on, and I have to bite my tongue several times to keep from revealing what I know.

News of the death and subsequent rumors go viral via students' electronic devices, so the principal makes a special announcement on the classroom TVs confirming the unfortunate news, pointing out that nobody knows any details yet, so please disregard any and all unofficial stories. He says grief counselors are available all week for anybody who might need to speak with an adult about the tragic loss of such a wonderful person and teacher. I'm touched to see several students, the majority of them very studious looking, in tears as they come to and from the counseling office. It all serves as a reminder of what an incredible reputation Marc Watkins had among his students and colleagues.

So why would anybody want to murder a man like him?

∞

Lewis Wilde is one of ten seniors who earned a prestigious spot in my sixth-hour Independent Study in American History class. A sign on Mr. Watkins's second-floor classroom door instructed his classes to report to the media center today, and when I enter the mammoth library I spot Lewis sitting with the other students in a side conference room.

I slide into an empty desk beside him and listen as one of the assistant principals explains to us that the search for a qualified educator to replace Mr. Watkins has already begun, although he agrees it will take time and somebody like Mr. Watkins will never truly be replaced. He runs out of things to say after ten minutes and suggests we spend some time brainstorming research topics for the semester project. It's silent as the ten of us look around at each other, wondering what to do, but voices soon fill the air as the people who know one another group up and try to talk history even though the history teacher is dead.

"This is insane," Lewis says, turning his desk toward mine and tucking his black hair behind his ears. "What do you think happened to him?"

"Beats me," I say, noticing again how perfect his green eyes and pale skin are. "Look, I'm sorry I drove off like that this morning. It's just . . . I don't know. It's hard for me to talk about my mom with people I don't know, but thank you for mentioning her. I pulled over to tell you, but you were already gone."

"Oh, that," he says. "There's a little shortcut to school my grandpa told me about. It involves some backyards."

And that's likely a total lie, I say to myself. I know this because the lovely Lewis glanced to his right when he said it. A little interrogation tip from Dad: people tend to avoid eye contact when lying and often look off to the right.

"It also freaked me out a little when you asked about our house," I say. "What happened there?"

"Do you really want to know?" Lewis says, holding my gaze now.

"You tell me, Lewis," I say, rolling my eyes. "Do I?"

"Well, I'm not telling you," he says, a slight smile crossing his face. "I just decided that. If you want to know, it's something you'll have to look into."

"Because I might not want to know. Is that what you're getting at?"

"Yeah," he says. "Something like that."

We listen to the chatter around us. The assistant principal has stepped out to speak with the media specialist in the library. Two male students sit silently nearby, jotting things down in notebooks, while the other six, all girls, actually discuss possible research topics.

"I think we're the only ones not on task," I say. "Have you thought of any topics you'd like to pursue?"

"Yes," he says, smiling. "Murder."

"That's not funny," I say, a sour feeling spreading through my stomach.

"I don't mean it to be," he says. "I've thought a lot about it. I'd like to examine some of the most famous unsolved murders in American history and explore the likelihood or unlikelihood of DNA evidence helping to solve them." He shrugs.

"Cool," I say, nodding. "That's actually interesting. Sorry I snapped at you."

"Don't worry about it," he says. "It's been a weird first day."

"Agreed."

"You want to know the craziest rumor I heard today about Mr. Watkins?"

"I'm afraid," I say, sliding off my glasses to clean the lenses. "But go ahead."

Lewis says, "I heard some kids at lunch saying his death had something to do with Perennial."

I almost vomit when I hear the word.

Help me, Alix. Perennial is all around you.

My glasses fall to the tiled floor. My pulse quickens. My body trembles. The safe and orderly world I cherish spirals instantly into chaos.

What's happening to me?

Dream Guy.

Perennial.

A murdered teacher.

Now a strange guy who appears out of nowhere this morning, this guy saying cryptic things about my house and a rumored link between Mr. Watkins and something called Perennial. I manage to hold down the vomit as I grab my glasses, gather my belongings, and stand, feeling dizzy and unable to look at Lewis.

"Alix, what's wrong?" he says. "You don't look so good."

"Don't talk to me," I say, noticing the sudden silence in the room. I've drawn an audience. Great. "I have to go," I say, lowering my voice to a whisper others hopefully can't hear. "And don't ever say that word around me again."

"Alix, I'm confused," he says. "What word? What are you talking about?"

"You know what word," I say. "Perennial."

I quietly exit the room.

CHAPTER 4

I cut through the library and straight past the assistant principal and media specialist, both of whom say nothing to me as I exit the massive media center. I'm in a terrified haze that I figure must be some sort of panic attack. My heart thumps wildly, and I'm dizzy to the point where I fear I might pass out in the hallway. Dad's voice is in my head, saying what he always says when I have an especially bad freak-out moment: *Breathe slowly and deeply, Alix. Be a master of your actions as opposed to a prisoner of your reactions.*

It takes a minute, but I manage to calm myself just as I reach my locker, where I get what I need and head down the wide, empty hallway toward the student parking lot in the back of the school. I'm skipping out early, and if a hall monitor or any other adult questions me I'll say I'm sick and ready to puke, which isn't too far from the truth.

Information. I need it. I need to know what happened in our house, if anything. Maybe Lewis is simply messing with my head. Regardless, I need to know what Perennial is and why I dreamed about it. Am I some kind of psychic? Is this some new ability I'm developing? I hope not.

God, just keep me normal. I don't want any weird shit in my life, okay? Now or ever.

I'm fifty feet from the rear entrance doors and only steps away from a hallway to my left when it happens. A large, fast-moving figure in dark clothing rounds the corner with lightning quickness and squeezes me in a bear hug that feels like a powerful vise. He lifts me off my feet and presses my face so hard against his chest that I'm unable to speak. I try screaming but manage nothing more than a muffled grunt.

He carries me a few feet and stops. I know how to fight. Dad has taught me hundreds of self-defense techniques over the years, but I can't do anything against this kind of strength. I try to at least squirm a little but can't move an inch. Something squeaks. It's a door opening. A few more steps and we're inside. The door thumps closed behind us.

Silence. Just my heavy breathing. Whoever he is, he's calm. I can barely hear his breathing. Smells like chemicals and soap in here. Probably a custodial closet. I stop resisting in order to conserve energy. If this sicko has any sexual intentions, all I need to make sure he never pees again without medical assistance is one free limb.

"Listen to me, Alix." Definitely a male voice, deep and scratchy, but I can tell he's exaggerating those aspects to mask his real voice. He tightens his grip around me. I grunt again as the wind escapes me. "Stay away from Perennial," he says, sending a fresh wave of nausea through me. "You don't want anything to do with it." He pauses. "Think of me as your guardian angel, but I can't help you unless you listen to me." He relaxes his grip slightly, but nowhere near enough for me to strike. "I'm leaving now. Don't make a sound until you count to ten in your head. I'll know if you cheat, and you won't like the consequences, understand?"

All I can do is emit another grunt. He must take that as a yes, because the next thing I know he shoves me. I stumble over what must be a bucket and crash onto a concrete floor lined with plastic and metal containers. Sharp pain ripples through me as he exits and slams the door, but I don't even count to one before I'm up and yelling for help.

I reach for the door handle and turn it. Locked. I repeatedly pound both fists on the thick metal with everything I have, constantly shouting for somebody to open the door. I want to burst into tears, but I realize that won't solve a thing. I have to keep myself together and get through this.

It takes a few minutes, but the door finally opens, and an elderly male hall monitor with bad posture and thinning gray hair stares at me, wide-eyed.

"You okay, miss?"

"I think so," I say, stepping out of what is indeed a custodial closet. "Somebody played a joke on me. It's nothing. Thanks for letting me out."

"Teenagers," he says, shaking his head as I slide past him and exit Beaconsfield High just as the dismissal bell rings.

∞

Tuesday night, sitting on the living-room sofa with my tablet, debating whether to dig deeper into what I want to know but am afraid to learn. Dad's working, but even if he was here I wouldn't tell him what's happening. He has enough to worry about with his job. The closet encounter was terrifying, but the more I think about it, the more I'm convinced my "attacker" actually was trying to protect me from something.

What is Perennial? What happened at 1326 Maple Grove Street in Beaconsfield, Michigan?

The slim computer in my lap is a potential gateway to answering these questions, but shouldn't I bury my curiosity and resist the urge to turn it on and search the Internet? Dad and I chose Beaconsfield so that I could enjoy a quiet senior year in a great school. Despite all the drama of day one, I should do what I've always done and what Dad's always suggested: keep my nose clean and stay out of trouble. I've always been good at that.

But what do you do when trouble finds you? I haven't asked for any of this. It's come to me, like an unwelcome illness. I want it to go away, which means I need to know what it is in order to figure out a way to get rid of it.

Information.

I Google "perennial Beaconsfield, Michigan." The search results are discouraging and consist primarily of perennial garden plants that thrive in Michigan. Not at all what I need, of course. I scroll pages and pages into the search results and even change the search terms a few times. Still nothing, not even a hint of what or who Perennial is.

After a quick mental break, I type our complete address into the search bar and add the word "history" after the zip code. All I see are real estate links from when the house was for sale. I click through some of these but don't find anything of interest besides how much Dad paid for the house, which was actually far less than what I imagined. After several pages of unproductive browsing and increased frustration, I decide to call it a night.

And that's when a link that reads "What Happened to William?" catches my attention. The title is so different from the other listings. What can a question like that have to do with this house? I squint to make sure I've read the text correctly. Sure enough, I have. I take a deep breath, click the link, and find myself staring at a two-year-old blog entry.

Then my phone vibrates with an incoming text.

The text is from an unknown number. The message reads: U SHOULD'VE LISTENED, ALIX.

I drop the phone, cover my mouth, and stare at the computer screen, hoping this is all one bad dream and that I'll awaken in the safety of my own bed at any moment.

CHAPTER 5

Part of me wants to scream and run out of the house, but all that will do is attract unwanted attention and upset Dad. I could calmly leave right now and drive to Dad's station, but his current undercover status means he doesn't really have a home base. There's the emergency cell number of his that I've never had to call or text, but he's reminded me more than once that the number is a last resort. In other words, I'm not to contact him unless it's a true emergency.

Hmm . . . let's see: a mysterious man shoved me into a custodial closet today and told me to stay far away from the elusive and mysterious Perennial. And now that same so-called guardian angel just sent me a threatening text because I'm trying to learn about the history of my new house.

I'd say that qualifies as a true emergency.

Still, I rely on Dad so much. Rely on him for everything really. Always have. I've never made a move without his blessing. Last night I had a dream that's proving to have some strange connections today. There's not much he can help me with there, and he'll think

I'm insane if I mention anything remotely related to psychic powers. Dad despises the paranormal world, especially psychics. He says psychics have harmed far more criminal cases than people are aware of. According to Dad, for every psychic who actually provides useful information to law-enforcement authorities, there are at least twenty-five who lead them in the wrong direction.

Think and breathe, Alix. Don't react. Just think. Handle it on your own. You're safe here. Nobody is in the house, and Dad should be home soon. Besides, you know where the emergency gun is if you ever need it.

I retrieve my phone from the floor and lay it beside me. No new texts. Good. Next I focus my attention on my tablet, where the two-year-old "What Happened to William?" blog post awaits me. Somebody obviously has my phone number and is tracking everything I do on my computer, meaning I won't use our wireless network or this tablet again, but the blog-post page has already loaded, so I might as well read the entire thing. After all, my guardian angel–stalker knows I've accessed it.

The post is from an obscure, short-lived, and quite anonymous blog called *Vagabond's Warrior*. I say short-lived, because "What Happened to William?" is the only post on the site. The blog has no page links and no mention of an author for the lone post.

This is what I read:

What Happened to William?

William Weed was no saint. He had serious problems. We all know that. But William is dead now, and there's nothing we can do to bring him back. The official story is William committed suicide in his own bedroom by firing a bullet through his brain—he was another addict who took the easy way out—but anybody who knew him knows that scenario is highly unlikely.

William wasn't suicidal. He was trying to break Perennial's hold on him. But Perennial won. William knew Oval City better than anybody, even Face. In the end, that's what killed him. William knew too much and got too close. Rumor is he had something big on Face, something to do with Aruna's disappearance.

Anybody reading this needs to know that somebody murdered William Weed. What happened at 1326 Maple Grove in Beaconsfield that night wasn't suicide. It was murder. Problem is places like Beaconsfield don't want murders on their hands. Best to make it a suicide, then. That's easier to explain and accept.

Bottom line: the Beaconsfield orchard of goodness and perfection lost an imperfect apple, and that suits the citizens of Beaconsfield just fine.

Somebody needs to dig Perennial out of the ground and expose it. Only then will the truth emerge. Only then can William and others find peace. I wish I could do the digging, but that's impossible due to circumstances beyond my control.

His photograph appears below the last sentence, the caption "We miss you, William" centered below the photo in a tiny font. He looks about eighteen, shirtless in black cargo shorts and sporting two full sleeves of colorful, fresh-looking tattoos. I squint in an attempt to detect a theme to his body art, but the picture is too small and not of the greatest quality. Although he's wearing sunglasses and a backwards black baseball cap, I can tell from his high cheekbones and muscular body that William had no trouble finding dates. I'd always pictured drug addicts as scrawny and weak, so I figure this photo must be from before he developed his habit.

Despite all the initial fear, a surprising calmness washes over me as I experience further connections to Dream Guy. Words like "Oval City" and "Face" dart through my mind, smaller pieces of a larger puzzle I can't seem to pull away from. As crazy as it sounds to my structured and analytical mind, I sense that Dream Guy was perhaps William Weed or a type of spirit energy of his making contact with me.

Two years ago something violent and awful happened in one of the five bedrooms in this house. As much as I'd like to push it all away, last night's experience with Dream Guy seems to make more sense by the minute. I'm deeply connected to real danger for the first time in my life, but I'm now convinced that I possess some sort of psychic ability that can help people. Of course, I'm basing all of this on one dream I had less than twenty-four hours ago. This could simply be a one-time experience, but there's no way I can ignore feelings this strong. I'm involved in something whether I like it or not.

It's terrifying, yes. But what's more terrifying is that I find the danger exciting as hell.

I give in to a sudden urge to click the "Refresh" button on the browser. The page reloads with something new, a blank white page with six words centered across the top:

You just broke ground. Keep digging.

Three loud raps on the thick front door take my breath away. I nearly drop the tablet onto the floor. I think about the gun again but first decide to crouch and dart across the huge living room toward the large window overlooking our palatial front yard. I glance at the clock on the TV and notice it's just after nine—not as late as I thought. The surprise visitor rings the doorbell, and I take a moment to peek through the lower corner of the drawn plantation blind.

Lewis Wilde stands on the long, white, well-lighted wooden porch that spans the length of the front of the house, Lewis wearing stylish dark jeans and a long-sleeve black V-neck tee, his wavy black hair looking salon fresh. My heart rate spikes at the sight of him. There's something about him that is unlike anything I've ever seen in a guy. I suppose "perfection" is the word. What worries me most is that he seems like the type of guy I might make regrettable decisions over. Good Lord, Mom would lecture me something awful if she knew I was having thoughts like this over a guy. As for Dad . . . well, I can't even imagine.

I'm just crouching here, gawking at Lewis's improbable beauty, when he looks my way with surprising speed and waves to me. All I can do is roll my eyes and stand, hoping my face isn't as red as it feels when I open the door and stand face-to-face with Mr. Supermodel.

"Hi, Lewis," I say, finding it easy to get lost in his aqua-green eyes.

"Hey, Alix." His minty breath blends with the late-summer smells of leaves, pine trees, and freshly mown grass. "I told myself I wouldn't come over here, but here I am. I would've texted, but I don't have your number." He pauses. "Is everything okay? I mean, one second you're listening to me explain my research topic, and then, *boom*, you're freaking out over some stupid rumor about how Mr. Watkins died."

"I owe you another apology," I say, forcing myself to look away from him as I step onto the porch. There's a surprising chill to the air. I wrap my arms around my shoulders as I scan the street for any sign of somebody watching. Satisfied, I turn and lean on the porch railing, saying to Lewis, "I overreact sometimes. I'm sorry. It's been a lifelong problem I've never quite gotten under control. Drives my dad crazy." I shrug and raise my eyebrows. "I know what happened, by the way."

"Everybody knows now," he says. "I can't believe somebody shot Mr. Watkins seven times at close range. The news said he was killed execution style. And how they found him in one of those abandoned buildings in Oval City . . ." He makes a disgusted face.

"I'm not talking about Mr. Watkins," I say, although I find the new details interesting, especially the mention of Oval City. "I'm talking about this house." I nod toward the front door behind him. "No wonder my dad got such a good price."

"You know about William, then?"

I nod and say, "I don't see why you didn't just tell me."

He steps toward me, barely three feet separating us now. I notice hints of muscularity beneath his tight long sleeves that were impossible to detect under the black Beaconsfield hoodie earlier.

Lewis says, "I didn't think today was the best day to tell you somebody was murdered in your bedroom two years ago."

"William's death was ruled a suicide," I say.

"Do you really believe that, Alix? I hope not, because it's a bullshit story, and deep down everybody around here knows it. The police buried it and made it go away. His death barely made the papers."

"Did you write the *Vagabond's Warrior* blog?" I ask.

"*Vagabond's Warrior*?" he says, squinting and giving me a look. "I have no idea what you're talking about."

"Whatever," I say, standing and distancing myself from him. "What I'm really wondering is how you know where my bedroom is."

That catches him off guard, and I can tell he knows he made a mistake. Trying to recover, he looks beyond me toward the yard and says, "Look, it's not what you think, okay? I'm not that guy."

"And what '*guy*' is that, Lewis? You mean the high-school perv who spies on female classmates to a get a look at them in their most private moments? Jesus, you remember who my dad is, right?"

"Like I said, I'm not that guy. Trust me."

Somehow I know he's telling the truth, so I shake my head and say, "I'm guessing you knew William."

"Yes," he says, his stunning eyes locked on mine again. "I knew William well. That's why I get pissed whenever somebody says he committed suicide." He lowers his gaze. "We called him Willis, by the way. His good friends did anyway."

"You said you just moved here and are living with your grandparents while your parents are in China," I say. "If you knew William—or Willis, that is—you couldn't have lived too far away."

"Our house is over in Eastland," he says, referring to Beaconsfield's eastern border city. Eastland isn't as wealthy as Beaconsfield, but it's definitely an upper-class suburb. "William and I met at the Oakland

County Alternative Academy during freshman year. We'd both been in a lot of trouble at our middle schools, so our districts made us start high school at the academy. We clicked right away. Eventually, I stopped using and got my act together. William didn't. I spent a year there and went to Eastland High as a sophomore. William dropped out of the academy and never went back to school." Lewis shrugs. "But we always stayed in touch. I tried to help him turn things around, but it was pretty clear he preferred me as a friend and not a peer drug counselor. I could have spent my senior year at Eastland High, but I guess you could say I needed a change of scenery." He shifts his gaze away from mine and looks around the stately neighborhood. "When I found out my parents were off to China for a year, I jumped at the chance to finish high school in Beaconsfield. I mean, who wouldn't?"

"What room did he die in?" I ask, aiming an outstretched arm toward the house.

"Your bedroom," he says. "I already told you that."

"And what room is my bedroom?" I stare hard at him. "Indulge me, okay?"

There's a silence during which we gaze at each other and I feel something important but unspoken pass between us. The cold air seems to intensify, sending a shiver through my body that reaches my bones. Lewis's dazzling lagoon eyes appear brighter than ever. A hint of a smile crosses his face.

"William died in the bedroom above the living room," he says, aiming an index finger directly above us. "The room that is now your bedroom."

I fold my arms across my chest and study him. "Who are you, Lewis?" I say in almost a whisper.

"What do you mean?"

"I've never had a day like this in my life," I say, feeling heat building behind my eyes. *God, don't cry, Alix. Keep it inside, girl.* "I play by the rules and keep my nose clean," I add, definitely fighting a flood of tears. "I've never been in trouble for anything."

He smiles in a way that scares me.

"Something's happening to me, Lewis," I say. "Good or bad, I don't know, but somehow I know you're connected. And I think Mr. Watkins is connected. The same goes for William Weed." I pause. "What can you tell me about Perennial, Oval City, Face, and Aruna?"

"Aruna? Nobody's seen her since before William died." Lewis's troubling smile widens, revealing a set of perfect snow-white teeth any dentist would love to advertise. Then he emits a short but disturbing laugh that only adds to his overall mysteriousness. "Look at it this way, Alix," he says, smile fading, "maybe you're finally discovering who you really are. And that's something you can't fight no matter how hard you try."

"You need to leave," I say, trembling. "Now."

"I know." He closes his eyes and seems to sniff the air. Then he opens his eyes and says, "I'm sure your dad will be home soon. We'll talk later. Don't worry. You're safe for now."

He extends his right palm toward the left side of my face. My heart pounds, but I don't fight it. Lewis Wilde stops himself at the last possible moment and pulls his hand away just before his fingertips touch my skin.

Then he turns and walks away.

CHAPTER 6

Dad walks in twenty minutes after Lewis leaves. I'm sitting at the kitchen table in a confused daze as I leaf through course information my teachers flooded me with today. I stored my tablet and phone upstairs in my bedroom, but bed is the last place I want to be right now. Truth is I'm afraid of falling asleep because of what I might dream about.

I smell the evidence of beer and cigarettes the moment Dad enters the kitchen. I've never been the partying type. I've tried different types of alcohol, but I hate the taste. More importantly, I hate the way alcohol makes me feel, and the smell of any kind of tobacco gags me. Call me boring, but I enjoy being the viceless geek I am. Dad knows all of this, meaning he's had a horrible day if he's blatantly exposing me to his occasional vices.

"You stink," I say, not looking up from my math syllabus.

"I know," he says, slightly slurring his words. Not totally drunk, but definitely buzzed. "Sorry, Alix. You're usually in bed by now on a school night. Anyway, I had a bad day. Really bad. The kind of day that makes me wonder if I can do this for five more years."

He crosses the kitchen and pours a tall glass of water from the refrigerator dispenser, leaving behind an invisible cloud of bar stench. I scrunch my nose and wave a hand in front of my face as he leans against the sink and stares at me through bloodshot eyes. He usually doesn't say much when he's in one of his dark moods, but tonight is different. I can tell he wants to share some things.

"The school is devastated about Mr. Watkins," I say. "The administration is doing everything it's supposed to do in a situation like this, I suppose, but it was surreal being there today. Nobody really knew what to say to anybody. Teachers included. My first day at Beaconsfield High was memorable for all the wrong reasons." I think back to the custodial closet experience. "Trust me."

"Marc Watkins is the reason for my bad day too," he says, rubbing his eyelids with his fingertips. "I'm guessing you know the details by now."

I nod. "Execution style. Multiple shots. Found in a building in some place called Oval City."

"How do you know the Oval City part?" he says. "That wasn't in the news."

"Oh," I say. "Um . . . I heard kids at school talking about it."

He buys it and says, "They tied his hands and feet together like he was nothing more than a hog."

"Thanks," I say, raising my eyebrows, "you could have kept that one to yourself."

"Sorry." He downs the water in one extended gulp.

Dad places the empty glass on the granite countertop and puts his face in his hands. At first I think he's about to cry, something he's never done around me, and which he didn't even do after Mom passed, but instead he lets out a frustrated grunt before tugging on his unsightly beard and emitting a loud exhale—Dad trying to calm himself.

"There's stuff you can't talk about but wish you could," I say. "I get it, Dad."

"I saw Watkins's wife and two little boys today," he says, shaking his head. "All three of them are beautiful. The boys are six and eight. It doesn't make sense why a solid guy like Marc Watkins, a guy who seemed to have it all, would go and . . ." He cuts himself short.

"Go and what?"

"Nothing," he says. "I can't say anything for certain yet."

"What is Oval City anyway?"

"You've never heard of it?" Dad sounding surprised.

"No," I say, shaking my head. "Not until today."

"That's probably a good thing," he says, managing a smile. "Remember when your mother and I used to take you down to Eastern Market on Saturdays?"

"Eastern Market," I say, smiling at the memories. "Oh my God, I love that place. All the vendors yelling out their prices. All those food smells. It's been so long. We need to go down one Saturday morning. It can't be more than twenty-five minutes from here."

"I'll keep that in mind," he says, "but what I'm getting at is that Eastern Market is a perfect example of what a lot of cops call Mythical Detroit. Most people who shop there are suburbanites. People like you and me. We feel safe as long as we stay along the Russell Street corridor and shop the market sheds or surrounding stores. Plenty of beat cops patrol there to keep everybody feeling safe too, especially the tourists. It's one of the last places in the city where you can see a cop on horseback."

"What does Eastern Market have to do with Oval City?"

"I'm getting there," he says. "The past ten years or so everybody's been talking about the rebirth of Detroit. I mean, Alix, I've lost count of how many stories the *New York Times* has done about young hipsters moving to Detroit to start their little artsy projects, urban gardens, and foodie restaurants for cheap. Hey, great. More power to them. I wish them the best of luck. But here's the thing," he says, Dad getting worked up now. "At the end of the day, Detroit, Michigan, is still one of the most violent cities in the country. Anybody who has ever lived here knows that, which is why people who live in Detroit— and I'm talking black, white, Hispanic, Arabic, you name it—they get the hell out and move to the suburbs as soon as they can, because the suburban garbage gets collected every week and the suburban police show up when people call them.

"Anyway, it's a warzone at night, Alix. Detroit is a dangerous, decaying, poison-filled city at night. Oval City popped up a few years ago. It's the bottom of the cesspool. It's right next door to Eastern Market too, on the other side of the I-75 Service Drive. There's an abandoned housing project there. It's a huge, oval-shaped space. The mayor promised to demolish the buildings when they closed the complex three years ago, but they're still there, a collection of gutted, graffiti-tagged, redbrick eyesores across the street from one of the city's biggest points of pride." He shakes his head. "Oval City's nothing but bottom feeders—addicts, dealers, prostitutes, violent offenders, you name it. If it's illegal, Oval City probably has it. At the moment it's the most dangerous part of Detroit."

"How come I've never heard about it?"

"Because it's a public embarrassment," he says. "Everybody talks about Eastern Market, Midtown, the Stadium District, the Riverfront—places like that. That's what we mean by Mythical Detroit. There's a myth of safety in Detroit now, but it's not a safe place, which is why I don't ever want you to set foot in that city unless I'm with you. Understand?"

"Yes," I say, nodding.

"Promise?"

"I promise," I say. "Why was Mr. Watkins in Oval City?"

"I don't know," he says. "But what we do know is that two different worlds are colliding in Detroit. We're seeing a lot of cases involving younger people new to the city who think they can ride their customized bicycles anywhere they want, even at night." He pauses.

"More than a few have paid dearly for their little joyrides to go see abandoned buildings. We had a young guy and his girlfriend beaten nearly to death in Oval City in the middle of the day last week. They were on bikes, scouting locations for some film project. You feel bad for what happened to them, but on the other hand . . . Well, have some common sense and don't ride bikes through Oval City, you know?"

"Why don't you guys just raid the place and clean it up?" I say. "Use a SWAT team or something."

"We've raided it more times than you know," he says. "But the monsters always come back. The problem won't disappear until the buildings come down." He rubs his eyelids again. "You get this sort of problem whenever individual neighborhoods are in transition. Usually, when legit money moves in, crime moves out. The problem with Detroit is that it's a huge city, and there's nowhere near enough legit money moving in, just random little pockets of progress here and there. The monsters don't feel threatened enough to leave, so they fight back to keep their criminal lifestyle, and they fight back violently, like it's one giant prison riot. It's not just Oval City either. It's the whole city." He leans his forearms on the counter, exhausted. "The bad guys are winning in Detroit, Alix. There's evil there. I see it every day." He studies me through glossy eyes, but I can't tell if the glossiness is from alcohol, fear, or sadness. Maybe all three. "When I think about you and your future," he says. "College. Career. Marriage. Kids."

"Ugh," I say, unable to bear the thought of childbirth. "Please stop."

"I'm serious," he says. "Your life's just beginning. I'd like to be part of it for as long as possible. I've never felt more at risk on the job than I do these days. Part of me wants to quit tomorrow. Another part of me can't stand the thought of the bad guys winning."

"What about just quitting the undercover stuff?" I say. "I know that's what you're doing whenever you grow a beard like that."

"That's the problem," he says. "In my line of work, when you're deep into something you can't just walk away."

"I understand," I say. "But what about when this . . . assignment or whatever you call it is over?"

He straightens and smiles. "You're reading my mind, kid. I'm thinking this might be the last one for me." He takes a few steps toward me but pulls up short. "I was about to give you a hug but I stink, remember?"

I laugh and shake my head. "Good night, Dad. Tomorrow will be better."

I'm leaving the kitchen when he says, "Alix?" I stop and turn. Dad says, "Is there anything else you want to tell me about today? As in your first day as a senior and all that?"

"No," I say, shaking my head. "It was just one strange day."

"If something was bothering you, you'd tell me, right?"

"Of course," I say. "Always."

He stares at me with his Dad-the-Cop eyes for a few moments, giving me a look that always means he's suspicious of something and trying to determine if I'm being totally honest. He's so good at this. It's his job to be good at reading people of course, which is why I hate lying to him. I'm always convinced he knows when I'm untruthful or hiding the complete story.

"Okay," he finally says. "Go get some sleep." He turns to refill his water glass.

I'm assuming Dad knows about William Weed dying upstairs two years ago. Part of me wants to ask him why he didn't tell me about it, but I know the answer. Death is often a sensitive topic, especially when your own mother passed unexpectedly one year ago. Dad is protecting me as usual. He sees no need to tell me about a troubled boy who allegedly took his own life in what is now my bedroom. Why stir up unneeded emotions about something that has no connection to our family?

Part of me also wants to tell him about the closet attack, the *Vagabond's Warrior* blog, and the scary text message, but as I listened to my father this evening, I realized Clint Keener is fighting battles far more troubling and dangerous than whatever it is I'm going through.

Me, I'm just a girl who had one weird dream and one very weird first day of school.

CHAPTER 7

He returns for the second straight night. As much as I feared falling asleep, I find myself thrilled as I float toward his presence through the now-familiar ocean of cloudy white light. There's a yearning inside of me, a yearning to feel his touch and see his physical form. I sense so many things coming from him—among the strongest, strength, weakness, kindness, anger, courage, and fear.

A flash of white light. I see the clearing and stop. He's here. Right in front of me. Inches away. His presence sends tingles through my body. Looking down, I'm surprised to see my own fully clothed body as opposed to last night's orb of white light. This excites me. Maybe he'll appear in his physical form as well.

Unfortunately, that doesn't happen, but communication is easier tonight. He knows how to message me without the initial inaudible sounds of our first session. I know he has to initiate the conversation, and as I wait I squint hard through my glasses in a failed attempt to catch a glimpse of what he looks like. Nothing, just that perfectly beautiful, warm white light as far as my eyes can see. I notice the smells too, a mixture of spring rain and delicate but fragrant flowers. If this is heaven, all the good people in the world have something wonderful to look forward to.

He's taking his time. I feel him watching me, looking me up and down. Conflicting thoughts rage inside me. Despite my clothing, I feel exposed, like he can see anything and everything he wants beneath the layers. But he likes me. I can tell. I have no experience in the romance department, but it feels good knowing that he's attracted to me.

Thank you, Alix Keener.

His voice. In my head. He's waiting for a response. Tonight his voice sounds like layers of different voices at different pitches, but every word is crisp and clear. It sounds as if a beautiful choir is speaking to me.

"Thank you for what?" I say, realizing my mouth is moving and I don't have to mentally message my responses.

For breaking ground. For starting to dig.

I take a few calming breaths to collect my thoughts. There are so many things I need to ask him.

"The *Vagabond's Warrior* blog. That was you?"

Yes. Don't worry about your tablet. It's safe to use.

"What about the text message? And the person who attacked me at school?"

I don't know about those things, but you'll always be in danger if you continue to dig for Perennial.

"There's the word again. What is Perennial?"

As I said last night, Perennial is all around you.

"Please stop being so cryptic," I say. "I never asked for any of this. Who are you? What do you want with me?"

Come on, Alix. You know who I am.

A long silence passes. I swallow hard. My heart pounds rapidly against my ribs.

"William?" I finally say, fear rippling through me at the thought of communicating with a dead person. "William Weed?"

The chorus of sounds comes to an end. I now hear a single, seductive, strong-sounding male voice: *Ah. Well done, Alix. Well done indeed.*

CHAPTER 8

Let me leave," I say, body shaking. I squeeze my eyes shut to avoid the sea of white light. "It's a dream, William. Wake me up and stay away from me."

His laugh is loud and unpleasant. I open my eyes and consider throwing a punch into the light.

I mean you no harm, Alix. I used the word "timing" last night. That's what you are. Perfect timing. Well, for me anyway. Hopefully, for you too. The verdict is still out on that.

"My bedroom," I say. "Where you died."

Where I died. Hmm. You make it sound almost peaceful.

An unseen force takes me by the wrists and squeezes hard, pinning my arms to my sides. I realize I'm being gripped by William's powerful hands, and his invisible body is so close to my own that I can feel his warm, pleasant breath against my face and neck, spiking my pulse at a dangerously high rate.

I was murdered in my own bedroom, Alix. You're the first person to use the room since it happened. I've been waiting two years for you.

I need your help. You're special. Vagabond gave me until the end of Friday.

"Until the end of Friday for what?" I say, wincing from the pain in my wrists.

There's a long silence.

I have until the end of Friday to figure out who killed me.

"Stop it," I say, trying to pull away but knowing I'm no match for his strength. "You're hurting me."

He releases me but stays close.

I'm sorry. The last thing I want to do is hurt you, but my emotions are running high right now.

"Who's Vagabond?"

Somebody you can trust. If you meet him, you won't like him. Nobody does. But you can trust him.

"What do you mean by *if* I meet him?"

I'm following Vagabond's orders. It means you have a choice. He gave me until the end of Friday, but I can't make you help me. You have a developing gift, Alix. ESP. Extrasensory perception. It's not like I can make contact with anybody I choose. Vagabond's interested in you. He wants to see how good you can become. That's why he let me make contact. He says it's no coincidence that you ended up moving into my bedroom. I know you like school. Think of this as a test. If you can help me find my killer, you'll pass, and I'll have peace in my world.

So many feelings and emotions race through me. Fear. Confusion. Disbelief. Overall, I'm still convinced this is all a dream. Problem is I want to experience William Weed for as long as possible, so instead of demanding to awaken in my own bed I decide to play along.

"So, I don't have to do it," I say. "I can say no and call it a day."

Vagabond doesn't want people who aren't interested in developing and enhancing their abilities. So yes, you can say no and never have contact with me again. Tomorrow your life goes back to its boring, predictable course. A boring senior year, followed by four years of boring lectures in Ann Arbor, followed by a boring job and a boring husband

and kids you don't want but will have because you want your father to
be a happy grandpa. That's really what your life has been and always
will be about. Pleasing your daddy.

"Screw you, William," I say, squinting and jabbing an index finger
into his light. It's useless of course. My finger strikes nothing solid.
"Maybe those are *exactly* the things I want, you idiot. Maybe you're
just jealous because you were nothing but a drug addict with stupid
tattoos and shitty parents." I pause. He doesn't message a reply. "No.
Wait," I say. "I bet your parents were awesome and you were just a
spoiled-asshole son who was too weak to say no to pills, needles, and
powder."

His translucent hand grabs the back of my neck and squeezes
hard. William's fingertips feel like they could easily dig through my
skin and crush my bones. I close my eyes and sense his open mouth
centimeters from my lips.

Listen to me, Alix.

There's increased anger in his voice as he continues squeezing
my neck.

I need your help. I'm just trying to convince you that everything
you think you've always wanted might not be your true destiny after
all. Will you help me find my killer or not?

He releases my neck, and I sense him backing away a few feet.

"What about the guy who threw me into a closet and told me to
stay away from Perennial?" I say. "And I'm pretty sure he's the guy
who texted me after I visited your clever little blog. He told me I
should have listened and stayed away."

You just answered your own question. If you say no, you stay away
and nobody bothers you anymore. But I need you, Alix. I need you
more than you realize. If my murder remains a mystery, a killer walks
the streets, and I live a tortured existence on this side. I was no saint. I
admit that. Vagabond despises me. I'm nothing but a pawn to him. He
says you're capable of great things and that your gift can possibly help

a lot of innocent people against evil. The only thing in it for me is that I might figure out who killed me.

"Where can I find Vagabond?"

You can't find Vagabond. Nobody can. Vagabond finds you.

"But who is he, William? Is he human? Is he something else?"

I'm afraid I can't say anything else. But your curiosity is obvious, meaning you've already agreed to help solve my murder.

"Fine," I say. "I'll need information from you. What do you remember about the night you died? Did you do something to piss off Face? Was Aruna your girlfriend?"

His loud, annoying laughter fills the space around us.

"Stop laughing, William. Please just shut up."

I clench my jaw and close my eyes until he stops.

I'm sorry, Alix, but you're grasping at straws. Desperation and ignorance make anybody unattractive, even somebody as beautiful as you. Besides, the game doesn't work that way. I can't give you any information. You have to solve the mystery using your brilliant mind and developing abilities. Vagabond's orders. Again, he needs to know how good you can become. If I reveal too much, the deal is off, and we all lose. I'm sorry, but you're on your own.

"I can see what you stand to lose, not knowing who killed you. But what would I lose? Nothing as far as I can see. As you said, I'll just go back to my nice, boring, predictable life." I pause. "Lots of people in this world would love to have something like that."

Nice try, Alix, but your interest in all this surrounds you like a bright, shining halo. This is the most important puzzle of your life. You have all the pieces you need. Go solve it. Our time is up for tonight.

"Wait," I say, not wanting to lose his presence and voice. "What about Lewis Wilde? He seems different. Can I trust him? He said you two were friends. It's the only question I'll ask you." I pause and take a deep breath. "Can I trust Lewis?"

I feel William's mouth close to the side of my neck. I close my eyes as his warm breath travels around my throat and the nape of my neck before settling on my lips.

Lewis was a good friend, Alix, but loyalty has different meanings to different people.

My eyes remain closed as his fingertips caress the sides of my face. A warm, tingling sensation washes through me in reaction to his touch. I imagine Lewis's hands doing the same thing and soon find myself thinking other things about Lewis that surprise me.

"I need to know you're real and not a dream, William," I say, unable to resist his hands as they travel gently down my neck, arms, waist, and outer thighs. "Please," I whisper, "I want to help you, but I need to know you're real. Lewis is real. Are you real, William?"

Of course I'm real, Alix. I'm William Weed. I'm your Dream Guy. Open your eyes and see for yourself.

∞

I gasp and awaken bolt upright in bed, my sheets and pajamas once again damp with sweat. I sense something at the foot of the mattress but can't see anything in the dimly lit room. I rub my eyes and slide my glasses on.

William Weed stands over my bed, hands folded in front of his waist, the slightest smile on his beautiful face. It's the William from the blog photo, and he's absolutely stunning, shirtless in his black cargo shorts, taller and even more muscular than I imagined. He's there for less than a second, not long enough for me to get a closer look at his tattoos, not long enough for me to ask him to remove the sunglasses and backwards baseball cap.

I blink once, and then he's gone. But William is real. I know this now. I've agreed to play a dangerous game, a game that can kill me if I'm not careful. As crazy and un-Alix-Keener-like as it sounds, this is a game I know I must play. As Vagabond told William, it was no coincidence I ended up living in his bedroom. Up until now my parents have planned my life for me. I loved Mom. I love Dad, and I would never do anything to hurt him. But something is happening to me—something that reaches beyond the so-called normal world. I have new, developing abilities I need to explore, abilities that can help people, abilities that both excite and terrify me. I have otherworldly abilities that can fight evil. The universe is enormous. In the grand scheme of things, humans are specks of dust. There is so much more out there.

Strange. Although I've never met Vagabond, I find myself eager to impress him. He's obviously part of something special. When it comes down to it, I'm really not much different from my father. Dad is a cop fighting the bad guys, and it looks as if I'm heading down a similar career path. Except something tells me my stage will be far larger than his. I need to solve William's murder. Not only for William, but because I want access to whatever special club Vagabond is considering me for.

Of course, it also occurs to me that I'm falling in love for the first time, and it happens to be with two different guys. One object of my affection is a mysterious fellow senior who lives down the street. The other happens to be a ghost who by all accounts was quite a bad boy when he was alive.

CHAPTER 9

Wednesday, September 5

The second day of school is surprisingly normal for a high school that just lost its finest teacher to a horribly violent death. I'd been checking the hallways all day for any sign of Lewis's amazing face, but I didn't see him until sixth-hour history class, where a long-term substitute named Mr. Frank Dobbins introduced himself at the front of Mr. Watkins's former classroom on the second floor and awkwardly explained his approach to teaching the course. Although he pointed out more than once that he was no Marc Watkins, he insisted he would teach the independent study just as Mr. Watkins would have done, a fact all ten of us appreciated. Basically, this means we get to select and research our own narrow, instructor-approved American history topic for the entire semester, which is exactly what independent learners want.

Mr. Dobbins, a tall, stocky man in his late thirties, looks professional in his navy-blue suit and reminds me of a retired football player. Despite the overall jock-like aura he gives off, he seems like a nice, fair teacher, as good a replacement for Mr. Watkins as any, I suppose. I also sense that the high intelligence levels of, and ultra-nerd vibes given off by, the ten select students in this class intimidate him. I find that awesomely funny.

"Any topic ideas yet?" Lewis asks.

We're near the back of the classroom, desks facing each other as we brainstorm research proposals during the last twenty minutes of class. Mr. Dobbins circulates the room, stopping and conferencing with students, tapping notes into his tablet now and then. For all I know he's checking sports scores or messaging a girlfriend or something.

"Nothing," I say. "I still like yours, by the way. I love the science link with the DNA too. Famous Unsolved American Murders and the Likelihood of DNA Evidence Helping to Solve Them." I smile. "Wow, Lewis. I can already see the title on the cover of some well-respected historical journal. I'm jealous I didn't think of it myself."

"I'm starting with the Donner Party."

"Gross," I say, laughing and adjusting my glasses. "Back in the nineteenth century, some California pioneers got snowed in, starved, and eventually ate each other, right?"

"Actually, there's a lot more to it than that," he says, his aqua-green eyes melting part of me every time they connect with my own. "The cannibalism is the mystery part. I'd like to figure out who ate who, if anybody, although DNA evidence is probably useless in the Donner Party case. Still, you have to admit that it's one cool story."

Mr. Dobbins gives us a strange look and moves on to another pair of students. When his back is to us, Lewis and I cover our mouths to muffle the laughter.

"On a somewhat related note," I say, gathering my composure, "I have a favor to ask you."

"About cannibalism?" he says, smiling.

"No," I say. "About murder." Lewis must sense my sudden seriousness, because his smile fades and he stares right through me. "I believe you about William getting murdered and not killing himself,"

I add in a hushed tone. "I think we should do something about it. But I can't do it alone. I'm asking you to help me solve his murder."

Lewis's gorgeous mouth opens slightly. Then he rubs his face with his hands as if he doesn't believe what he's just heard.

Clasping his hands in front of his chest, he looks me dead in the eyes and says, "Alix, you have no idea—" He cuts himself off, shakes his head, and studies the room to ensure nobody is listening in. "Listen to me," he continues, quieter now, gaze back on me. "You have no idea what you're talking about, okay? Willis was into bad stuff with bad people. I know because I was there once, remember? I got clean, and he didn't. There's a reason why I told you that stuff on the porch last night about the Beaconsfield police covering up his death. I wanted you to mention it to your dad, okay? He's the cop, Alix. Not you. And he's not a Beaconsfield cop either. Everybody knows Clint Keener does hardcore undercover federal shit, so I was thinking he might have some power to look into Willis's so-called suicide." He shakes his head as if it's full of cobwebs. "Jesus, are you insane or something? Drug people will kill you if you start sniffing where you're not wanted."

"Wait a second," I say, struggling to keep my voice low. "What about all that stuff about me finally starting to discover who I am? You said that last night, right after I mentioned Oval City, Aruna, and Face. It felt to me like you were trying to convince me to get involved." I pause and think about William. "Like it was my destiny or something."

Lewis closes his eyes and tilts his head back. "All one big misunderstanding, Alix." He exhales deeply and opens his eyes. Around us students begin gathering their belongings in anticipation of the dismissal bell. "I'm sorry if I misled you. I didn't mean to. I was simply hoping you'd mention things to your dad." He pauses. "Well, everything except me knowing where your bedroom is." He smiles. I don't. "Right," he says. "Wrong joke at the wrong time. Sorry."

"Maybe I don't need my dad on this one," I say, drawing a few glances from my peers. I wait for them to look away before whispering, "I know what I'm doing. Trust me. But I can't do this without your help." I dig into my pocket and drop a yellow sticky note with my phone number written on it onto his desk. He glances at it but leaves it lying on the desktop. "I'm going to Oval City tonight," I say. "I'd like you to be my tour guide."

"Bullshit you are," he says, pointing an index finger at me. "If you go there, there's a good chance you might not come back, especially if you're nuts enough to drive that new Explorer."

"Then wish me luck," I say. "I'm leaving around eight. With or without you."

The dismissal bell rings. Lewis and I stare at each other as the class files out.

"Just one question," he says, standing. "Why? You live in Beaconsfield, Michigan, and you're sitting in one of the best high schools in the country. I get the sense you can choose the university of your choice. You don't seem like a drama queen. You say you lose it and flip out every now and then, but who doesn't? What I'm saying is that you have a perfect life with an amazing future in front of you." He shrugs. "So why does a sweet, beautiful, wholesome girl like you want anything to do with something as ugly as Oval City or the death of William Weed?"

I ponder his solid questions for few moments. Then I say, "Like I told you last night, there's something happening to me. I'm questioning things for the first time in my life." I pause. "And it has everything to do with what happened in my bedroom two years ago. We need to bring justice to William. People can't just get away with murder."

When the room empties, Mr. Dobbins gives us a good-bye wave before entering a tiny office connected to the front of the classroom and closing the door. Lewis reaches for the sticky note and shoves it into his front pocket.

"So, I'll hear from you later?" I ask.

Lewis nods. Barely.

I'm turning to leave when he says, "Alix?"

I stop and turn in the doorway. "Yes?"

"Bring a weapon," he says. "Nobody goes to Oval City without one."

My heart pounds, my knees are on the brink of buckling, and it takes everything I have to keep a straight face as I nod and walk away.

CHAPTER 10

I'm too nervous about tonight's trip to Oval City to go home to an empty house, so I drive through the snobby downtown Beaconsfield shopping area and make an impulsive decision to stop at Zeppelin Coffee, the small, independent coffeehouse where Dad buys his fancy coffee-geek beans and accessories. In a city full of high-end chain stores and expensive boutique shops, Zeppelin Coffee is easily the coolest retail outlet.

The downtown streets are old and narrow, paved with newer red bricks that are supposed to look old but don't. Despite that poor design decision, downtown Beaconsfield is actually quite beautiful. Enormous planters overflow with cascading flowers and hang from every lamppost. Mature trees line the streets. Old brick structures mix with newer, modern designs, creating a mixed-use area of high-end residences and ground-floor retail space that draws huge numbers of shoppers and gawkers from all over metro Detroit. If you could remove all the arrogant rich people, the place would be perfect.

There's never daytime parking available at the metered street spots, so I drive through a tight alley around back and barely manage to wedge the Explorer into one of five tiny spots reserved for Zeppelin. Maneuvering an SUV through spaces originally designed for much smaller vehicles is a real pain sometimes.

It's a hot and humid afternoon. Walking through the deserted back lot, I wipe sweat from my brow and decide I'll order a large, unsweetened iced coffee. What's odd is I'm not a coffee geek at all. I've only had a handful of iced coffees in my life, but for some reason I feel like I'm supposed to be here right now. It's as if I'm following somebody else's program, a feeling I've never had before and suddenly don't like.

I'm approaching the shaded, narrow concrete walkway that separates the coffeehouse from the neighboring building when my attention shifts to a green Dumpster to my right, directly behind Zeppelin Coffee. The blinding white light and subsequent vision slice through my mind like the clearest, most vibrant HD film imaginable.

I stop in my tracks and place my palms on either side of my head. It all happens so quickly. It's new. It's terrifying. It's exciting. Imagine a bright flashbulb filling your head and revealing a crystal-clear display. It's showing the future, I realize. Seconds from now. I'm seeing what others can't.

There's a girl hiding behind the Dumpster. I see her in my head. She has no clue I know this, but she's waiting for me. She wants to surprise me. Is she a threat? I can't tell, but she does seem desperate.

Wait. There's more. She's sick. Really, really sick. She needs help.

I know who she is. I've never seen her face before, but her name pops into my head after another blast of the mental flashbulb.

"Aruna?" I say, lowering my hands and preparing to defend myself as I step toward the Dumpster. There's still no sign of her, but she's back there. "Aruna? It's okay. You can come out."

She stumbles out from behind the Dumpster and nearly falls onto the walkway, before managing to lean a deathly thin arm against the Dumpster for support. Aruna's shoulder-length dark hair is disheveled, matted, and dirty. She's way too pale. Her glassy eyes and lack of coordination make it clear she's in another world, stoned beyond belief. She's wearing a wrinkled black tank top and tight, tattered black jeans. I see small red marks up and down her arms. Needle marks, I realize. Right now she's the most un-Beaconsfield-like creature in Beaconsfield.

And this once-beautiful girl is dangerously close to death.

"Hey there, special new girl," she says, slurring her words. Her voice is annoyingly high pitched, and whatever she's high on makes her giggle at the end of her sentences. "Face said you'd know who I was." Another giggle. "But how did you see me? I thought I was hidden pretty damn well, if I do say so myself."

I'm trying to read her and hoping for another vision, but I get nothing. Five feet separate us. She's not carrying a bag or any other accessory, and her tight clothing doesn't reveal any hidden weapons. Still, her unstable state worries me, so I clench my fists and keep them at my sides.

Aruna notices and says, "No, no, no, special girl. You got me all wrong. I'm not here to fight. You'll get plenty of that later." Giggle. "I'm just a messenger. You know what they say—that thing about not shooting the messenger or whatever. That's me, okay?"

"Aruna, you need help," I say. "Can I take you to a doctor?"

She laughs so loudly that I figure it's only a matter of time before a nearby employee or resident comes back here.

"Help?" she says, stifling her laughter. "I'm beyond help, special girl." She removes her hand from the Dumpster and manages to stand under her own power, although she's swaying badly.

"From what I'm told, you've been missing for two years," I say. "Isn't there somebody you can call? There must be people who care about you and want to know you're alive."

"Shh, shh, shh," she says, shaking her head and raising an index finger in front of her mouth. "Some people prefer not to be found. You know what I mean? Besides, everybody's dead to me, special girl. Everybody except Face. Face takes care of me." She glances at her toothpick-like arms. "He gives me what I need."

"My name's Alix," I say. "Alix Keener."

"Well, then shut up and listen, Alix Keener." Giggle. "Face has a message for you. Stop now and you'll live. Continue digging and you'll die." She smiles, revealing a set of yellowed and blackened chipped teeth. "They know where you live, Alix. You live in Willis's old room. The room he died in."

The white light explodes in my head as soon as she mentions his bedroom. *My* bedroom. I see a vision that upsets me, but it occurs to me that this is a vision of the past, not the future. I see that William and Aruna had a history. I see them together in his bed, a thin, white sheet covering their sweaty bodies, the two of them lying on their backs beside each other, smiling and staring at the ceiling, Aruna's glazed eyes looking like red spider webs. It's obvious what they just finished doing—something I've never come close to doing—but I find it odd that William has his backwards baseball cap and sunglasses on. I glimpse his tattoos for the first time. William has an ornate green, blue, orange, purple, and red Japanese dragon running down the length of each arm. Each dragon has its open mouth just above his wrist. The dragons are beautiful, and I wonder how he paid for such quality work.

"Now, tell me something," Aruna says, leaning her left arm on the Dumpster again and ending my vision in the process. She does something different this time though. I watch closely as her left hand reaches behind the Dumpster and out of view. "Face says you can talk to the spirits. He says you've been talking to Willis. Is that correct?"

"Aruna, if you don't want my help, then I think we're done here. Would you like me to tell anybody you're alive?" I say. "Barely."

"Oh my," she says, laughing loudly again. "The bitch has a sense of humor. I'll be sure to let Face know. He'll like that." She pauses and somehow manages to hold my gaze, Aruna not looking as stoned now. "Thing is I know exactly what you're thinking, Alix. We all do. You're thinking you're safe because of who your daddy is. You're thinking if things get too scary, you can just run to Clint Keener the lawman and turn everything over to him. Truth is you're nothing but a bored little virgin schoolgirl who thinks a few visions have made her invincible and ready for an adventure on the wild side." She emits a soft grunt and spits onto the asphalt. "You're hoping the water doesn't get too hot, but honey, let me tell you something: you're one step away from feeling the boil. Alix Keener, you will crash and burn to your death if you try to expose, weaken, or disrupt Perennial in any way." She brushes a matted clump of sweaty hair away from her eyes. "And girl, you better believe me when I tell you there isn't a damn thing your daddy will be able to do to keep you safe."

"As I said, Aruna, it looks like we're done here."

I tighten my fists, sensing she's about to try something desperate, something stupid. She's right, though: part of me does wish either the police or my dad would show up right now to take her away, but I know that isn't going to happen. I'm terrified at the thought of violence, but I'm well aware the road I'm embarking upon is loaded with it. Right now I'm thankful to Dad for all those years of self-defense lessons.

"Just one last thing," Aruna says, lowering her head and looking sad and exhausted now, her left hand still hidden as I walk a wide arc to my left to get around her and onto the path. "Face wants you to have this."

She's barely eight feet away and charges me with surprising speed for a strung-out druggie, Aruna raising her left arm over her shoulder, sunlight glinting off of something sharp and shiny in her hand: a knife about seven inches long and easily capable of ending my life at seventeen. Dad's fight lessons pay off for the first time in my life.

I don't have time to think. All I can do is react. I raise my right arm and chop the outside edge of my hand directly below Aruna's knife hand. I have a terrible vision of her future as I deliver a sharp left jab to her chin. Aruna grunts and hunches over, stunned. Next I grab her left wrist and the back of her neck and force her out away from me, twisting her knife-holding hand inward and up, which allows me to bend her left wrist back as far as I want while simultaneously landing a hard kick to her right knee. Aruna screams from the pain and drops to her knees, her grasp on the knife easily weakened enough for me to pry the weapon from her hand. She's lucky I didn't break her left wrist, because that would've been my next move if she refused to release the knife.

I back off to create some space between us, keeping the silver weapon in my right hand as Aruna breaks into tears and rolls onto her back. She's rubbing her wounded knee with one hand and cradling her aching wrist against her chest. Her crying turns into childlike wailing. I feel bad for her, but I had to defend myself.

I hold the knife behind my back, stand over her, and say, "Aruna, you need to get away from Face. You tell Face that any man who sends a girl to do his fighting isn't a man at all. He's a pathetic piece of shit."

"I'm so sorry, Alix," she says, genuine terror on her face as her crying stops and she looks into my eyes. "I mean it. I'm so sorry. He makes me do these things. But you don't understand. He has powers too. He does things normal people can't. I'm so scared, Alix. I can't get away. He'll find me and kill me. The only way to free me is to kill Face." She breaks into a fresh round of tears. "But I don't think he can die. He's too different."

"Did Face kill William?" I say, noticing a pristine black four-door Mercedes pulling up and stopping perpendicular to the Zeppelin lot, blocking any chance I have of getting out of here in the Explorer. Full black tint covers the sedan's windows. The vibe coming from this car is one of pure evil, so much so that I feel the hairs on my arms stiffen and rise. "Hurry, Aruna," I say, shifting my gaze between the car and her. "Your ride is here. Did Face kill William?"

"William," she says, tilting her head to stare at the car, which just sits there, engine humming quietly beneath the blazing sun. "God, I'm in so much trouble, Alix." She looks at me. "I don't know how William died, and that's the honest-to-God truth. But he's something, isn't he? So bad and yet so, so good." She forces a smile. "You know what I mean. I can tell. Could you do me a favor and tell him I said hello and that I miss him and that I'm sorry I lost it?"

"Lost what?"

The car engine revs. I'm in no position to challenge this vehicle. Whatever or whoever is behind those windows holds far more power than I do. So what I do is walk slowly backwards toward the Dumpster, eyes glued to poor Aruna as she struggles to her feet and limps slowly toward the Mercedes, where she opens the driver's-side back door and collapses into an empty backseat. The door closes automatically, and the driver pulls quickly away, leaving behind a filthy cloud of brown dust that blankets my Explorer.

Looking behind the Dumpster, I find the silver knife's well-worn black-leather sheath resting on a rail just beneath the Dumpster's top hinges, so I sheathe the knife, slide it into my back pocket, and allow my shirt to fall over it as a screen.

I'm coughing from the dust cloud as I walk the narrow path leading to the front of Zeppelin Coffee.

CHAPTER 11

I'm holding back tears as I enter Zeppelin Coffee and wait in a short line, heart thumping wildly. I'm struggling with the overwhelming urge to call Dad's emergency number.

What would I say to him?

"Dad, a girl who's been missing for two years just tried to knife me in Beaconsfield right behind your favorite coffeehouse. Then she got into the back of a mysterious black Mercedes and drove off. By the way, I'm developing some freaky psychic abilities and am currently communicating with the ghost of the beautiful bad boy who died in my bedroom. He needs me to figure out who killed him, and . . . oh yeah, the girl who just tried to kill me seems to know all of this and warned me that Face has powers as well. Speaking of Face, I think he killed William and runs something called Perennial, whatever that is."

What else? Hmm. "Oh, William is a pawn of some guy named Vagabond, who wants to see if I'm a good enough psychic to gain access into some special club of his. Also, last but not least, I'm pretty sure Oval City is the epicenter of this mystery, which of course means I have to go there. Tonight."

Yeah. Right.

Dad has never hit me before, but a psycho rant like that might do the trick. At the least, Clint Keener—a calm man of reason, a man of the law, a man who firmly believes that the key to a bright future is a solid education and a willingness to live according to society's time-tested rules—would handcuff me and commit me to the nearest psychiatric facility until the doctors deemed me fit to reenter the normal world.

But not everything in the world is normal, Dad. In fact, everything I thought was normal has blown up in my face in less than forty-eight hours. I'm on my own undercover investigation now, an otherworldly investigation you would never understand.

And this is why I can't whisper a word to you about my new world.

The young woman seated at the circular table for two off to my left catches my attention. She's sipping a large iced coffee and playing with her phone. She's not looking my way, but she's the reason I'm here. Somehow I know this. She's incredibly beautiful too, with rich, deep mocha skin, and long, layered hair. Her dark clothes are tight but stylish. She looks about my age, maybe a year or two older. There's an aura of confidence around her, a type of positive energy she exudes that makes me want her on my side.

A flash of light explodes inside my head. Two blurred words in bold black print hover within the white cloud of light. Her name.

I leave the line and walk over to her. She knows I'm two feet away but still pretends not to notice.

"Excuse me," I say. She looks up from her phone with big brown eyes that have surely melted more than a few men. "I'd like you to know that you have the coolest name I've ever heard."

"Is that right?" she says, smiling. "And what is my name?"

"London," I say. "London Steel."

"Get your coffee and sit down, Alix. Vagabond says congratulations, by the way."

"For knowing your name?"

"No," she says, "for passing your first test back there."

∞

She doesn't say anything for a few minutes, just keeps typing away on her phone. I sit there, sipping my iced coffee, feeling the uncomfortable pressure of Aruna's knife in my back pocket. The place is busy and loud now, adults and teenagers dropping in for late-afternoon drinks. I realize Dad could walk in any minute, meaning I should get rid of this knife as soon as possible.

"I'm sorry," London finally says, forcing herself to pocket her phone. "I blog a lot. It's kind of addictive."

"No problem," I say. "What do you blog about?"

"Good question," she says, mulling it over. "I guess you can call me an Internet job recruiter. I'm a type of headhunter, as adults in the business world call it. Special jobs for only the most highly qualified people."

"People like me."

"It's looking good so far," she says. "What you did back there was impressive. Being an effective psychic is rare enough, but where'd you learn to fight like that?"

"My dad's a cop."

"Ah," she says. "That would explain it." London smiles.

I smile back. "Was that even Aruna back there?"

"Oh, it was definitely Aruna. Poor thing." London shakes her head. "We knew Face had her. We just didn't know if she was dead or alive." She raises her eyebrows. "Now we know."

"She's in danger."

"Aren't we all?"

"That's not what I mean," I say. "I had a horrible vision when I first made physical contact with her during the fight." I swallow hard and promise myself to hold back the tears. "She'll die soon. It'll be Face, and it won't be pretty."

London, serious now, says, "I know your abilities are new to you, Alix, as in two-days new, but is there anything you can do to save her?"

"No," I say. "I saw her dead. I saw Face standing over her. That means he'll kill her. Just because I can see the future doesn't mean I can change it."

"What else did you see that involved her?"

"I knew she was behind the Dumpster. I knew when she was about to attack." I pause. "And I saw her in bed with William just before he died."

"Whoa," she says, raising her hands as if they're stop signs. "You saw a *past* event too?"

"Yes," I say. "It surprised me. Actually, everything's surprised me lately."

"Wow," she says. "No wonder Vagabond's interested in you. A brilliant young mind and a two-way psychic who can kick ass when she needs to." She laughs. "That's hot, girl." She raises a hand for a high five across the table, which I gladly give her.

"When will I meet him?"

"Vagabond?" she says. "That's up to him. Right now, though, I want you to take my hand and hold it." She lays her strong right arm on the table. I stare at it before glancing around the coffeehouse. Nobody is watching us. "It's okay, Alix," she says, sensing my nervousness. "You can trust me, and you know it. Hold my hand and tell me what you see."

She wears a shiny but simple silver ring on her right ring finger. I sense there's something special about it, so I make a point of pressing my palm against it as I wrap my right hand around hers and rest it in the center of the table. We stare at each other, London's gaze intense now. At first I can't get a reading, just strange warmth from the ring and incredible strength in her elegant hand. She works a lot with her hands, I realize, but I don't know what kind of work she does.

Moments later the mental flashbulb fills my head with brilliant white light. Seconds after that, images, footage, and words about the life of London Steel overload my brain. It's the strongest reading yet, which is exactly why she gave me her hand. The power is greater with physical contact. I experienced that with Aruna as well. I tell myself to harness the power and understand it.

Don't run from it. Embrace it and think of yourself as a messenger of good.

The reading on London is amazing but terrifying. Sometimes I see what amount to short video clips of a past or future event, always sharp and clear, often violent, never more than a few seconds in length. Sometimes a series of vivid but bizarre battle images shoot through my mind like a high-speed slide show. Other times I see what I begin calling "word clouds," like I did with her name and Aruna's, the words always slightly blurry and printed in bold black against a white background.

I'm crying. I feel warm tears rolling gently down the sides of my face. What I'm seeing is a violent fantasy world of fire and light, a world of fabulous human warriors and hideous, grotesque shape-shifting demons, the two sides engaged in an epic struggle to defeat each other.

"It's okay," London whispers. "It's hard. I know. Just take it all in and observe. Don't react. Observe. It's all real, and you're becoming part of it."

The vision ends, but fear keeps me holding her hand. I wipe tears away with my free hand as words begin flowing out of me almost automatically, like a well-rehearsed script.

"London Steel is your real name," I say, trying to regain my composure. "You're nineteen and from Canada." I scrunch my nose. "Canada. Eww. Sorry about that."

"Ha!" she says. "London, Ontario, believe it or not. Anyway, nice one. Keep going."

I squeeze harder. She does the same.

"You're very into genealogy," I continue. "Your family history in the US dates back to the so-called lost colony of Roanoke in what is today North Carolina. Before that, West Africa and Europe. The ugly institution of American slavery had a huge impact on your family."

"Excellent," she says. "What else?"

"The silver ring on your hand."

"Damn, you are good." She smiles. "What about my ring?"

"I'm not sure exactly," I say, telling the truth. "It's powerful. Other members of your family have worn it in the past, but not everybody. It's like you have to qualify for it somehow. But it's not always a good thing. Sometimes you hate the ring, but most of the time you can't imagine life without it. Other families have rings too, but not many. I'll never have one, and I'm glad." I pause and fight off more tears. "The ring allows access to another world. You've done horrible things, London, but only because you've had to. You're some sort of warrior," I say, shaking my head slowly. "Nobody would ever guess it by looking at you, but you've killed before. Many times. There's plenty of blood and gore in your recent past. And future, I'm afraid. But deep down you like it. You love the thrill of battle. The taste of it. The smell of it. Everything." I pull my hand away, exhale deeply, and lean back in my chair. "That's enough," I say. "What the hell was all that about?"

"You just passed another test," she says, retrieving her phone. "And with flying colors, I should add." London leans across the table and motions me forward. I lean toward her, and in a whisper she says, "I sure hope you solve William's murder, Alix, because you're incredibly gifted, and I would love to work with you. You just read me like a book and got a glimpse of what my real job is." She smiles. "You can help us in so many ways. There are sacrifices involved, but it's Vagabond's job to explain all that." She places her right palm on my left cheek in an almost motherly way. The warmth of the silver ring feels pleasant against my skin. "I wish I could help you in Oval City, but this is your test. You're on your own. Evil isn't just somebody who does a very bad thing. Evil is much deeper than that. You know that from what you just saw." She lowers her ring hand and squeezes my left hand with the kind of strength guys never dreamed girls could have. "Oval City is evil, Alix. That's why bad things happen there. Do you understand what I'm saying?"

"Yes," I say, nodding. "I'm scared, London."

"I know," she says. "There's nothing wrong with being scared. I'm scared every day. Vagabond says courage is being scared to death of something but confronting it anyway." She pauses. "Trust your abilities, but don't trust anything or anybody else."

"Okay," I say. "Thank you, London."

"I'll say the last part again," she says. "Don't trust anything or anybody else. *Anybody*." She stands, pushes her chair in, and grabs her clear plastic drink cup. "I know you'll do great," she adds, smiling and laying a hand on my shoulder. "Good luck."

"Here," I say, covertly retrieving Aruna's silver knife from my back pocket and palming the sheath as I offer it to London. "Take this. You're the warrior. Not me."

"Actually, I think you should keep that," she says, pushing my hand back toward me. "It might come in handy. Besides, my personal arsenal is good to go." She winks. "Good-bye, Alix, but not for long. We'll see each other soon under very different circumstances. I just know it."

I turn in my chair and watch London Steel exit Zeppelin Coffee. She moves with the confidence of a runway supermodel, the only difference between her and a supermodel being she doesn't look like she has an eating disorder. What I find funny is that every male in here is basically foaming at the mouth as they watch her leave.

CHAPTER 12

A small yellow envelope with my name written on it in black marker waits for me on the driver's seat of my Explorer when I leave Zeppelin. There's no sign of forced entry into the vehicle, so I have no clue how the tiny package arrived. I check the back of the SUV to make sure nobody's hiding there. All clear.

I get in and start the engine, savoring the chilly air as the air conditioner cools the hot, sticky interior. The envelope is sealed. I press on it in different spots. It feels empty. I decide to open it using my thumbnail to break the seal.

I don't see anything at first, but as I poke my index finger around to widen the inside of the envelope, I see what looks like purple powder at the bottom. I adjust my glasses and squint for a better view. Sure enough, that's exactly what it is: purple powder, about an inch of it, loose and dry. I waft my hand from the open end of the envelope toward my nose. The substance has no smell that I can detect.

I freak for a few moments and reseal the envelope as I remember news stories about politicians and some of their staff people getting sick and sometimes dying from opening mail laced with poisonous powders. Thankfully, I feel fine after a few deep breaths, so I place the envelope beside Aruna's knife in the beverage holder and drive home.

∞

I'm home before five, and the next few hours seem to last forever. Dad texted that he'd arrive home later than usual, meaning anytime after ten and before sunrise. Lewis texted that he has a car we could use, which is perfect, because if Dad's working the Watkins case there's a good chance he's in or near Oval City and would recognize my Explorer in a heartbeat. I figure if we leave at eight we should be home by ten. Besides, I'm basically thinking of tonight as a scouting mission, a quick trip to get the lay of the Oval City land.

I try doing math homework to pass the time, but that's pointless because I keep looking at the silver knife and yellow envelope, constantly thinking about Aruna, London, William, and Lewis. The whole idea of school seems trivial in comparison to my emerging psychic abilities and my commitment to solve William's murder.

Despite the danger that awaits us in Oval City, I can't stop thinking about how attracted I am to William and Lewis. I mean, William Weed is a ghost! It's impossible to have a real relationship with a ghost! William can be my Dream Guy anytime he wants, but I need to try and push aside my thoughts about him and focus on Lewis. Lewis Wilde is real. He's a living, breathing, beautiful, gorgeous, and godlike human. He's strong and disciplined too. I respect him for getting himself clean and off of drugs when he was at the alternative academy as a freshman.

I wonder what drug or drugs he was on. Cocaine? Heroin? Weed? Wait. Can you be *on* weed, or do you just say you smoke weed? Do you *do* weed, as in *do* drugs?

God, Alix, you're such an innocent person when it comes to illegal substances. Like using that term right there, "illegal substances." Who says that besides cops? There you go. Dad's influence again.

Anyway, I bet Lewis got into a lot of fights when he was on drugs. I know there's a body full of muscle beneath those long-sleeved V-neck tees he wears. I bet he looks amazing with his shirt off, maybe even better than William. Maybe.

As crazy as it sounds, I start to think of tonight's trip to Oval City as my first date with Lewis. I'd considered wearing some sort of basic disguise just in case we come across my dad, but now I realize I want to look as good as possible for Lewis. My heart felt like it was about to bust out of my chest when he called me sweet, beautiful, and wholesome in sixth hour today.

I spend the hour between seven and eight doing something I've honestly never done before: trying to make myself attractive to a guy. I figure it all starts with the hair, but what can you do with short, spiky dark hair besides make it . . . well, short, dark, and spiky? So I ditch the hair and remove my glasses. I actually think my brown eyes aren't so bad. I'm no London Steel, of course, but I make a note to ask Dad about getting me checked out for contact lenses. Until then the chunky black frames stay on my face, because life is one big, blurry movie without them. As for makeup, it's out of the question: my face breaks out whenever I wear it.

God, I am such a loser.

My only real option for changing my appearance is clothing, and this is where I go to my closet and make a decision to try something new and very un-Alix-like. London looked absolutely stunning in her tight, stylish black outfit. I don't own anything like that, but Mom bought me some things a few months before she died, things I've never worn. She was a big fan of denim, so I try on the faded denim skinny jeans she thought I would like—skinny jeans complete with strategically placed tears in the knees and lower thigh. They're tight but surprisingly comfortable. I want Lewis to see that I actually have legs, and these pants definitely have a sexy fit. As for a shirt, I go with a dark denim button-up with long roll-tab sleeves, button cuffs, and a curved hem, leaving the top button undone just to remind him that I'm a girl. When it comes to shoes, I have to go with black Chuck Taylors, because I have a feeling running is common in Oval City.

Lewis knows my dad isn't home, so he knocks on the door at eight. He's punctual. I like that. I slide Aruna's knife into my back pocket, liking how the back hem of the shirt conceals the sheathed weapon. I open the door, and we stand there for a few awkward moments, the two of us staring at each other. He's still wearing what he had on in school, but it doesn't matter. With those hypnotic eyes, that dark, wavy hair, and pale, exquisite face, he can wear anything and look good. He steals a glance at my pants and then quickly returns his gaze to my face.

"You look great," he says. "Good call on the Chuck Taylors too." He smiles and looks over my shoulder. "Are we leaving right away?"

I'm speechless and feel like a fool for not inviting him in.

"Oh, here," I say, turning sideways. "I guess we have a few minutes. Come on in." He leaves behind the smell of mint and a light soapy cleanliness. Perfect. I look outside to an empty driveway and street. "Where's your car?"

"Down the street."

"Why?" I say, the door closing behind me.

"Isn't it obvious?" He stops and turns in the middle of the spacious living room. "I didn't want your dad to see it."

"What if he pulled up right now?"

Lewis shrugs. "Then I guess you'd have to hide me."

I stare at him and feel afraid of what I need to tell him.

"Alix, it was a joke," he says. "What's wrong?"

"Lewis, Aruna's alive."

There's a silence.

"What?" he finally says. "How do you know?"

I tell him all about our encounter and fight in the parking lot behind Zeppelin, leaving out the psychic parts, including Aruna knowing I'm psychic and communicating with William. I also leave out the parts about Face having powers and me seeing Aruna's inevitable death, although I do tell Lewis how awful she looked.

"Do you know her family?" I say. "Is there anybody we can tell?"

"Aruna's older," he says. "She's at least twenty-two by now. I don't know much about her. She was Willis's girl, not mine. She's been on the streets since she was a kid. Willis said she ran away from a sicko stepdad. I'm glad she's alive, but it sounds like she's Face's slave." He pauses. "How did she know you would be at Zeppelin?"

"I have no idea," I say, which is true, but I'm fairly certain Face had something to do with it. "But it looks like I have my weapon." I withdraw the knife and show him before quickly tucking it back into the sheath.

"Okay, this is pretty huge." He rubs his forehead, Lewis thinking hard about something. "If Face sent Aruna to intimidate you, it means he's afraid of you, which means you're not telling me everything, because Face isn't afraid of anybody." He stares at me. "What are you leaving out, Alix?"

"Nothing," I say, hating the feeling of lying but knowing I'm not ready to tell him everything yet. As with Dad, if I start babbling to Lewis about psychic visions and a violent world of evil demons and courageous human warriors . . . Well, I'll have no chance with him. "Maybe Face knows about my dad or something. Or maybe somebody in sixth hour heard us talking today and told Face." I pause. "The Mercedes could have followed me and dropped Aruna off on the street as I pulled around back. That would have given her time to hide on me."

He considers all of that and seems to accept it. Good.

"Okay, so what's your goal tonight, Alix?" he says. "Why are we going to Oval City? Have you even asked yourself that question?"

"Of course," I say. "We're going to Oval City in search of proof that William was murdered. Based upon that obscure blog post I came across yesterday, combined with what you've told me about William and today's run-in with Aruna, I think Face killed William because William had information that could bring down Face."

"I agree," he says. "But what do you expect to get tonight? Do you think you can just go around asking for Face in Oval City and find him? Even if you did, what then? Do you just walk up to him and say, 'Hey, Face, I know you killed William Weed. It's time to turn yourself in'?" Lewis shrugs. "Look, I admire your courage and sudden determination to solve William's murder, but you have to think things through. If not, you have a good chance of getting hurt. Or worse. Personally, I don't see why you won't tell your dad everything you know. Especially now with the whole Aruna thing."

I lose it and yell, "I don't need my dad right now, okay, Lewis? Stop talking about him. Please!" He stares at me, expressionless, as I take a few deep breaths and finally calm down. "Look, I'm sorry. I'm not saying we need to find Face and solve the mystery tonight. But I need to see what the area looks like. I need to know where William hung out. You know Oval City. I trust you to show me what I need to see. Nothing more for tonight."

"Okay," he says, nodding. "That's better. I can do that." He raises his eyebrows and clasps his large hands together in front of his waist. "You ready to go?"

"Yes," I say, nerves already rocketing through me. "But there's one more thing you need to see." I point toward the kitchen behind him. "Somebody put a present in my Explorer when I was in Zeppelin. It's on the kitchen table."

I follow Lewis into the kitchen, where he picks up the yellow envelope and gives me a look before opening the flap and examining the contents. Seconds later he closes the flap, drops the envelope onto the table, and backs away. It's the first time I've seen him look afraid.

"What is it?" I ask.

Looking quite vulnerable, Lewis says, "Alix, the thing about being a recovering drug addict is that you're a recovering drug addict for the rest of your life."

"That purple powder is a drug?"

"Oh, it's a drug," he says. "But not just any drug." He points at the envelope. "The purple powder in that envelope is more addictive than cocaine, meth, heroin, or anything else I've ever tried. I'm surprised I was able to beat it. Most people get hooked the first time they try it and never quit. That's what happened to Willis, Aruna, and who knows how many others around here." He shakes his head. "They couldn't beat it, and it destroyed them." He looks at me and says, "Whoever gave you this wants you to try it. They want you hooked too. So you have to promise me you'll never try it."

"I promise," I say. "Lewis, I've never done drugs in my life. I'm not about to start now, especially with something like that." I study the envelope. "What's it called?"

There's a long silence.

Then Lewis says, "That purple powder keeps Oval City and Face in business. Rumor is Face invented it, but nobody knows for sure." He takes another step back, as if the envelope might come to life and attack him. "You wanted to know what Perennial is," he says, studying me and pointing toward the envelope. "Well, Alix, you're looking at it."

CHAPTER 13

A drug," I whisper to Lewis. "Perennial is a drug."

"Bingo," Lewis says, still eyeing the kitchen table as if it's a violent monster. "And the stuff in that envelope is pure. I can tell by the color and texture. People started calling it Perennial on the streets because the high lasts so long, like a permanent high. And it's such a good high you want it to last forever, which means you have to always have more. *Boom*. You're addicted before you know what hit you."

"Perennial," I say, recalling the definition. "Permanent. Present at all times."

"Face is the kingpin," Lewis says. "He's got a monopoly on something that's about to go viral. Last I heard, the only way to get genuine Perennial is to buy it in Oval City, which means if they took the trouble to put it in your car, Face or somebody is afraid of you." He walks toward me and does something that both surprises and thrills me. He takes my hands in his own and stands less than a foot away. "Alix, I'm going to be honest and tell you that part of me wants to snort everything in that envelope right now, which is why you need to take it and flush it down the toilet. Can you do that for me?"

"Sure."

"Like, right now," he adds, giving my hands a gentle squeeze before releasing them and heading to the safety of the living room. "I'll meet you outside. We need to leave."

When he's safely out front, I do exactly what he asked and flush the small yellow envelope full of Perennial down the toilet of the first-floor bathroom. The purple powder reminds me of grape Kool-Aid as it swirls and disappears down the porcelain bowl.

∞

"So what does it feel like?" I say. We're hustling down the sidewalk to wherever Lewis parked his car. The night air is cool but humid, the street quiet on a Wednesday night. "The Perennial high, I mean. What's it like?"

"It's hard to explain," he says, scanning the neighborhood. "What's the greatest physical feeling you've ever had?"

"I don't know," I say. "I feel good most of the time. I suppose you could say I enjoy a natural high."

"Come on, Alix." He groans.

"What?" I say, nudging his elbow with my forearm. "I'm not very exciting that way, okay?"

"You have a knife in your back pocket that you took away from a girl who was trying to stab you. I'd say you're exciting."

"Well," I say, smiling, "that might be true, but you're looking at somebody who doesn't drink, smoke, or do drugs, remember? I don't know what any of that stuff feels like."

"Fair enough," he says. "Then what was the happiest moment in your life?"

"Hmm," I say, thinking. "Not to sound corny, but the happiest moment in my life was probably two years ago when I took a summer trip to Niagara Falls with my parents."

"You're kidding, right?" he says, laughing.

"No. I'm not."

"Wait a second," Lewis says. "Two years ago? You were in high school and went to Niagara Falls with your parents?"

He continues laughing, but in a sweet way that makes me smile.

"I know," I say. "It's not very teen-angst-like of me, is it? Look, what can I say. My parents are pretty awesome." Lewis's laughter fades to silence. He is surely remembering that my mom is dead. "Have you been there?" I say. "To Niagara Falls?"

"Not yet."

"It's beautiful," I say. "The falls are huge—even bigger than they look in pictures. People say the Statue of Liberty always looks smaller in person. Niagara Falls is the opposite. There's this tourist boat called the *Maid of the Mist* that takes you right up to the falls. They give you a plastic poncho to wear, and you need it because the mist really does soak you. Anyway, there was this moment on the boat where I just stopped and watched Mom and Dad's mist-covered faces as they took it all in and smiled at each other. I'd always known they loved each other deeply, but the looks of happiness on their faces that day made me so happy to have them as parents." I feel warm tears rolling down my face and wipe them away. "Then Mom and Dad looked at me looking at them, and we all laughed and shared this incredible moment. Nobody said a word, but the feeling of love in our family on that trip is something I'll never forget for the rest of my life." I wipe more tears away. If Lewis notices, he doesn't say anything. "It was the last time we took a trip together. One year later she was gone."

Lewis takes my left hand in his right and squeezes gently as we walk.

"I'm sorry," he says. "But at least you have the memories. Those will never go away. I envy the hell out of you, Alix. Most kids don't talk about their parents like that."

"I know," I say. "Believe me, I know."

"So," Lewis says, "imagine this. If you could take that moment on the boat, the happiest moment of your life, and make it last forever, you sort of get the idea of what a Perennial high is like. That's how good the stuff is." He stops at the quiet corner of Maple Grove and Covington, where a run-down black Ford pickup rests in front of a stately house across the street. "There's my truck." He takes the keys from his pocket and jingles them. "Looks like it's showtime."

"Is it yours?" I ask as we cross the deserted street.

"My grandpa's a retired Ford engineer and has a lot of cars. He tinkers around on them all day." Lewis unlocks the doors with the key-chain remote. "Don't let the looks of it fool you. This thing runs great. He called it his Detroit truck. It's the only thing he drove if he had to go into the city. He made it look beat-up on the outside so nobody would ever think of stealing it." Lewis shrugs. "It might not look very Beaconsfield, but it's mine until graduation."

"I love it," I say.

We get inside the truck, where the smell of cleaning chemicals greets us. The interior is pristine and like new. Lewis starts the engine, which comes to life instantly and also sounds brand new. Lewis's grandpa sounds like a cool guy, so I make a mental note to ask Lewis if I can meet him soon.

Right now, of course, we have other business to tend to.

"You were wrong a minute ago," I say as Lewis pulls forward and makes a right onto Maple Grove.

"About what?" he says, playing with the radio before powering it off completely.

"About the Perennial high," I say, glancing at the passenger-side mirror and noticing a pair of headlights far behind us. "I don't think any man-made drug can ever replace the natural power of love. At least not the kind of love our family had."

Lewis doesn't respond to that. It's silent for a few minutes. A few turns later, I notice the same car still trailing us.

Lewis notices too. He tightens his grip on the steering wheel and says, "I think somebody is following us."

The vehicle is closer now, maybe a hundred feet back, headlights almost blinding as they reflect off of the glass.

"Speed up and turn on the next street you see," I say, heart pounding. "But use the opposite turn signal."

"What?"

"Just do it," I say. "It's something my dad taught me."

Lewis accelerates, doing at least forty-five in a twenty-five zone. The vehicle behind us speeds up and gains some ground on us.

"There's a right coming," Lewis says, activating the left-turn signal.

"Make the turn at the last possible moment, okay?"

"Alix, what if it's a cop?"

"It's not," I say. "I can tell by the headlights."

Lewis does as instructed, hitting the brakes hard just before turning right onto another residential street lined with enormous yards and large homes. Moments later the mystery vehicle makes the same turn at high speed.

"Shit," I say. "We're in trouble."

"You're sure it's not a cop?"

"Trust me," I say. "Besides, the lights and sirens would be on by now."

"He's going too fast," Lewis says. "There are little kids around here."

The vehicle is fifty feet away and closing quickly.

"Just breathe, okay?" I say. "Whatever you do, don't pull over. You need to get to a main road and park in a public place full of people. Can you find one fast?"

"No problem," Lewis says, eyes darting to and from the rearview mirror and the road. "But what if he—"

"Watch out!"

Lewis never sees the stop sign as we approach the residential intersection. The last thing I see is another pair of headlights to my immediate right, followed by a brief glimpse of a car colliding head-on with the rear passenger side of the truck, the awful sounds of metal grinding against metal ringing in my ears as we spin out of control.

Then it falls eerily silent inside the truck as everything fades to black.

CHAPTER 14

A lix?" the garbled voice says. "Oh my God. Alix, are you okay? Please just open your eyes! I'm so sorry. I never saw it coming."

I feel my left shoulder shaking and realize somebody's trying to wake me up. Lewis. The accident. I'm alive. Thank God.

"Hey," I say, opening my eyes. "I think I blacked out."

"Oh thank you, God," Lewis says, running his palm against the side of my face. "Are you okay?"

"I think so." I test my arms and legs, all of which feel good, but then I look at Lewis and realize he's still driving. "Wait. Why are we moving? Lewis, did you flee the scene of the accident? That's illegal. You can get in big troub—"

"Alix, just listen and let me explain," he interrupts. "The truck did a one-eighty, and we stopped in the middle of the street. The car that hit us kept on going. The one that was following us turned left and followed the one that hit us. They took off fast, which makes me think they were working together. Nobody was around, and I was worried they might come back, so yeah, I left the scene. Just like they did."

"Okay," I say, shaking the mental cobwebs out of my head and wondering how sore I'll be in the morning. "Don't worry about it. How long was I out?"

"Not long," he says, eyes glued to the road as his free hand rubs my shoulder. "A minute. Maybe less."

"What about the truck? How will you explain the damage to your grandpa?"

"I'm not sure," he says. "I'll think of something, but I'm actually glad this thing was built before airbags became standard. It's running fine, but I think you're missing the point."

"Which is?"

"Somebody's trying really hard to keep you out of Oval City."

∞

We head southbound on the I-75 Chrysler Freeway and exit at Mack Avenue less than twenty minutes later. Turning left on Mack would take us into the relative safety of the Eastern Market district, but tonight we have a different kind of Detroit tourism in mind, and Lewis gives me a dubious look as he passes Mack and stays on the Chrysler Service Drive.

Anybody familiar with Detroit knows about the woeful state of its city services. If you live in Detroit and need emergency police and/or medical assistance at your residence, you'll wait anywhere from thirty to sixty minutes before help arrives. If you need streetlamps repaired, you'll wait a lot longer. Poor city services are probably the main reason the city's population continues to plummet. One thing I remember from my sophomore Michigan history class is that nearly two million people lived in Detroit in 1950, but only about seven hundred thousand call this troubled city home today. Dad says even that figure is misleading, because most of the people who live here only do so because they can't afford to leave. Detroit is an angry city. Morale is in the basement.

For all the little pockets of urban renewal that have popped up over the past decade or so, Detroit is essentially a disassembled jigsaw puzzle. There are a lot of different pieces to the city, but nothing brings them together anymore. For example, it's not a pedestrian-friendly city. Like Dad said, you can walk in certain areas and feel safe, but those areas are few and far between. You can take the city bus if you don't own a car, but the city bus is a city service and therefore notoriously unreliable. In fact, it's common for the buses not to show up. There are no subways or trolleys. There is this creaky old elevated train thing called the People Mover, but it only runs in a small area of the downtown business district. It's useless to most residents and therefore empty most of the time. I guess you could say the Detroit People Mover has never really earned its name.

I'm thinking about all of this as we head down the service drive because it *is* downright dark and creepy around here. My stomach is doing flips as we turn right on a street called Wilkins, where Lewis parks the battered truck curbside. There's nothing around but darkness, overgrown fields, and abandoned buildings tagged with graffiti. I don't see any cars, and I find it hard to believe we're sitting in the middle of the modern Motor City. Honestly, it feels more like some postapocalyptic war zone in Eastern Europe or something. The only evidence of any life is the low hum of vehicles whipping along I-75 in the distance and the twinkling lights of the waterfront buildings along the Detroit River to the south.

"Is this Oval City?" I ask, scanning both sides of the desolate street.

"There," Lewis says, cutting the headlights and pointing across the street, where four gutted housing towers stand in the distance like hollowed-out giants. Single-story structures dot the barren landscape as well, but it's the graffiti-laden towers that grab your attention. "It's hard to believe a lot of good people used to actually live here."

"I don't see a single light."

"You won't," Lewis says, head on a swivel as he moves uneasily in his seat. "Unless it's a flashlight or a fire."

"You okay?"

"Not really." He clears his throat. "I haven't been down here in almost three years. I was always stoned out of my mind too. This is the first time I've been near this place sober."

"How do you feel?" I reach for his hand and hold it.

"Thankful but terrified," he says, guiding my hand to the side of his soft but masculine face and allowing it to rest there. It feels as if I'm touching the world's most perfect sculpture.

"Lewis, can I ask you a question?"

"You can ask me anything, Alix."

"Is something happening between us?"

He thinks about it and finally nods, saying, "Yes. I think we both know something's happening between us."

I stare deep into his eyes, thinking that if my life ended at this very moment I would die the happiest seventeen-year-old girl on the planet.

"Look . . ." I trail off, unsure what to say. "I don't know . . . it's just that I'm so new at this, okay? I'm new to all of this." I laugh and shake my head to make sure I'm not dreaming. "I'm sitting here in the middle of a dangerous city I promised my dad I would never go to without him. I'm with a guy he's never met, a guy who just fled the scene of an accident, and I even flushed illegal drugs down the toilet of my own house today."

"Don't forget about the knife in your pocket, badass."

"Exactly!" I say, laughing.

Lewis laughs too. "So you're on some quest or something, okay? Just let it happen. I'm here to help you and keep you safe. You wanted to see Oval City because you know it has something to do with

William's death. Take a good look. There it is. And this is as close as we're getting today, so can we leave now?"

"Yes," I say, still touching his face. "Thanks for showing me."

He tilts his head to the right and leans toward me. Time seems to slow as he brings his lips closer to my own. I follow his lead and lean forward to meet him. He places his palms on either side of my face. My whole body tingles with the kind of excitement I've only felt in my dreams about William. An amazing feeling of warmth spreads through me as I realize what's about to happen.

"Lewis?" I whisper, our lips inches from touching.

"Alix?" he says, smiling.

"No games, okay?"

"What do you mean?" His warm, minty breath washes over me.

"You know what I mean," I say. "Something tells me you have a lot of experience in this department. I don't. So don't play games with me."

"I would never do anything to hurt you," he says. "I promise."

I close my eyes and wait for him to take over.

And that's when something loud crashes onto the top of the truck with an enormous bang, causing us to flinch and pull away from each other.

"Good evening, young lovers."

Terrified, I look to my right, where a filthy homeless man with a long, unkempt white beard stares at me through the open window. His rickety shopping cart is full of plastic bags, dirty clothing, and old pillows.

"Spare some change for a struggling fellow human?" he says, the foul odors of sweat and urine wafting into the truck.

"Not tonight, old man," Lewis says, turning his head and looking out his window toward Oval City. I figure the man's smell is too much for him. "Get lost, okay?" he adds. "And don't touch my truck again."

The homeless man crouches and peers inside the vehicle. My heart rate spikes. I think about reaching for the knife but then realize the man isn't looking at me. He's watching Lewis. Well, the back of Lewis's head anyway.

"Lewis, it's okay," I say, digging into my front pocket and fishing out two dollars. "Here," I say to the man. "Take this."

I offer him the cash, but he doesn't take it. It's as if he doesn't even see it. Instead, he's ultrafocused on Lewis.

"I know you," he says to Lewis. "Why would you bring a sweet girl like this down here?"

"You don't know me, old man," Lewis says, head still turned. "I haven't been here in years."

"You're lying," the man says. "I saw you here last night. I recognize your voice. Why won't you show me your face, boy?"

"Because you smell like death, okay?" Lewis says, angry. "You might remember me from three years ago, but I wasn't anywhere near this place last night." Lewis finally turns toward us, eyes narrowed as he glares at the man. "And by the way, it was her idea to come here. Not mine. So take the cash she's being so nice to offer you and get the hell away from us."

We hear a round of disturbing laughter and a few blasts of what sound like firecrackers coming from deep within Oval City.

"We need to leave, Alix," Lewis says. "Pocket the money if he doesn't want it." He starts the engine and puts the headlights on.

The man finally turns his attention toward me, giving me an inquisitive look as he reaches for my humble donation. I notice a sharp twinkle to his blue eyes. Despite his smells and sad career choice, there's wisdom behind those eyes. It occurs to me that this isn't your typical mentally ill homeless person. I misjudged him and assumed the worst.

"Alix?" the man says, taking the cash and squeezing my wrist lightly as he does so. "You must be the one they're waiting for. Funny, but I thought you'd be a guy."

It happens the moment he touches my skin. My throat goes dry as white light explodes inside my head, blinding me. The vision is unlike any so far. Instead of seeing this man's past or future, I see something new and troubling, a wall of searing orange and red fire, the intense heat of which seems to prickle my skin.

The vision only lasts a few seconds. When I open my eyes, I'm sweating and breathing heavily. One thing I sense for certain is that the fire represents evil.

"You're not human." The words come out involuntarily, as if somebody else is speaking through me. I whisper the sentence so that Lewis can't hear me above the truck engine.

"Whatever you say, Alix." The old man smiles and snatches the two crumpled singles from my palm. "Thank you. Have a nice night."

He turns and proceeds to push his squeaky shopping cart west down Wilkins Street in the direction away from the freeway, the man laughing and whistling as he ventures farther into darkness.

"I'll be right back," I say, and I ignore Lewis's protests as I open the door and hop out of the truck.

I don't follow the strange homeless man. Instead, I succumb to a strong urge to set foot on Oval City soil, crossing Wilkins Street in front of the truck and hearing Lewis get out behind me, Lewis calling my name and following me as I step onto the overgrown brush bordering Oval City.

This afternoon I experienced visions of Aruna's past and future. Afterward, my reading on London Steel revealed things about our world that only a handful of humans ever see. And now, with the otherworldly reading on the homeless man, I know that good and evil exist. London hinted at the cause of evil. Demons. Demons possess human souls and make them do evil things. I know this now. What did London say about evil in Oval City? Something about it causing bad things to happen there. I believe her, because nothing but searing fire shoots through my head as soon as I set foot on Oval

City land. Evil lurks below and above Oval City. Evil gave rise to this land, and evil shall remain here until it's defeated.

Perennial. Face. Oval City. They're all evil. They all thrive here. I now understand that solving William's murder is only part of my test. What Vagabond really wants me to do is destroy the evil that is Oval City, which means I have to figure out a way to do something the city of Detroit hasn't been able to accomplish for years.

The blunt truth hits me like a massive asteroid: if I want to bring justice to William and get rid of Face, Perennial, and all the sadness and horror Oval City has caused, I have to somehow figure out a way to destroy Oval City.

But how do you destroy an entire city block?

"Are you insane?" Lewis grabs my shoulder and snaps me back to reality. "This is a good way to get yourself killed. And what was all that weird talk between you and the homeless freak anyway?"

"I was right," I say, turning toward him.

"Right about what?"

"Everything's connected."

"You're acting weird," he says. "That guy spooked you. We're going back to Beaconsfield."

"No," I say, grabbing his hands. "Listen to me. There's been a slight change of plan. I need you to drive me through Oval City. I need to see all of it. Just one quick pass, okay? And please don't argue about it. I know it sounds crazy, but I know what I'm doing. Trust me."

Lewis is about to say something but changes his mind. Instead, he simply shakes his head and walks back toward the truck.

CHAPTER 15

Lewis makes a U-turn on Wilkins and a right onto the service drive. We still haven't seen another vehicle, but we begin to see more people. Lewis says they're Perennial addicts coming to Oval City to score the purple powder that is destroying their minds and lives. It's hard to see faces in the darkness, but the majority are young males. Like Aruna, they're far too thin. Lewis says Perennial suppresses your appetite. Perennial addicts don't think about food. All they think about is securing the next dose of Perennial. Lewis says he gained thirty pounds in three months once he quit using.

He turns right on the next block, another dark street, this one called Alfred. I notice him double-checking the door locks as he powers up the windows nearly all the way, leaving barely two inches of open space for us to take in the sounds of young lives gone downhill. A few addicts turn and eye the truck, suspicious and probably thinking we're cops. They squint from the headlight glare, a depressing display of sad, pale, hollow, and paranoid faces.

"They look like death," I say.

"Some of them aren't too far away from it," Lewis says. "Whatever you do, don't open your door for anybody. We're doing this as fast as possible."

The four empty apartment towers are so close they could step on us. Lewis turns left onto a street called Brewster Loop and tells me it's the street that gives Oval City its name.

"Also known as the Gateway to Hell," he says. "Brewster Loop is the only way in and out by car. Get ready, Alix. It's showtime."

He accelerates as we pass the first tower on my right, and I instantly understand why my father's job is so depressing and stressful. Groups of shady, dangerous-looking men eye the truck, evil grins plastered across their faces as they wave us over. Lewis says they're some of Face's low-ranking Perennial dealers, who assume we're kids from the suburbs here to buy.

As we pass the second tower, my eyes gloss over with tears when I notice a few scantily clad, strung-out young women standing on the various corners, their glazed eyes giving away their addictions. Each girl reminds me of Aruna, and I can't help but wonder where she is and how she's doing.

"Hookers," Lewis says. "The dealers get them addicted and make them sell themselves."

"I know how prostitution works, Lewis." I wipe tears from my eyes as we round the halfway point of the oval. "It's just that I've never seen prostitutes in person before. What makes them try it in the first place? The drug, I mean. What made you start?"

"Everybody has a different story," he says, constantly shifting his gaze from one side of the street to the other. "I think it goes back to how you talked about your parents on that Niagara Falls trip. They raised you right. My parents didn't raise me that way. All they did was drink and fight. I was angry and looking to get back at them. That's why I started using." He pauses. "Or take somebody like Aruna and her sicko stepfather. Who wouldn't want to run away from a situation like that?" We approach the third tower, where dark figures pass by several of the blown-out windows on the higher floors. "Girls like Aruna run away to the big city and end up with bad men who take advantage of them."

"Are you saying William was bad?"

"No," he says. "William had demons, but he was the best thing that ever happened to Aruna, and Aruna was definitely the best thing that ever happened to him. They were beautiful together, Alix. She was helping him get clean, but then Face came along and blew it all apart."

A bloody-faced man wearing a white tank top and cutoff blue jeans stumbles out of the entrance to the third tower and collapses in the middle of the road in front of us, where he rolls onto his back and screams toward the sky, his face contorted in pain. Lewis has to hit the brakes hard to avoid running the man over.

"Oh God," I say. "We need to help him."

"No," Lewis says. "We need to get out of here." He swerves left to maneuver around the man, taking half of the truck up the curb and onto the dead grass, Lewis pointing toward tower three and saying, "See what I mean?"

I watch in horror as three men emerge from the entrance, each of them carrying what looks like a police-style club. Two of the men spot the man in the road, rush to him, and continue a violent beating that obviously started inside the tower. The third man just stands there, staring at the back of the pickup as we pass. I crane my head to the far right, watching him as he reaches for something in the back of his waist.

It's a handgun. I don't even have time to warn Lewis. He raises the weapon, and a burst of orange erupts from the gun barrel as he fires at us, followed by a loud crack and the sound of a bullet piercing the metal of the truck somewhere in the rear.

"Lewis, he's shooting!" I yell, turning and ducking low in my seat. "Get us out of here!"

"Told you this was a bad idea," he says. "Hold on tight."

Lewis lowers his head and steps hard on the gas pedal. The sudden acceleration throws me back into my seat. I keep my head just high enough to see out my window as we quickly approach the fourth and final tower.

"They're not going to kill that man, are they?" I say.

"Maybe," Lewis says. "I don't know."

"I can't get his face out of my mind. All that blood and the way he was screaming."

"We're lucky they didn't kill *us*."

"Take me home," I say. "I need some time to think."

"I'm sorry you had to see that."

I spot another cluster of men in front of tower four as we approach. I'm guessing Lewis is doing at least forty-five miles per hour, which is probably why the men turn and watch us as we get closer. I stay extra low and pray they don't shoot at us. I glance at Lewis, who has both hands white-knuckled to the steering wheel, eyes focused on the road.

As we fly past the men, they don't engage us in any way.

But what sends my world spinning is the sight of my dad glaring directly at my window as we pass.

CHAPTER 16

You're sure it was him?" Lewis says. "We were going pretty fast."
He speeds across the I-75 overpass on Wilkins and makes
a hard left onto the northbound service drive. We're next to Eastern
Market now and safely out of Oval City.

"It was him," I say, heart thumping as if I've just sprinted a mile.
"I'm positive."

"Think he saw you?"

"I don't know," I say, rubbing my forehead. "I'm screwed if he
did, though." I check my phone for messages or calls. Nothing. "My
head was barely three inches above the window. I don't think he saw
me, but the way he glared at us." Shivers ripple through me. "It was
like he could see me even if I was invisible."

"I doubt he saw you," Lewis says, merging off the service drive
and back onto the freeway. "Try not to worry about it. He's an undercover guy doing his job. It's not like he was looking for you. He was
just staring at a fast-moving truck. He probably figured I was a buyer
hightailing it out of there."

"I don't know how he does it, Lewis," I say, trying to take his advice and not think about Dad spotting me. "His job, I mean. How can you see that kind of stuff on a regular basis and not go crazy? And why wasn't he helping that poor man in the street? He had to have heard his screaming. And all the prostitutes, dealers, and addicts we saw. They didn't seem to be afraid of anything. Why can't my dad just round up the troops and arrest everybody? Or burn down Oval City?" I put my face in my hands and groan.

"It's frustrating, I know," Lewis says, reaching over and taking my hand in his. "But the only way to stop it is to get the kingpin. If your dad is working undercover in Oval City, he wants the same thing we want."

"Face," I say, sitting up as the realization sets in. "My dad's trying to bust the Perennial ring."

"I think it's a safe bet based upon what we just saw."

"I wonder if they suspect him in William's murder."

"Probably not," Lewis says. "That's a closed case as far as law enforcement is concerned. Suicide, remember?"

"You're right," I say. "Still, if my dad's working to bust Face, then the difficulty level on this whole thing just skyrocketed." I massage my temples with my free hand. "Ugh. Lewis, I'm getting a headache."

"Understandable," he says, squeezing my hand. "You know what I'm thinking about right now?"

"What?"

"How I'm going to explain the truck damage and bullet hole to my grandpa."

He looks at me, and we both smile. Then, despite the disturbing evening we've experienced, we break into laughter. I suppose it has something to do with the fact we're both glad we survived Oval City.

"God, Lewis," I say, "do you think I'm going crazy?"

"You really want me to answer that?"

"Oh, shut up," I say, giving him a playful jab to his right shoulder. I see the exit sign for the upcoming Beaconsfield ramp and finally manage to relax a bit. "Why do they call him Face anyway?"

"Ah," he says, nodding. "I was wondering when you would ask about that. It's sort of a joke really. Nobody knows his true identity, so people on the street started calling him Face. He always wears a freaky mask when he meets people for business."

"Wait a second," I say. "You're telling me nobody's seen Face's actual face before?"

"Nobody I know," he says. "I've never met the guy. I just bought Perennial from his dealers for a long time."

"But you said Face destroyed William and Aruna, so surely William knew his identity. And Aruna, she's Face's . . . I don't know, girlfriend or slave or whatever, so she has to know who he is, right?"

Lewis says, "If William knew who Face was, he never said a word about it to me." He shrugs. "As for Aruna . . . you'd have to ask her about it."

"Well," I say, shaking my head. "That doesn't make this any easier either. Face could be sitting right next to me and I wouldn't know it."

"Are you implying something?" Lewis says, giving me a wink.

"No, I didn't mean it like that," I say. "And then there's Mr. Watkins."

"What about him?"

"There must be a reason they found him near Oval City."

"There is," Lewis says. "It's a good place to dump a body."

"No, not that," I say, thinking hard. "He was linked to Perennial somehow. It's just something I feel."

"Maybe Mr. Watkins was Face."

"Not a chance," I say. "According to Aruna, Face is alive and well. Although she did mention losing something of William's, and that she was sorry about it."

Out of the corner of my eye, I notice Lewis flinch.

"She said what?" he asks.

"Aruna said she lost something of William's and feels bad about it." I study him. His eyes are locked on the road. "I didn't think much of it because she was so high, but does that mean anything to you?"

He squeezes his eyes shut for a moment. "No," he says, opening his eyes and exhaling deeply. "All I can think is that maybe she lost some of his Perennial or something." He shakes his head a few times. "I have no idea. Look, I don't think you're crazy, Alix, but I do think you need to be careful with every move you make from now on. You never know who's watching you. You saw the ugly side of life tonight. I'm guessing there's an Oval City in every major city in the country." He signals for the Beaconsfield exit and heads up the ramp. "What I'm wondering is if you're ready to tell me what's really motivating you to solve William's murder."

I remain silent for a few minutes as we travel through the land of the wealthy en route to my house. All of these beautiful homes and wide, tree-lined streets sit less than twenty minutes from a one-block war zone of evil. Do I tell Lewis about the dreams and visions I've experienced during the past forty-eight hours? Do I mention London Steel battling demonic beasts? What would he say if I told him William is reaching out to me in my dreams at the request of Vagabond, who I haven't even met yet but is clearly the architect of this whole test I'm trying to pass? Yes, Lewis exhibits his own strange behavior at times, but he's human and I'm in love with him. I can't tell him everything, but I decide to test the waters a bit.

"Remember last night on the porch," I say, "when I told you something was happening to me and I knew that Oval City, William, Face, Aruna, and Perennial were connected?"

"Of course," he says, turning into our subdivision. "And don't forget about Mr. Watkins and me. You had us on that list too."

"I know," I say. "And so far I'm right. Maybe not so much on Mr. Watkins yet, but what I'm saying is that every person and place on my list connects to everything else on the list." Nerves spread through me as I decide how much to tell him. "How do you think I figured all that out in one day?"

"Beats me," he says, turning onto a quiet Maple Grove Street. "You mentioned a blog. *Vagabond's Warrior* I think it was. Or something like that."

"That definitely helped," I say. "But let me ask you a question." I clear my throat and take a deep breath as Lewis parks curbside a few houses away from mine. "Lewis, do you believe in ESP?"

"ESP?" he says, cutting the headlights and turning toward me. "What, you mean like psychics?"

"Yes," I say, gazing straight into his gorgeous eyes now. "Specifically the ability to use only your mind to see past or future events in somebody's life, even if you've never met them before."

"Like the psychics who channel the minds of murder victims and help police find their killers."

"Exactly," I say, nodding. "Do you believe in that sort of stuff?"

"Are you trying to tell me you're psychic, Alix?"

"No," I say, smiling. "Not necessarily. I'm just wondering if you believe in those things."

"Paranormal things."

"Sure," I say. "Paranormal. The unexplainable. Whatever you want to call it. Are you a believer?"

Lewis takes my hands and says, "I guess you could say I have an open mind on the subject."

"Good," I say, feeling pleasant warmth spread through me again. "Me too."

"Right now, though, I think we should get back to where we were before Mr. Homeless interrupted us."

"Hmm," I say, tilting my head as we lean toward each other. "I think I agree."

Our first kiss is perfection. I take one last look at his dark, wavy hair and aqua-green eyes, and then I thank God for blessing me with such a stunning human to kiss. I lay a palm on his pale face, admiring the high cheekbones for a moment before closing my eyes at the last possible moment before our lips touch.

Lewis's lips are soft and moist, his breath pure mint. As we open our mouths, his strong hands move down my ribs and settle on my waist. A wonderful heat spreads through me, surprising me with the parts of my body it reaches. He's like a living William Weed, my Dream Guy in the flesh. I feel my shoulders relax and my knees weaken. I have to remind myself to breathe. Lewis times it expertly, ending the kiss but keeping his lips close to my own.

"I was right," I say. "You definitely have experience in this area."

He smiles. "You're not so bad yourself."

"Really?"

"Really." He reaches for my glasses. "It might be easier if we take these off."

"Oh, you are a smooth one, Lewis Wilde," I say, reaching for his hands and lowering them back onto my waist. "Nice try, but the glasses stay on tonight." I smile. "You're welcome to kiss me again, though."

"Fair enough." He runs his hands along the sides of my ribs and places his warm palms on either side of my neck.

It happens as soon as his lips touch mine for the second time. I'm ready for another incredible kiss, but I see the explosion of white light instead. I'm not afraid of the light anymore, so I actually manage to enjoy the kiss and further melt into Lewis's arms and lips as I await whatever vision I'm going to have about his past or future. It occurs to me that I really don't know much about him, so I'm looking forward to what my abilities choose to reveal about his life.

The fear sets in when the white light morphs into another wall of searing orange and red fire.

There it is, just as it happened with the homeless man. Something isn't right. I sensed the homeless man wasn't human. I sensed he was evil in human form. But how can Lewis be evil? He's dangerous, yes, but in good ways that have me hooked on him. Maybe I was wrong about the homeless man. Maybe I'm losing my abilities already and am no longer able to glimpse somebody else's past or future. Maybe the fire represents the fizzling out of my abilities. If that's the case, Vagabond's probably already given up on me and I'll never meet him. Would that be so bad? Not really. I never asked for ESP. It just happened. Deep down I want nothing more than to return to life as it was before yesterday morning.

But as much as I pray for the fire to go away so that I can enjoy my time with Lewis, the flames blaze even brighter and hotter in my head, forcing me to break the kiss and pull back.

"What's wrong?" Lewis asks, concern on his chiseled face.

"Nothing," I lie. "It was wonderful." Not a lie. I wipe my brow, surprised to feel a light coating of sweat. "It's just that I'm afraid of what might happen if we keep this up."

He stares at me. I can sense his disappointment. I'm disappointed too, but I have to figure out what the fire visions are all about. I focus hard on Lewis, thinking back to how he suddenly appeared out of nowhere in the middle of the street yesterday, and then how he pulled his disappearing act when I drove off. I again wonder how Lewis knew the detail about the police finding Mr. Watkins's body near Oval City. I'm still not certain how he knew where my bedroom was either, and the more I think about it, it's surprising how unconcerned he is about the damage to his grandfather's truck.

And then something else occurs to me.

"The homeless man," I say.

"What about him?" Lewis says.

"He seemed certain that he saw you yesterday in Oval City."

"Don't tell me you believe a nut like that."

"He said he knew your voice."

"Alix," he says. "He's an insane old man. He's probably senile and confusing his memories. If he remembers me, it's from years ago. I promise." He closes his eyes and groans as he purposely but lightly knocks the back of his head against the padded seat. "You're killing a beautiful moment."

"I'm sorry," I say. "Sometimes I'm too paranoid, I guess. But you need to answer something for me."

"Like I said, you can ask me anything."

"You know where I live," I say, reaching for his hand and hoping the fire doesn't return. It doesn't. "You even know where my bedroom is." I smile at the wink he flashes me. "Seriously, though, I have no idea where *you* live. I know you're from Eastland and living with your grandparents somewhere around here. But what's their address?"

"Alix," he says, rolling his eyes, "they live at 3116 Bloomfield, okay? Do you want to go over there right now and meet them? They're probably sleeping, but I'll take you if you're doubting what I'm saying."

"No," I say, relieved and committing those four numbers to memory—3-1-1-6. They total eleven, so that's how I'll remember them. "It's fine," I add. "I believe you. I just needed to know. And yes, I'd like to meet them, but not tonight. My dad can come home at any time." I open my door. The dome light illuminates the truck's interior. "Thank you for tonight, Lewis. I mean it. Thank you."

"My pleasure." He caresses my palm with his fingertips. "Can I interest you in one more kiss?"

"It's tempting, but you're too dangerous."

I step out, close the door, and walk in front of the truck toward the sidewalk.

"Hey, Alix?"

I reach the sidewalk and turn.

Lewis says, "Don't forget."

"About what?"

He smiles. "You have a knife in your back pocket."

"You're right," I say, patting my pocket, relieved the weapon is still there. "Thanks for the reminder." I remove the silver knife from its sheath and show it to him before quickly tucking it back where it belongs. "Hey, Lewis?"

"What's up?"

I smile. "Good luck explaining the truck to your grandpa."

He nods and gives me a wave. Then he turns the headlights on and drives slowly away, leaving me with the feeling he's one of those people who the more you think you know them, the less you really know about them.

If William is my Dream Guy Lewis is my Mystery Man.

I stand there on the sidewalk, rubbing my warm lips and watching the back of Lewis's truck until the taillights fade to tiny red smudges in the dark street.

I can't imagine being with a better kisser than Lewis Wilde, and as much it scares me to think about it, I really can't wait to be alone with him again.

CHAPTER 17

I step into my house just before ten and sense danger as soon as I close the door behind me. Once again I place my hand on my back pocket to double-check that I still have Aruna's knife. Satisfied, I flick on the living-room light and breathe a sigh of relief at the sight of an empty room. The relief doesn't last long, however, because I suddenly have that same feeling I experienced behind Zeppelin in the moments before Aruna made her appearance.

Somebody is inside this house, and it isn't my dad.

I step cautiously into the room, hand on my back pocket, fear overwhelming me.

"Aruna?" I say, now frustrated at the lack of a clear vision and suddenly hoping my abilities return full force. "Is that you, Aruna?"

No answer—just the sound of my heavy breathing.

I decide to take Dad's advice on this one. Since there's a gun in Dad's office and the intruder might already have it (or one of his or her own), it's too dangerous for me to stay here, so I decide to quietly and quickly leave the house to call the police.

And I'm taking my first step backwards toward the front door when it happens.

A dark figure is directly behind me, waiting. I see it in my mind, just like I saw Aruna hiding behind the Dumpster before she made her appearance. Problem is I'm too late this time. This person is too good. This person has abilities that dwarf my own. At the same time, something weird happens with Aruna's silver knife. I feel it vibrating in my back pocket like some trapped animal trying to break free. Then I remember London's comment about the knife possibly coming in handy.

It's some sort of warning, I realize. The knife is warning me.

But it all happens too fast. The next thing I know, a muscular arm wraps around my neck and I'm in a choke hold that could easily kill me in my own living room.

I drop to my knees, unable to breathe as the pressure of the person's arm threatens to crush my trachea. A shiny, black, spandex-like material covers the arm, but there's disgusting slimy moisture on it that I feel against my throat. The knife responds too, now vibrating with more intensity. It's as if the knife is struggling along with me and pleading for me to reach back and grab it. Problem is I can't take my hands off of this person's arm. I'm using every ounce of strength I have to get this anaconda off of me, but it's no use.

I'm on the verge of blacking out when I hear a male voice in my ear that goes against everything good in this world. It's a low, dirty, guttural voice—the voice of evil. The sound of it sends the most intense wall of fire through my mind yet.

Slowly and calmly, he whispers the following: "I want the knife, Alix. It doesn't belong to you."

He releases his death grip and shoves me forward onto the wood floor.

I land face-first, roll onto my back, and grab my aching throat, coughing and crying as I struggle to get my wind back. A tall, muscular figure stands above me, intense black eyes glaring at me with hatred. The strange black material covers the man's entire face and body, feet included. He wears no shoes. He reminds me of a ninja who just emerged from a swimming pool.

"Who are you?" I say, dreading the thought of another choke hold. "*What* are you?"

The knife continues to go bonkers in my pocket.

What happens next confirms that London's world of violent battles against demonic beasts exists.

With inhuman speed, the "man" hunches forward onto all fours. His back arches like that of a cat. I hear a series of disgusting popping sounds that remind me of tree branches snapping in half. He's getting larger, I realize, and his arms have become his front legs. Wide-eyed, I watch in horror as his black eyes turn into yellow slits. At the same time, long silver claws protrude from the four "feet" that now resemble gigantic black paws.

It finally occurs to me that the spandex-like material isn't fabric at all. It's the creature's skin.

His slimy, eel-like face is now twice as large as its original form. The beast reminds me of a steroid-bloated hairless cat without ears or a tail.

The monster launches itself toward me, stopping inches from my face, its head moving slowly from side to side. The yellow eyes seem to stare right through me. Terror paralyzes me. I'm unable to respond to the knife's continuing protests in my pocket.

The voice again: "Give me the knife, Alix, or you won't like what I do to you."

The creature has no mouth, I realize, just those awful eyes and hideous face. The words simply emerge from it somehow.

This is impossible. It can't be happening. But it is. This thing is all too real and from someplace I want nothing to do with.

"Will you go away and leave me alone if I give it you?" I ask, finally managing to muster some words.

The beast's mouth suddenly appears like a new fault in the earth's surface. A dark horizontal crack forms across the lower middle part of its face. Black ooze seeps from the crack as the creature opens its mouth, revealing a set of sharp yellow teeth that look as if they could slice me in half with ease. Each daggerlike tooth is nearly the size of my head.

What happens next nearly makes me vomit.

A thick, slimy, bloodred tongue uncoils from the back of the beast's mouth and protrudes several inches beyond its teeth. The creature then runs the tip of its grotesque tongue down the side of my face and neck, leaving behind a trail of yellow ooze that smells like rotten garbage. All I can do is close my eyes and try not to go insane from the terror.

"You taste good, Alix," the monster hisses, running its tongue over my nose and glasses. "Now, give me the knife and I'll be on my way."

I manage a deep breath and, eyes still closed, think back to my reading on London. As those awful battle images danced through my mind, London told me to take it all in. She said it was real. She said I was becoming part of it.

As I again recall her tip about the knife coming in handy, I realize that right now it's official. I'm part of London's world, and as awful, violent, and unreal as her world is, this is happening, and I need to summon the courage to deal with it.

Courage.

Again, London's words come to mind. *There's nothing wrong with being scared. I'm scared every day. Vagabond says courage is being scared to death of something but confronting it anyway. Trust your abilities, but don't trust anything or anybody else.*

My mind somehow clears, and although I'm still lying on my back and experiencing intense pain from the choke hold and fall, I know exactly what I have to do. As the creature's wet tongue explores my forehead and hair, I keep my eyes closed and carefully slide my right arm behind my waist, where I manage to grasp the handle of the silver knife. The knife continues its odd behavior and settles into my grip as if my hand is a high-powered magnet. I lie there a few moments, fear building again as the beast raises a front leg and brings one of those nasty silver claws dangerously close to my throat.

"Here's your knife!" I yell.

My words surprise the beast. It lowers its leg and begins to withdraw its tongue, but not before I grab that disgusting tongue with my outstretched left hand. I get an excellent hold on it too, the tongue feeling like warm raw meat as I use it as leverage to pull myself up to a seated position. The beast squeals like a wounded pig, fighting me hard as I raise the knife high over my right shoulder with blinding speed I never knew I had. I close my eyes and scream as I plunge the knife through the thick center of the monster's tongue. The blade cuts through the skin as if it's warm butter and embeds itself into the wood floor. A warm, putrid liquid sprays my face. When I open my eyes, I see a geyser of yellow ooze erupting from a fist-sized hole in the trapped creature's pinned tongue. The monster shrieks like mad and begins shaking violently. I grab the knife and pull it out of the floor and through the mangled tongue.

"Go to hell!" I yell, wiping hot, stinky yellow ooze from my glasses and raising the knife for another strike.

But I don't have to strike again. Instead, I feel an intense heat emanating from the wounded creature. I see the explosion in my mind just before it happens. Knowing what's coming, I grip the knife tightly and roll backwards as far as I can, watching from the entrance to the kitchen with a morbid sense of fascination as the crawling, skinless, demonic cat-beast explodes into a brilliant blue, yellow, and orange fireball the size of a large boulder and vanishes before my eyes.

I sit up, heart pounding as I look around the now-silent room. It's as if the whole thing never happened. The knife has stopped moving, and I somehow know this means the danger has passed. I pocket my valuable weapon and sit there on the wood floor in a daze, reaching up to wipe leftover monster ooze from my face only to discover there's no ooze to wipe. Weird. I'm not even sweating. I touch my throat. It's not the least bit sore from the choke hold. All evidence of what just happened has disappeared. I'm bewildered, confused, and convinced I'm going mad.

"Go away," I whisper, breaking into tears and burying my face in my hands. "Please, God. Just make it all go away."

For the next few minutes, I cry harder than I have since the day Mom died. One moment I think I have everything figured out and I'm confident I'll bust Face for William's murder and destroy Oval City. The next moment I remember I just destroyed a shape-shifting monster with a magical knife I have no business carrying. In between I think about my overwhelming feelings for Lewis but face the fact I still have serious questions about his sudden presence in my life.

"I need help," I say through the tears. I'm sitting on the living-room floor, face still in my hands. "I'm alone and I need help."

Knowing I'm all out of tears, I dry my face with my hands, remove the knife, and stare at it, examining it closely for the first time and noticing a series of wedge-shaped designs etched lightly into one side of the solid silver handle. But upon closer examination I realize the markings are more than beautiful designs. They're symbols, dozens of them, a series of small triangles with vertical and horizontal lines connecting them. The history student in me feels a strong urge to go upstairs and research the markings, and I'm getting ready to stand and do that when I again experience the sensation that somebody is in the room with me.

Moments later the white light erupts inside my head and I see an image of a well-dressed man with piercing blue eyes and a freshly shaven head. His dark suit is impeccable. He's handsome but older, more like a father figure. Grandfatherly even. I open my eyes, drop the knife onto the floor, and stare at it, unable to garner the energy needed for another fight.

"I give up," I say, shaking my head. "Whoever you are, just do what you have to do. Take the knife. I give up."

Nothing happens, but I know the man in the suit is close by.

"Take the knife!" I yell, pushing it across the floor as if it's a hockey puck.

The weapon hits something five feet away and stops with a dull metallic thud. I raise my gaze slightly and see a pair of immaculate dark-leather men's shoes.

A voice: "That's a shame, Alix. Because overall you've shown great promise thus far."

I close my eyes and refuse to look up. He speaks quickly but calmly, his accent falling somewhere between Australian and English. The aura he gives off is one of pure white light. There is no fire to this man, and there's no need for an introduction. William warned me I would not like this man, but I know he represents good.

Right now though, I don't care what he represents, because I'm done with this.

"Vagabond?"

"Hello, Alix." I hear him kick the knife. The weapon slides across the floor and stops inches from my knees. "You're allowed to feel sorry for yourself on occasion, but don't you ever voluntarily relinquish that knife. You're only beginning to understand how special that weapon is. Now, please stop being so submissive and rude. You look incredibly sad and weak at the moment. I despise those two qualities, so stand up and open your eyes. We have a lot to talk about."

I do as he says, opening my eyes and standing across from him, but I make a point of leaving the knife on the floor. Vagabond looks exactly as he did in the vision, a walking male model for some high-end suit store catering to men aged sixty and up. He folds his hands in front of his waist and studies me with eyes so blue they're hard to look at.

"Say it," he says.

"Say what?"

"Exactly what you're feeling."

"I just did," I say. "I quit. I'm done. I can't handle any of this. I never asked for it. I don't want it." I pause. "Okay, maybe I wanted it at certain points, but not after what just happened with that . . . that thing I just killed."

"Nobody asks for abilities like yours, Alix," he says, glaring at me. "What you and certain other humans can do is incredibly rare, a combination of luck and genetics, but mostly luck."

"Lucky is the last thing I feel right now."

"I understand," he says. "What you're feeling—that roller coaster of emotions—it's normal and expected at this stage. London Steel had to deal with it. Roman King had to deal with it. So did the others."

"Roman King?" I say, squinting. "That name rings a bell. Who is he?"

"A recent addition to my team." Vagabond smiles. "I'm sure you two will meet soon." He claps his hands together once. "Right, then. Shall we get on with it?"

"Get on with what?"

"A little chat, Alix. There's a lot you need to know."

"No," I say, shaking my head. "There isn't. Maybe I wasn't clear, but I'm done, okay? I feel bad for William, but I'm sure you already know who killed him, so why don't you just take it from here and leave me alone?" Vagabond stands there as stone-faced as a statue. "Leave, Vagabond. Do you have any idea what my dad will do to you if he walks in and finds you here?"

"Unfortunately, you're proving more stubborn than expected," he says, taking a step closer and towering at least six inches above me. "Listen closely to three things, Alix. First, for reasons you don't yet understand, I have no idea who killed William Weed. As far as

I'm aware, you're the one person on this planet who possesses the abilities to solve that mystery, so stop trying to avoid who and what you really are. You might not like it, but you're an incredibly gifted two-way psychic who will do a lot of good in this world . . . and beyond." He pauses. "Second, if your father walked into this room right now, all he would see is you talking to yourself. And how do you suppose Mr. Clint Keener would feel about that?"

I have no answer for him.

"He wouldn't like it, would he, Alix? In fact, Clint Keener would probably give you yet another lecture about controlling your emotions and not overreacting to anything that happens to you in life." Vagabond shrugs and brushes nonexistent lint from his suit-coat sleeves. "It's good advice actually. As an undercover lawman, your father is a master of observing before reacting. I wish he had the kind of abilities required to join us." He raises his eyebrows and smiles. "Unfortunately, *he* doesn't. But *you* do."

"You're telling me you have no idea who murdered William?" I ask.

"Correct."

"It was Face," I say, rolling my eyes. "Everything points to Face."

"Are you one hundred percent positive it was Face?"

"Yes," I say, but then I look away and shake my head. "Well, no, not really, but Face runs Perennial and Oval City. And he took Aruna from William and brainwashed her with that drug."

"So many pieces, Alix," Vagabond says. "But you need to put them together to prove who did it." He smiles again. "After all, William is counting on you. Friday night will be here before you know it."

"Screw you," I say, jabbing a finger toward his face. "He said I wouldn't like you. He said *nobody* likes you. I can't believe you're using him like this just to test me."

"William Weed was a worthless drug addict whose spirit happened to be in the right place at the right time," Vagabond says. "I started scouting you the day you moved into his bedroom. I sensed you had the abilities needed to fight Fire. It took a few tries, but once William made contact two nights ago I knew you were special. You have no idea what you're capable of, Alix. Solve his murder by the end of Friday. William will finally rest in peace, a murderer will be off the streets, and you will finally understand how powerful you are." He clenches his fists and holds them against his chest. "I need you, Alix. London Steel needs you. Roman King needs you. Everybody who fights for Light needs you."

"No," I say, swallowing hard and wondering exactly what he means by fighting *against* Fire and *for* Light. "I'm finished, Vagabond. Look, I feel bad for William, but as you just said, he was nothing but a worthless drug addict, right? This is not who I am. I'm Alix Keener, a gifted student and college-bound senior. I'm not Alix Keener, para-normal psychic and killer of fantasy monsters."

"I'm sorry, Alix," Vagabond says. "But the blunt truth is that you're all of those things."

There's a long, tense silence during which we stare at each other and refuse to look away.

"You told me to listen to three things," I say. "You mentioned two. What's the third?"

Vagabond nods and smiles. "Well done," he says. "You're a good listener. I neglected to mention the third item on purpose, but now, since the satisfaction of solving a murder *and* helping an untold number of people fight evil in the future doesn't seem to appeal to you, I'll add one last reward."

"What is it?"

Vagabond studies me for a few moments. Then, as if finally mak-ing up his mind, he takes a deep breath and says, "Alix, how would you like to see your mother one last time?"

Just when I thought I was out of tears, fresh ones stream down my face.

"You can do that?" I whisper.

"I can do that," he says, extending his hands toward me. "But you'll have to earn it, so stop crying, pick up your knife, and take my hands. There are things you need to see and hear."

I wipe my face, grab the knife from the floor, and sheathe it in my pocket. Then I step toward Vagabond and place my hands into his. His skin is pleasantly warm.

The last thing I see is his smile. Then everything flares to the blinding white light I've come to know so well.

CHAPTER 18

Vagabond and I stand across from each other in a vast and seemingly endless expanse of clear and pleasant white light. The space is familiar. It's the same setting where I've encountered William for the past two nights. Although we're standing on something that feels solid, the surface is invisible. All I see is the wonderful white light in all directions.

"Is this heaven?" I ask, adjusting my glasses and gazing around.

Vagabond looks even more striking in this setting, his dark suit and deep-blue eyes in stark contrast to our white surroundings.

"I suppose many people would call it that," he says. "But you can get here without being religious."

"I don't get it."

"What is religion, Alix? Who created it?"

"I didn't know this was going to get so deep," I say, smiling.

"Your sense of humor is back," he says. "That's good. Look, you're the gifted student. You said so yourself. Answer my questions."

"Religion," I say, mulling it over. "Okay. I suppose people created religion to try to understand why we live and die, how we should behave during our lives, and what happens to us when we die."

"Agreed," Vagabond says. "Are you religious, Alix?"

"I don't go to church or anything," I say. "But I believe in a higher power, and I believe there are positive consequences for good behavior and negative consequences for bad behavior. You know, the whole karma thing in Hinduism and Buddhism and how it can impact your next life. That seems right to me."

"So you were raised Christian but believe in reincarnation, then?"

"I didn't say that," I say. "What I'm saying is that I respect all religions. I mean, when it comes down to it, all religions are basically the same. If you live a so-called good life, you can expect some type of reward when you die. If you live a so-called bad or sinful life, you can expect bad things to happen wherever you end up next." I pause. "Actually, since all religions are essentially the same at their cores, I would argue there's really only one world religion."

"I see," Vagabond says, scratching his chin. "Very nice, Alix. You're even smarter than I thought. This is good." He pauses, thinking. "Here's a scenario to ponder. What about the few remaining primitive rain-forest tribes out there? They've had little to no contact with the modern world and therefore know nothing about organized religion outside of their own nature worship. Or maybe they're just trying to survive and don't even think about what happens when they die." He holds out his arms and gestures around the wonderful space. "Can people like that—people who don't know about our notions of heaven, hell, gods, goddesses, demons, and devils—get to a place like this after they die?"

"Sure they can," I say. "Let me put it this way, Vagabond. People have been around a lot longer than organized religion. In my opinion, it's all pretty simple. If you're a good person, good things happen to you when you die. If you're an evil person, you can expect to be haunted by evil for eternity. I don't care how many gods somebody does or doesn't believe in. Every sane human understands the difference between good and evil—even primitive rain-forest people; even the earliest humans for that matter. So yes, I think everybody is capable of living life in a way that makes it possible for them to be in a place like this when they die."

"What about atheists?" he says. "Those who reject the idea that gods and goddesses exist?"

"Atheists?" I say, raising my eyebrows. "I think atheists are misguided. We should bring all of them here to prove it."

Vagabond breaks into laughter and claps his hands several times, applauding my joke, I suppose.

"Oh bravo, Alix," he says. "Bravo indeed."

"Okay," I say. "So what's with the religious line of questioning?"

"Right," he says. "Basically, everything you just said is correct. But allow me to make it even simpler. Two forces drive the universe and have been in constant battle since the beginning of time. Humans have put many labels on these two forces in an attempt to understand and explain them throughout history, but as you just said, when it comes down to it, it's pretty simple. You know what I'm referring to, don't you?"

"Yes," I say. "Good and evil."

"Bingo." He clasps his hands together in front of his waist again. "Good and evil. Humans are interesting, Alix. They tend to think they're the most important organisms in the universe, but when it comes to the big picture, people are nothing but specks of dust in a massive cosmic landscape. But," he says, pointing at me now, "there's one thing about your kind that forces me to keep a constant eye on you." He pauses. "Would it surprise you to learn that human beings are more susceptible to evil than any other form of life in the universe?"

"I've never really thought about it like that," I say, finding it fascinating that he just confirmed the existence of extraterrestrial life. "But I can't say it surprises me. Not after seeing Oval City tonight."

"Ah, Oval City," he says. "We'll get to that sickening pit in a moment, but let me ask you another question. Do you believe in demons, Alix Keener?"

I think back to the horrible beasts I saw during my reading on London, and it's as if I can still smell and feel the cat-beast creature I destroyed only minutes ago.

"After today, Vagabond, I think evil takes many different forms, including demons, yes."

"Be careful," he says, serious now. "Demons aren't just a *form* of evil, Alix. Demons are the *source* of evil. You *must* remember that. From now on your life depends on it. Allow me to phrase it another way. I can tell you for a fact that demons are responsible for every evil act in human history. Who is the most evil person you can think of, dead or alive?"

"Adolf Hitler," I say, needing no time to think about that one. "Or if you need somebody more recent, Osama bin Laden." I squint and adjust my glasses again. "Are you trying to tell me those guys were possessed by demons?"

"Yes," he says. "That's exactly what I'm telling you. You love history, so here's some interesting information. If you do the research, you'll discover that the concept of demonic forces causing evil is found in every human civilization in history, going all the way back to ancient Mesopotamia, the world's first civilization. Demons are real, Alix. They're here. They've always been here. And they want one thing. They want power over as many human souls as possible."

"Demonic possession," I say, nodding. "I read somewhere that demons thrive and gain energy by taking over the minds of humans."

"Precisely," he says. "Demons prey on human souls and cross over into the earthly realm via portals. Portals are two-way highways between the Fire world and yours. Thankfully, demonic portals are rare, but the longer they remain open, the more damage the demon or demons can do. Demons would like nothing more than to possess

every human being on the planet and use Earth as a breeding ground
for evil." He pauses. "My job is to make sure that never happens."

"Hell," I say. "The Fire world. That's what you're talking about,
isn't it?"

"You're using a Christian reference, which is fine, but remember
what you said a minute ago. At their cores, all religions are the same
in that they recognize good and evil. Demons are universal, Alix.
They don't discriminate according to religion. Demons want human
souls, plain and simple. Christian. Muslim. Buddhist. Hindu. Shinto.
Pagan. It doesn't matter." He gazes at his shoes, thinking. Then he
says, "Unfortunately, all the years of fighting between religions
have made humans easier targets for possession. I've never understood why you people fight wars over religion. Demons love it when
humans go to war. It's like recess for them. You'd be a much stronger
lot if you could all just get along. Trust me."

"If portals are so rare," I say, "how do they open in the first
place?"

"Good question," he says. "The answer is simple. Portals open
when humans get stupid and summon evil. Sometimes it's an
accident, like when a séance gets out of control and the person con-
ducting it doesn't know how to handle the situation. Usually, though,
ignorant humans open portals on purpose. Satanism. Ouija boards.
Black magic." He shrugs. "Things like that."

"How do portals close?" I ask.

"I'm afraid it's even harder to close a portal than it is to open
one," he says, a troubled look on his face. "Alix, the only way to close
a demonic portal is to destroy the leader demon who is using it."

"That thing I just killed," I say. "The freaky human-cat hybrid.
Was that a demon?"

"Yes," he says. "A minor one. A type of scout, really, not even
close to a leader demon. That particular type is known as a Brawler.
You'll meet others soon. Heaters. Crawlers. The whole lot. Anyway,
that nasty little Brawler was testing you. You did well, but it tricked

you. Now the leader demon knows you have powers and can actually use the knife. In a way, the weapon was made for you. You didn't get it by accident. I can assure you of that."

"Oh my God. Face," I say, thinking back to my fight with Aruna. "Aruna said he had powers. She said she didn't think he could die. She also said he *wanted* me to have the knife. I thought she was just saying that to intimidate me, but she was serious." I press my fingertips against my temples as it all sets in. "Vagabond, Face is the leader demon, isn't he? The portal is somewhere beneath Oval City. London basically said bad things happen in Oval City because it's evil, and I sensed evil belowground when I was out there tonight."

"You're doing well, Alix," Vagabond says, looking pleased. "Pieces are coming together, aren't they?"

"Perennial," I say, thinking hard. "Lewis said it's the most addictive drug he's ever tried and that it's about to go viral." I stare at Vagabond as the realization strikes. "Perennial is how Face controls people."

"Who's Lewis?" Vagabond says, squinting.

"A guy from school," I say. "Lewis Wilde. He knew William. He's a friend of mine." I find myself imagining Lewis's soft lips brushing against my neck. "Well, more than a friend, actually," I add, feeling my face turn red.

"I see." Vagabond looks concerned. "My advice is to not trust anything or anybody except your abilities."

"London said the same thing."

"Good. I trained her well."

"Vagabond, do you think the real reason Face created Perennial was to make it easier for him to possess souls?"

"If that's the case, then we have a major problem, don't we? Imagine a possession drug like Perennial spreading worldwide." He shakes his head, clearly horrified at the thought. "It probably comes as no surprise to learn that certain people are easier to possess than others. For example, you and your father are good, tough, disciplined, strong-willed people. Demons steer clear of folks like you. Demons are like wild animals on the hunt. They don't like to waste energy, so they look for easy targets. Sometimes they get hold of somebody for a long time. You mentioned Hitler and bin Laden. They're good examples of long-term possession. Serial killers fit that mold too. But what about the faithful husband and father on Main Street, the one who hasn't done anything wrong in his life but one day has too much to drink and hits his wife? Sure, he feels awful about it afterward and swears he'll never do it again, but the fact is that he did it. And how does he explain his behavior?" Vagabond shrugs. "The answer, Alix, is that he *can't* explain his behavior. Why? Because the man experienced short-term possession. A demon momentarily hijacked his soul and moved on after the evil deed was done. That's how the vast majority of possessions work. They're temporary, short-term events."

"Like when a drunk driver collides head-on into an oncoming car and kills an innocent mother and wife," I say, looking over his shoulder and remembering.

"Your mother's death," he says. "Yes, the man who killed your mother was experiencing short-term possession. Don't get me wrong. That doesn't excuse his behavior. It just goes back to what I said about strength and character. That man had weaknesses that allowed a demon to get to him." He gazes down for a moment before looking back at me. "I'm not trying to sound insensitive, but it's actually a good thing that most possessions are short term. It means the demons have to constantly jump from soul to soul. That's why true evil has never taken over the entire human population. You'll be happy to know that although good and evil are everywhere, good has a much higher winning percentage." He offers a sympathetic smile. "It's the rare long-term possessions that worry us."

"And if Perennial spreads worldwide," I say, imagining the horrible scenario, "it weakens God knows how many human minds, ruins lives, and makes its victims perfect targets for long-term demonic possession." I cover my mouth with my hands. "That's what Face is really up to, isn't it?"

"Possibly," Vagabond says. "And if Face succeeds, evil wins and the entire human population becomes nothing but weak, helpless cattle under the control of barbaric demons."

"A breeding ground for evil," I say, recalling his earlier comment.

"That's right," he says. "Earth becomes a breeding ground for evil. A sort of home base for the Fire world."

"But why me, Vagabond?" I ask, puzzled. "Why London? Why Roman King? Why us?" I close my eyes and take a deep, calming breath. "I understand that you're not human. I also understand that you're one of the good guys. So why can't you, and the others like you, just team up, kill all the demons, and call it a day?"

"I wish it were that easy," he says, "but demons have one huge advantage over us. Alix, I'm a messenger for something called the Army of Light, a type of otherworldly network that's been at battle with the demonic Army of Fire since the beginning of time."

"Light and Fire," I say. "Good and evil."

"Exactly."

"Heaven and hell."

"All synonyms for the same two things," he confirms. "Fire and Light."

"What are you, then? Some sort of angel warrior?"

"I suppose you could say that," he says. "Although I prefer the title of messenger."

"Fine," I say. "So what's the huge advantage Fire has over Light?"

"This is what it all comes down to," he says. "Listen very carefully, because our time is almost up and you won't see me or your mother again unless you pass your test." He clears his throat. "Unlike demons, the Army of Light is unable to cross over into the human realm. That's why we rely on humans with strong paranormal abilities to fight the demons that have crossed over and destroy their active portals. That's why you're special to us. Do you understand how important you are? There are very few people like you. Light is counting on you, Alix. With your growing abilities, you can do so much good in the world." He steps forward and takes my hands, squeezing gently and sending wonderful warmth through me. "This is not a dream, Alix. This is serious business. It's a lot to throw at you, yes, but we don't have time to waste. Do you understand what I'm saying to you and how important it is?"

"Yes," I say, wishing it all *were* a dream and that I would awaken in the comfort of my own bed. "I need to tell you something, though. I already told you I sensed evil beneath Oval City."

"Correct," he says. "The answers you seek are all there."

"But the visions," I say. "They don't always follow the same pattern. They almost always begin with a blast of white light, but I've had two where the light changes to fire, and I can't get any sort of reading on the person. Does that mean anything to you?"

"I'm afraid not," he says. "It's still a new and developing ability in you. My advice is to just let it happen. Don't fight it. You'll figure it out eventually."

"And you'll keep your promise about my mom?" I squeeze his hands hard.

"I will," he says. "I promise. But you have to solve William's murder first."

"This is a lot bigger than solving William's murder," I say. "We both know that now, so you don't need to keep it so simple. I'm starting to see why William and the others don't like you. What started as me solving a murder now has me battling demon scouts and trying to kill a leader demon on his home turf. What happens if I fail?"

Vagabond doesn't respond. Still holding my hands, he stares over my shoulder. Another troubled look crosses his face. It's as if he's having a vision of his own. A scary one.

"What is it?" I ask. "What are you seeing?"

"Alix," he says, "you've already seen and learned things that have changed your life forever, but there's more to come. There always is.

It's vital that you take your father's advice and try to remain calm in any situation you find yourself in. You have the abilities. You have the knife. That's all you need. Understand?"

"Yes." I let go of his hands and remove the silver knife from my pocket, liking the feel of it in my hand and enjoying the way the beautiful white light reflects off of the shiny steel blade. "The cat-beast I killed in my living room," I say, rotating the knife from side to side. "I didn't really kill it, did I?"

"No," Vagabond says, a slight smile on his face now. "You can't kill a demon, Alix. You can just destroy the bastards and send their negative energy back where it belongs."

"And the fireball thing it did when I stabbed it," I say, lowering the knife. "Do they all do that?"

"They do," he says. "We simply call those Fires. You scored your first one tonight. Try to keep track of them. Warriors like London and Roman have a friendly contest going over who can get the most."

"And what about these symbols?" I offer him the knife handle for inspection. "All the lines and triangles. What do they mean?"

"Hmm," he says, taking the knife into his large, strong hands and examining the handle closely. "Interesting. It's good news, actually, but I'll let you do the homework. In the meantime, I do know something about you."

Vagabond steadies his playful gaze on me.

"What are you talking about?"

"Clasp your hands together in front of your chest as if you're praying."

"What?" I say. "Why?"

"Just do it," he says. "Trust me."

I do as he asks, but for the first time tonight I *don't* trust him. In fact, my heart pounds as I hold my clasped hands out in front of me. Then Vagabond's enormous left hand comes up with blinding speed as he grasps both of my hands in his palm. His strength is inhuman. My hands are prisoners to his palm, unable to move. I don't feel any pain, just the uneasy feeling of knowing I'm not going anywhere until he decides to release my hands.

He raises the silver knife in his right hand and stares at me.

"What are you doing?" I say, wide-eyed. "Let me go. Please!"

"Easy now," he says. "Relax and observe, remember?"

"What's going on?"

"I need to show you just how special you are," he says, smiling. "Just breathe. This won't hurt a bit."

I'm helpless as Vagabond raises my joined hands until they're level with his chest, which puts them directly in front of my own eyes. He tightens his grip on the knife, white light glinting off of the blade as he does so.

"Alix Keener," he whispers, a blank look on his face now. "You, my friend, are pure Light."

"No!" I yell, seeing it in my mind just before it happens.

Again, I'm too late.

A blur of silver as Vagabond slices expertly through both of my wrists. I watch in horror as my severed hands fall into the white light and vanish, leaving two bloody stumps at my wrists. I close my eyes and scream, but then I realize there's no pain.

When I open my eyes, Vagabond is gone. It's just me surrounded by the beautiful white light. I feel the knife in my pocket, back where it belongs, but when I look at my hands, they're not there. Instead, two softball-sized orbs of white light shine brilliantly from my wrists. A feeling of immense power surges through me. It's as if the orbs are generators of immortality.

Moments later, flaring white light blinds me like an Alaskan blizzard. Moments after that, the light clears and I find myself back home, sitting on the cold living-room floor and staring into space on a Wednesday night.

It occurs to me to check my hands. They're both there, attached and healthy.

CHAPTER 19

William Weed makes dream contact for the third consecutive night. I don't even remember falling asleep. All I recall is being exhausted after my memorable little field trip with Vagabond and sitting there on the living-room floor, wondering if maybe it was all a dream but knowing it wasn't. It took everything I had just to get myself up the stairs and into my bedroom. I'd planned on using my tablet to research the knife symbols, and I remember sitting down at my small desk and opening my favorite browser, but everything's blank after that.

I must have crashed at my desk, because right now I'm back in the clear, crisp white light, surrounded by the smells of spring rain and delicate flowers. The setting might be the same, but rain and flowers are William's smells, not Vagabond's.

So many things race through my mind as I await his appearance. Despite the fatigue from such an eventful evening, I feel my powers getting stronger and remember the overwhelming energy boost I experienced when the orbs of light replaced my hands. Visions and blurry word clouds slice through my mind like a film montage. I sense this is the last time I'll see William. I feel bad for how Vagabond has treated him, and as much as I try to fight it I realize at this moment that I still have strong feelings for William Weed. He's my Dream Guy, a fantasy that happens to be all too real. I need to make the most of our last encounter.

I also feel guilty. It seems like I'm cheating on Lewis, but I haven't even done anything with William. I just happen to have an epic crush on a bad-boy ghost while at the same time having my first real boyfriend. What's strange is that I didn't think about William romantically at all when I was with Lewis tonight. Yes, I'm committed to solving William's murder and taking down Face and Oval City, but tonight I felt like I'd gotten over the stronger feelings I had for William during our first two dream encounters.

But right now butterflies swarm through my stomach as I anticipate his arrival. I feel like some weak, awkward middle-school girl who has a crush on the teacher. Seriously, it's like this place has some sort of William Weed pheromone that renders me helpless and makes me long for his presence.

So you can imagine the sheer joy I feel when William appears in his physical form tonight. He materializes out of nowhere, William Weed standing three feet away from me, again appearing as the William from the *Vagabond's Warrior* blog photo. He's shirtless and heavily muscled. Black cargo shorts. Sunglasses. Black baseball cap backwards on his head. A dazzling Japanese dragon tattoo runs down the length of each arm. My earlier vision of the tattoos—the one where I also discovered William and Aruna had a sexual relationship—proves dead accurate. The dragons burst with fresh greens, purples, oranges, blues, and reds, their ornate mouths opening at his wrists as if preparing to swallow his hands.

"William," I whisper, fighting a strong urge to reach out and touch his statuesque body.

"Hey," he says, smiling and revealing a perfect set of snow-white teeth. "Something tells me you've had an eventful day."

"You're actually talking," I say, thrilled to hear his voice emerge from his mouth. "I mean, it's you speaking through your mouth this time." I realize how dumb that sounds and try to recover. "Sorry," I say. "It's just nice to hear *and* see you at the same time."

"Yeah," he says, looking himself over as if he can't believe it himself. "I wasn't expecting this either. Maybe Vagabond allowed it. This is my last visit, Alix."

"I know," I say. "I sensed it."

"You know how this works," he says. "I can't confirm or deny any information you give me, but I'm curious as to what you've learned. Do you think you know who killed me yet?"

"Yes," I say. "Face."

He considers that for a few moments.

"And why would Face want to kill me?"

"Because he was jealous of you having Aruna," I say. "I know you two were close." I pause. "Very close." William smiles at that, a reaction that sends pangs of jealousy through me. "And I know Aruna was helping you quit Perennial, so I obviously know all about the purple powder and how it's the lifeblood of Oval City."

"Sounds like you've made progress," he says, stepping closer and looking me over from head to toe. "Those jeans look great on you."

"Oh," I say. "Yeah, thanks. My mom bought them for . . ." I trail off, totally flustered. "Never mind. Look, William."

"It's Willis," he says. "People close to me called me Willis."

"I like William better."

"Fine. Call me William." He smiles. "Something's different about you, Alix. Besides the jeans, I mean." He takes another step, William less than a foot away as he leans in and smells the air around me. "You seem a lot more confident tonight. That's pretty damn impressive for an innocent girl who's in real danger for the first time in her life." He brushes his fingertips against the side of my face. I don't fight it. "Personally, I think it's sexy as hell," he adds, slowly removing his hand from my cheek.

"Right," I say, still shocked with how helpless I am around him. "Truth is, Lewis has been a big help."

"Lewis," William says, shaking his head and looking down at his feet. "I bet he's been a big help."

"I thought you two were good friends," I say. "He told me about freshman year and the alternative academy."

"We were good friends," he says, "but I resented him for getting clean. I never understood how he was strong enough to quit Perennial. That powder, Alix—it's incredible. Lewis reached out more than once to try and help me, but I made it clear I didn't want him around." He pauses. "We lost touch toward the end. It's how addicts are. We push everybody away. All we care about is figuring out how to score more drugs."

"Let me ask you a question that has nothing to do with your murder," I say. "Were you clean when you died, or were you still using?"

He thinks about it, surely not wanting to break any of Vagabond's rules. Then he holds his hands out, palms up, a clear signal he wants my hands to join his. I don't hesitate. His hands feel wonderful. They're strong hands, but also soft, gentle, and warm. As my hands venture up to his wrists I find myself fascinated with the beauty of the colorful dragon mouths. I wrap my fingers around them, knowing instantly that William wants me to read him. He can't talk to me about anything relating to his murder, but he's discovered a loophole that he thinks might work.

"I want to help you, William," I say, not wanting to let go of him. "But I don't know if this will work. I mean, you're already . . . well, you know."

"Dead?" he says. "I'm aware of that. Just try, okay? This is the one and only chance you'll get with me. Vagabond will never know." He smiles. "Think of it as testing your powers on the deceased."

I apply more pressure to his wrists and stare at him. I wish I could remove his baseball cap and sunglasses, but somehow I know those are two permanent accessories of his. Nothing happens at first, and I really don't mind. Just touching him feels incredible enough. Seconds later, though, the white light flares in my mind, causing me to squeeze William's wrists hard. I feel him steadying me as I'm blinded by the light.

Then I squeeze my eyes shut.

The vision places me in a bedroom. It's my bedroom. No. Wait. It's my bedroom as it looked when William had it. I'm invisible here. It's night, the room dark and silent. William is sleeping alone, his bed in the same spot as mine. I sense that Aruna hasn't been here in many days. She's gone from his life for good. That checks with what Lewis said about her disappearing before William died.

What else?

William is incredibly sad about her absence. And he's clean. In his last few months of life, he'd broken free of Perennial's evil grasp. This is amazing, but it's also part of the reason he's so sad right now. Aruna helped him beat the drug, and now that she's gone he's very close to relapsing.

But that won't happen, because . . . oh, God . . . that won't happen because this is the night he dies.

Another flare of white momentarily blinds me.

I'm back in the room. Chaos. It's like watching movie footage somebody shot while running with a handheld camera. A large, tall, dark man is on top of William, straddling him, his back facing me. Everything is blurry. William. Lying on his stomach. He's struggling like a trapped animal, but even somebody with his strength is helpless in this position.

The man removes what looks like a large, clear oven bag from inside his coat and places it expertly over William's head. Then he violently pulls what looks and sounds like some sort of cord along the open end of the bag. I hear the bag seal itself around William's throat and watch in horror as he struggles unsuccessfully to break free.

Several seconds later, the killer holds William's motionless body in place for a few moments before turning him over onto his back and propping his corpse up, giving the eerie appearance that William suffocated himself on purpose while sitting up in bed. Just when I think the worst is over, the murderer quickly withdraws an object from his back pocket and places it into William's lifeless right hand, the killer holding the object in place so that it doesn't fall. It's a handgun, I realize. *William's* handgun. Somehow I know this. The murderer knew where to find the weapon, and now he's raising the gun in William's hand and bringing it toward the side of his bag-covered head.

A loud cracking sound and a burst of orange from the gun barrel. William's head slumps to the left. The killer gently lowers the gun hand.

A staged suicide. William Weed was murdered. There's no question about it now. I just watched it happen. But why can't I get a better view of the killer? Is it Face? It has to be. I don't know anybody else who has a motive.

Another explosion of white. The reading is over.

A deep exhale as the vision fades, and I'm back in front of William. He's holding me tightly, my fingers digging into his wrists.

"That was intense," William says, massaging my forearms. "What did you see?"

"I saw your murder," I say, wiping a tear away and catching my breath. "A man put some kind of suicide bag over your head. Then he shot you in the side of the head but made it look like you killed yourself." I close my eyes in a failed attempt to wipe the horrible images from my mind. "It was all so planned out, William. He wanted it to seem like you tried suffocating yourself and then shot yourself in the temple just before you passed out. To the police, it looked like the gun was a backup plan and you used it because the bag took too long to do the job." I open my eyes and shake my head. "It was awful. What kind of a deranged psychopath does that to another human being?"

"Face," William says, squeezing me harder. "Did you see him, Alix? Was it Face?"

"I don't . . ." I close my eyes, frustrated. "I don't know, William. I can't say for sure. It was too dark. Everything was choppy and blurry. But who else would have wanted you dead?"

He looks away but doesn't say anything.

"What?" I say. "There's something you want me to know, but you're not allowed to say it. Screw Vagabond. Just tell me what I need to know!" He shakes his head and stays silent. "Who else wanted you dead?" I yell, shaking his arms but knowing he won't cross Vagabond. "Look, even if it was Face, how would I know? Lewis says nobody even knows who Face is. Is that true? If you saw Face, would you know it?"

"Yes!" William snaps, breaking his arms free from mine. "I know who Face is, okay, Alix? Not many people do, but I'm one of the unlucky few."

"Then you know what he really is, right?" I ask, curious as to how much he knows about Fire and Light.

"I'm not sure what you're talking about," he says, rubbing his forehead. "All I know is that Face is a goddamn freak of nature who took away Aruna. She got me clean, Alix."

"She got you clean and then Face kidnapped her," I say. "You know Face's true identity, and that's why he killed you. He couldn't take any chances. You were off Perennial and thinking clearly for the first time in who knows how long. Face is the only one with the power and skills to make it look like a suicide. Face killed you, William. I'm sure of it."

"But you can't prove it yet, can you?"

"No!" I shout. "It's not like the courts allow psychic visions as evidence." I put my hands on my hips and groan. "It goes way beyond that anyway."

"What's that supposed to mean?"

"Never mind," I say, looking down and shaking my head. "There are things you can't tell me, and I've learned some things I can't tell you."

"I'm sorry, Alix," he says, "but I have to go soon."

"I know," I say, calming myself and taking his hands again. "Look, I'm sorry about how Vagabond is treating you, but I'll figure it all out by the end of Friday. I'll prove Face killed you, and I'll put him out of business forever." I think about my conversation with Vagabond and Face's possible grand plan. "I *have* to put him out of business forever."

"I know Vagabond's using me to test you," William says. "And I'm okay with it. I just want to know who killed me. If it was Face, then take his ass down, Alix, but don't get yourself killed doing it."

"I'll do my best," I say. "Look, you do know Aruna's still alive, right?"

"And still with Face," William says, nodding. "I know. And I know she's been back on Perennial since right after I died."

I think about my vision of her impending death and find it hard to look at William.

"What's wrong?"

"Nothing," I say, unable to bring myself to tell him the truth. "Don't take this the wrong way, but can you two ever be together again? She misses you, William. She told me so herself. I saw her today."

"You saw Aruna today?" William says, squeezing my hands hard. "How is she?"

"Not good," I say. "Face sent her to scare me out of investigating Perennial." I pause. "It didn't work."

"It's official," he says. "You've definitely gained some confidence."

"Can you answer my question?" I say. "Can you and Aruna ever be together again?"

"Did she look that bad?"

"You wouldn't want to see her like she is."

"I'm not positive how it works," he says. "And I'm not saying I want her to die anytime soon, but yes, I guess there's a chance that we can be together when she dies." He pauses. "It's just that . . ."

"Just what?"

"I don't know," he says. "It's been so long. Two years. I'll always care for Aruna, and I definitely hope she gets away from Face, but I'm not sure we could ever have what we had when I was alive." He shrugs. "What I'm saying is that I don't think I'm in love with Aruna anymore."

There's a long silence. We're still holding hands. My gorgeous Dream Guy is being candid in his last moments with me. I feel so bad for William. It must be so lonely wherever he is, not knowing who killed you and realizing you've grown apart from somebody you once loved. His life ended violently. William never even had a chance to say good-bye to anybody.

"I understand," I say, rubbing his muscular forearms. "I really do."

"I know you do," he says. "I'd much rather stay here with you, but it's time for me to go."

"Are you sure this is your last visit?"

"Yes," he says. "According to Vagabond it is anyway."

I feel heat building behind my eyes. "Maybe I can figure out how to channel you and we can talk again someday."

"I would love it," he says. "I don't know if I should say this, but if I wasn't dead I have a feeling I could fall pretty hard for you."

"Thank you for saying it, William." And it does feel wonderful knowing he feels that way about me. My knees seem to melt, but despite my smile and all the happiness his kind words bring, I fail to hold back tears. I don't want William to leave, but I know the time has come. "You know something, William?" I say. "You're the sweetest, hottest ghost I know."

William laughs. "If I don't do this, I'll always regret it."

"Do what?"

"This."

His soft, moist lips are on mine before I can react. Part of me wants to pull back, but I'm in William's world, and he simply has too much power over me. He kisses just as well if not better than Lewis, something I never dreamed possible. My whole body relaxes as William's strong arms wrap around my waist. He smells and tastes like spearmint, and there's a brief but funny moment where I consider the possibility that William and Lewis might use the same soap and toothpaste.

Warm tingles rocket through my body, hitting all the right places as William begins gently kissing my neck. I wrap my arms tightly around his upper back, eyes closed, my breathing heavier now. I'm aware of his hands moving further up alongside my ribs, and as much as I tell myself that this is okay because it's just a dream, I can't help but feel increasing guilt about Lewis. I have to do something quick, because as much as I want William to keep this up I know we're minutes away from going too far.

"Aruna," I say, pulling away but allowing my hands to rest on his wide shoulders.

"What about her?" William says, now looking at me through his dark sunglasses.

"She said something else," I say, catching my breath. "When she was talking about you today, she said she was sorry for losing something. I asked her what she'd lost, but she didn't answer." William continues staring at me, not a hint of emotion on his face. "Does that mean anything to you?"

"No," he says. "Maybe she meant me. She was sorry for losing me."

"Maybe."

"Good-bye, Alix," he says, placing his palms on either side of my face. "You're an incredible person. Thank you for helping me. I know you'll figure it all out." He gives me a quick kiss on the lips and removes his hands. Smiling, he says, "And I sure hope you figure out a way to channel me, because I think we'd both like to see each other again."

I nod and reach forward, longing for one last touch of his amazing body. But William Weed vanishes just as quickly as he appeared, his physical form flaring and joining the brilliant white light just before my fingers touch his dragon tattoos.

CHAPTER 20

I awaken at my desk with a loud gasp and nearly fall off my rolling swivel chair. It's as if I can still smell, feel, and taste William all around me. I rub my eyes and scan the dark bedroom just to make sure he hasn't crossed over like he did after the second dream.

As much as I secretly wish he had crossed, I'm relieved he hasn't. There's no sign of him, just his wonderful smell and the lingering feeling of his lips against my neck. I reach up and touch the spots where he kissed me, part of me feeling guilty, another part looking forward to Lewis kissing me in the same places.

It's nearly midnight. Dad isn't home yet, and again I worry that he saw me inside of Lewis's truck in Oval City. I check my phone for messages. There are none, not even a text from Lewis, which I find slightly disappointing. The good news is that the more time passes without me hearing from Dad, the less likely it is he saw me with Lewis tonight.

I remove the silver knife from my pocket and lay it on the desk beside my tablet. What a day! Events pass through my mind quickly.

Lewis. Aruna. The silver knife. London. An envelope of Perennial. A car accident. Oval City. *Dad* in Oval City. Vagabond's revelations about Fire and Light. Face is a leader demon. A portal beneath Oval City that I'm somehow supposed to close. Vagabond cutting off my hands and revealing wonderful orbs of white light. A final and quite memorable visit with William.

And his murder still to solve!

Whew. I should pass out from exhaustion right now, but I've felt incredibly alert and strong since my meeting with Vagabond. Somehow I'm still running on a full tank and sense that I'll continue feeling this way until my mission is complete.

Vagabond is correct. My abilities are new and developing. I shouldn't question or fight them and should just let them happen.

I turn on the desk lamp and find myself staring at a framed photo of Mom, Dad, and me in Niagara Falls two years ago. We'd just finished the *Maid of the Mist* ride, the one I told Lewis about earlier tonight. The three of us are soaked and still wearing our blue *Maid of the Mist* ponchos, huge smiles on our faces as we stand on the jetty. Mom's long brown hair sticks to the sides of her face in giant clumps, her brown eyes full of life. She was the kind of person you think will never die. That's why part of me died the day she did. And now Vagabond comes out of nowhere and promises me one last visit with her.

That bald bastard better keep his promise.

"Hi, Mom," I say, touching her face with my index finger. "I know you're out there, and I know you can hear me. I don't know if you realize it yet, but we're going to see each other soon. I promise, okay?" I sit there, finger pressed against the picture frame, biting my lower lip and hoping for some kind of vision of her. That doesn't happen, but I know she's in the Light world. She was the nicest, most generous person one could imagine. "By now you probably know I'm different," I continue, finding surprising comfort in speaking to her picture. "There's a lot of weight on my shoulders right now. I didn't ask for any of it, but I'm different, and that's something I have to live with now—and forever. We're not a religious family, but right now I feel like I need to pray. And I'm not praying to God, Mom. I'm praying to you. Please, I need your help. Over the next forty-eight hours, I'm going to experience hell. You and Dad are the smartest people I know, but Dad can't know about this, so I'm praying to you to guide me and bless me with the strength, courage, and wisdom I need."

I pull my finger away and clasp my hands to my chest in prayer.

"You're the reason I'm doing this, Mom," I say, glancing at the silver knife before returning my gaze to her picture. "Helping William find peace and destroying a demon bent on possessing the world are pretty damn important, but Vagabond didn't have me until he said I could see you." I unclasp my hands, kiss my fingertips, and press them against the picture frame. "I love you, Mom. I love you, Dad."

I turn my attention to the knife and the network of triangles and lines on the handle. The more I look at the weapon, the more I appreciate its craftsmanship. The knife doesn't weigh much—less than a can of soda—and the pristine condition of the silver makes it look brand new. Even after today's events, there isn't a single smudge or stray mark on the blade. It's as if the weapon heals itself after every encounter.

The symbols on the handle remind me of dozens of tiny golf tees arranged neatly in horizontal and vertical patterns. Every line has a triangle connected to one end, and every triangle except for one has a line connected to it. Viewed as a whole it's a cool design, but I know there's meaning to the symbols.

I decide to snap a photo of the knife with my phone and run the picture through Google Goggles to see if I get any visual search hits.

That's when something weird happens. The knife doesn't appear in the pictures.

I take four photos of the thing, two with the flash on and two without, and all that shows up in the pictures is my desk. According to my phone's camera, the knife is either invisible or doesn't exist.

"Unbelievable," I say, rubbing my forehead out of frustration.

I raise the knife in my right hand and stare at it. People talk about clothing that has a perfect fit. It's like that with this knife. It's a perfect fit for my hand. Vagabond said Face gave me the knife through Aruna to test me. Now that Face knows I can use it, he wants me out of the picture, and he wants the knife back. He even sent one of his freaky demon Brawlers to get it.

Which means he'll likely send more, because Vagabond said I would meet other scouts called Heaters and Crawlers.

Great.

Not wanting to think about that, I lay the knife on the desk and take a picture of it with my tablet just to be sure my phone camera isn't acting weird. It isn't. The tablet's camera produces the same result. There's no knife in the picture.

So if my dad walked in right now, would he be able to see the knife? Yes, I decide, because Lewis and Aruna saw it, and they're not paranormal demon warriors like London Steel and . . . me.

If the knife symbols are indeed a form of writing, I should be able to find an Internet keyword match fairly quickly, and I'm getting ready to conduct that research when, out of the corner of my eye, I see the knife moving.

It's barely perceptible, the blade moving less than an inch clockwise. I'm lucky I noticed it. I didn't accidentally bump the desk, so I figure it's one of those "house settling" movements Dad says are common in old homes. Regardless, I check beneath the desk, relieved not to find some hideous demon scout lurking at my feet.

My desk rests along the wall opposite the bedroom window. I turn to look. The window is halfway open. A gentle breeze blows through the screen, so the wind probably moved the knife.

Focusing on the tablet again, I'm typing the phrase "written languages with symbols" into Google when I hear a faint hissing sound from outside. The knife moves again too, faster and longer this time, doing a complete one-eighty and stopping when the handle faces me, symbol side up. The hissing stops as well.

"Okay," I say, sliding the tablet away and staring at the knife.

Fear ripples through me. I turn quickly in my chair in an attempt to surprise anything that might be waiting for me. The room is empty. I exhale deeply and even manage a smile.

"You can relax, Blade," I say, swiveling back to the knife and liking the nickname I just gave it. "It's a possum or something. Besides, we're on the second floor. Don't worry."

I reach for the tablet and hear it again, the hissing louder and closer now, sounding as if it's just outside my window. There's a rustling sound too, like an animal is moving through the shrubs in the front yard.

The knife begins vibrating on the desk in the exact same way it did in my pocket during my encounter with the Brawler. The movements make sense now. The knife is more than just an awesome weapon. It's also a type of warning system. It lets me know when trouble is near and when it's ready for action.

The hissing and rustling stop outside, but my heart pounds rapidly as the knife's movements intensify. It's going bonkers on the desk, vibrating like it's in the middle of a violent earthquake.

White light slices through my mind. My body reacts as if it's on autopilot. I know what to do. Somehow I just know, and it all goes back to Vagabond cutting off my hands and revealing the white light.

Light.

I open my right hand and lay it palm up on the desk about a foot away from the knife. I stare at the weapon and smile as it rockets toward my open hand under its own power and secures its handle in my palm. I wrap my fingers around it, enjoying the pleasing warmth it sends through my hand and arm.

I feel invincible. Yes, my abilities are definitely growing.

Another blast of white light.

Something that looks like a goat face flashes through my mind, followed by what resembles a starfish spinning like a fast-moving helicopter. Weird.

I stand and kick the chair under the desk, knife held in front of me at chest level as I turn and walk toward the window, squinting from the annoying yellow streetlight glare slicing into the room.

I'm three feet away from the window. It's still silent outside, just the soft, cool breeze hitting me as I approach the screen. It smells like late summer out there—dead leaves, freshly cut grass, and a bonfire somewhere nearby.

I reach the window. Nothing happens. It's a large window that slides open horizontally. The ledge is at my knees. Keeping the knife in front of me and ready to strike, I lean toward the screen for a look at the front yard below, shielding my eyes from the streetlight glare with my opposite hand. There's nothing evil down there, just impeccable landscaping, an emerald-green lawn, and a large maple tree off to my right.

The knife hasn't moved on its own since landing in my hand, so I consider the fact that this might be a false alarm. After all, my abilities are still in the beta stage, so I figure a bug is bound to pop up every now and then.

"I'm telling you, Blade," I say, scanning the yard, "there's nothing out—"

Heaters.

The word cloud shoots through my mind, but I'm too late.

The obnoxious streetlight prevents me from seeing it. Chaos as something hisses and shrieks loudly from the maple tree area and smashes through the window screen with incredible speed and momentum. Everything goes black. I'm falling backwards and can't breathe.

It's on my face. Something hot, stinky, and slimy is on my face, screeching with delight as it wraps what feel like short, muscular arms around the back of my head and squeezes, applying the kind of pressure that makes your skull feel like it's about to shatter.

The knife. Going berserk in my right hand. It wants to strike, but I'm on the verge of blacking out from pain and can't see anything. If I attempt a wild, blind strike on this thing, there's a chance I'll end up stabbing my face.

I drop to my knees and try screaming. No sound comes out. The smell is disgusting, like rotten meat in a desert. It feels like some high-powered suction device from hell is removing my face. I bring my free hand up in an attempt to pry the creature off of me. I get a brief grasp of what feels like a hot, fleshy horn, but then something sharp clamps down on my fingers, sending a searing pain through my hand.

The damn thing just bit me. That's my thought as I manage to pull my aching hand free from what I assume is its mouth.

The beast screeches louder now, surely thrilled with drawing blood from me. My only hope is the knife. Using the knife is risky, but I'm seconds away from dying in my bedroom. Whatever this thing is, it's probably not expecting my wounded hand to make another move, so that's exactly what I do, reaching up with my bloody left hand and making a desperate grab for the fleshy horn thing.

I get a great hold on it this time too—so good that the creature can't bite me. I feel it trying, but my hand is too high up, confirming my hunch that I'm definitely holding some sort of horn protruding from its small head.

I've distracted it enough for it to ease up on the pressure its short limbs are applying to my face and head, giving me enough time to bring the knife up and strike quickly but carefully with a waving motion a few inches in front of my face.

I feel the blade slice cleanly through something. I hope it's not my own flesh. The beast emits an awful high-pitched wail and removes itself from my face with a nasty suction-like sound. I gasp loudly, sucking in the night air and wiping my face free of what turns out to be more of the same thick yellow ooze the Brawler introduced me to.

Demon snot.

"What the hell!" I yell, opening my eyes and sensing the Heater still in the room, hopefully dead or at least badly injured.

That's when I realize I'm holding something in my left hand.

It's the horn. I cut off a Heater horn! There it is, a pink, membranous horn several inches long and ending in a dangerous, knifelike tip. Yellow tendons and fresh demon ooze dangle from the severed end.

"Yeah!" I yell, dropping the horn, adrenaline pumping and all senses on high alert as I stand and scan the room for the creature. "Come on out, you little wimp! Is that all you have?"

I see no sign of the beast.

Blade has calmed down in my right hand, barely moving now. I check the window screen and see an opening the size of a dinner plate. Maybe the Heater retreated back to Oval City or wherever it came from.

Using the streetlight glow as a light source, I scan the room again, every wall and every inch of floor. Nothing. I even grab my phone and use the flashlight app to check under the desk and bed. Again, nothing.

"It's gone, Blade," I say. "Nice work, buddy."

My left fingers sting. I inspect them with the phone light. The bite doesn't look anywhere near as bad as it feels, just a small red mark on two of my fingertips. Still, I'll need two Band-Aids, which means I'll have to lie when Dad asks me what happened.

Blade vibrates in my hand.

"What?" I say. "I told you. It's gone."

Blade doesn't believe me and continues to move.

"Okay, okay," I say. "One last look."

I aim the phone around the room again. Floors. Walls. Bed. Desk. I even check the ceiling this time, waving the phone in a wide arc, the yellow light sweeping across and illuminating nothing but drywall and plaster.

Until I see something in the upper corner of the room to the far left of the window, where the two walls meet the ceiling.

"Gross," I say, finding it hard to believe what I'm seeing.

It's some type of miniature goat-beast. That's why I had the vision of the goat. It has a small but hellish face about the size of a beverage coaster and gray skin full of sickly wrinkles. A pair of marble-sized red eyes pulsate brightly like a heartbeat. The large, open mouth is terrifying and way out of proportion with the small head. Dozens of yellow, daggerlike teeth, moist with demon ooze, line the perimeter of its mouth. One pink horn remains, protruding inches from one side of the Heater's forehead before curling up into the knifelike tip. There's a gaping hole where the other horn should be, which probably explains why the Heater isn't moving.

I've seriously injured this disgusting creature.

Despite the horrifying face and head, it's what I see attached to the Heater that scares me most. It has no body or neck that I can detect, but it does have what look like five muscular goat legs with hooves attached to the back of its head, the minilegs arranged in a perfect circle the size of a Frisbee.

"Gross," I repeat, squinting and stepping closer for a better look.

Blade starts moving faster now.

"Relax," I say. "I think it's about ready to fireball."

I'm wrong. The red eyes suddenly flare as the Heater creeps slowly along the top of the wall like a giant spider, the five legs all working together in a way that makes it clear the beast can move in any and all directions. I grip Blade tightly and keep my distance from the window. If the wounded Heater wants out, I'll gladly allow it to leave.

The creature stops when it's above the window frame and watches me with those disturbing, pulsating red eyes as its five legs begin rotating slowly in a clockwise direction. The vision of the spinning starfish suddenly makes sense. That's what the rotating legs remind me of: a spinning starfish.

Something tells me not to stare directly into its eyes, so I look away and gaze at the opening in the window screen instead. I think back to how quickly the beast came out of nowhere and shot through the screen.

Which means it can somehow fly. The legs. They must work as a type of propeller.

As if the Heater is reading my mind, it starts rotating its legs so quickly they become a blur, and the goat-beast rockets off of the wall, red eyes throbbing with delight, open mouth closing in on my face.

Again, my body seems programmed to react. I use my own surprising speed and complete a half turn and backbend that allow me to swing the knife up and over my body with great force. There's a sickening sound that reminds me of a shovel hitting fresh dirt.

The Heater has impaled itself on the knife, the silver blade plunging like a barbeque skewer through the Heater's eye. I stand and stare at the shrieking, shaking beast, holding it at arm's length as hot yellow ooze squirts like a geyser from its fading red eye.

"Sorry," I say, "but you deserved it."

Increased heat emanates from the Heater. I know what's coming, so I shield my face and turn sideways just as it fireballs into a basketball-sized explosion of red, orange, and blue.

I just scored my second Fire.

What worries me is that this one was kind of fun. Hmm . . . maybe I *was* born to slay demons.

The room falls silent, just the breeze slapping my back. Blade stops moving, the knife looking cleaner than ever as I sheathe it in my back pocket. I scan the room for any hint of the Heater fight. There's nothing. No demon snot. No sign of the severed horn. No hole in the window screen. No stinging bite marks on my fingers. It's as if it never happened.

But I know it did. So does Blade.

Then the front door suddenly opens and slams downstairs. Footsteps in the living room.

Seconds later, footfalls on the stairs. Now, footsteps in the hallway leading to my room.

I reach behind me and lay a hand on Blade's handle. Somebody or something stops outside my closed bedroom door.

I'm breathing dangerously fast. The doorknob turns quickly.

"Alix?" Dad says, opening the door and flicking on the bedroom light.

"Dad?" I say, letting go of Blade and knowing how bad this looks, me standing in the middle of my bedroom at midnight. In the dark. Fully clothed.

What bothers me is how angry he looks. This is rare. This is full-fledged pissed-off Clint Keener, Dad glaring at me in a way that scares me.

"Let me ask you two questions," he says, pointing at me. "And I'll know if you're lying, so be honest."

"Dad, what's wrong?"

"Shut up, Alix."

What he asks sends my head spinning for answers.

"What the hell were you doing in Oval City tonight?" He pauses. "And why are you dressed like that?"

I gaze down at my dirty Chuck Taylors and realize he's referring to the skinny jeans. All I can do is tell the best lie I can muster and hope he doesn't notice the silver demon-slaying knife in my back pocket.

CHAPTER 21

Dad, I don't know what you're talking about," I say, forcing myself to look him in the eyes. "But I promise you I was nowhere near Oval City tonight. Why would I even think of going to a place like that?"

"Don't lie, Alix." He turns and punches the door. The hinges don't break, but the door slams against the bedroom wall with a jarring crash. I take a step back. "I saw you in a pickup truck in Oval City," he says, turning toward me and shaking the sting out of his hand. "You were in the passenger seat, and you were ducking down so nobody could see you. I saw you, Alix. Who was the boy driving the truck?"

He steps further into the room. I've seen my father angry plenty of times, but I've never seen him this mad. I might be able to slay demons, but I'm no match for an enraged Clint Keener. It's killing me to lie to him, but sometimes you have to lie in order to protect the people you love.

"I'm not lying!" I throw my hands in the air. "I went to the library after school, stayed there until eight, and I've been home since. I'm telling you the truth, Dad."

He's biting his lower lip, Dad trying to calm himself as he rubs his red fist with his opposite hand.

"Alix, it's midnight on a school night. If you weren't out with a boy tonight, explain to me why you're wearing jeans like that."

"Okay," I say, rubbing my temples with my fingertips. "You're right. There *is* a boy I like, but I'm telling you the truth about not being in Oval City. I swear to God, Dad. You must have confused me with somebody else." I stare at my jeans and then back at him. "Mom bought me these right before she died. I've never worn them. I was thinking of wearing them to school tomorrow, and I couldn't sleep, so I decided to get up and try them on." I pause. "I just want to look good for somebody I like, okay?" He doesn't say anything, which means he might be buying it. "Is that too much to ask? You always joke that I should stay away from boys, but I think you might actually be serious. I'm a senior in high school, Dad. I'm almost eighteen years old. I've never even had a boyfriend, so do you really think I would jump into some guy's truck for a trip down to Perennial ground zero?"

I realize my mistake as soon as I say the word. "Perennial."

"Perennial?" he says, jaw clenched and looking like a man I don't know. "Alix, what do you know about Perennial?"

"Nothing really." I close my eyes and shake my head. "I heard about it at school, something about a drug that's a purple powder. People can only buy it in Oval City. There was a rumor that Mr. Watkins's murder had something to do with Perennial." I shrug. "Crazy, I know. But that's what I heard."

"Jesus." Dad puts his hands on his thighs and exhales loudly. "I'm beginning to think we should have stayed in Wayne." He straightens and continues rubbing his punching hand. "Okay, it *was* dark, and the truck *was* going fast, but the passenger looked a lot like you, so is there anything you want to tell me?"

"It *wasn't* me," I say. "You're really stressed out with everything, Dad. I'm not a drug addict, and I'm not one of those thrill-seeking Detroit hipsters you talk about." His face relaxes. It's as if I can see the anger melting away. "I'm a girl, and I'm not stupid, so let me do the things girls like to do."

"I know you're not stupid."

"Then please just trust me," I say. "So I know what Perennial is. Big deal. Everybody at Beaconsfield High knows what it is, but it doesn't mean we're all on it, and big deal if I like a guy and might want to go on a date. It doesn't mean I plan on getting pregnant and skipping college."

"Whoa," he says, raising his hands. "Easy, Alix. Easy."

"Sorry." I force a laugh. "You know what I mean."

Dad manages to laugh too. Good.

"It's the Watkins case," he says, rubbing his forehead. "It's driving us all nuts."

"Is there anything you can tell me?"

"Not really, but you know how it works. The longer it takes for something to turn up, the greater the likelihood the case goes cold and somebody gets away with murder."

"It's that bad?"

"It's that bad," he says. "Whoever did it planned it well." He pauses. "That stays between you and me, okay?"

"I understand."

"So, what's his name?" Dad asks. "This boy you like."

"Lewis." I'm relieved to say something that's actually true. "He's a sweetheart."

"Last name?"

"Dad." I put my hands on my hips and cock my head. "What, will you go all NSA on him and track everything he does?"

"I'm considering it," he says. "That's a joke."

"Wilde. His name is Lewis Wilde."

"You like a boy whose last name is Wilde?" He shakes his head and stares at the ceiling. "I don't know about this."

"Very funny."

Dad surveys the room. I watch his eyes come to rest on my desk and realize he's looking at the Niagara Falls picture. The sadness that crosses his face is hard to look at. Behind the long beard and tough-guy exterior is a sensitive man who has been lost for the past year.

"It's my favorite picture of us," I say. "Sometimes I use it to talk to her."

He nods and walks to my desk for a closer view of the picture. As he does so, I position myself so that I'm facing him and effectively screening the silver knife from his view.

"I was thinking of going to see her Saturday morning," he says, still staring at the picture. "Would you like to come with me?" He glances my way. "Maybe we could hit Eastern Market afterwards. How does that sound?"

"Really?" I say, loving the sound of it. "Yes. I'm totally in."

He takes another look around the room. I can tell he's trying not to cry.

"I'm sorry I was so angry." He walks back toward the hallway. "Sorry about the door too. You know what I'm going through."

"You scared me. I've never seen you that mad. I thought you might actually hit me."

"I would never do that," he says. "Even if that *was* you in Oval City, I would never hit you. I never have and never will."

There's a long silence.

"Let me ask you a question," I finally say. "The man who killed Mom. Do you think he's evil?"

"That's a strange question."

"I know. Maybe I'm just overtired, but do you think he is? Evil, I mean?"

"No," Dad says. "He's a disgusting alcoholic who's paying the price for making a horrible mistake."

"That's kind of how I look at it too." I pause. "Do you believe in evil, Dad?"

"You *are* overtired," he says, smiling. "What's bringing this on?"

"Mr. Watkins, I guess," I say, although I'm thinking more about William's murder than the death of Marc Watkins. "I'm just wondering what makes people commit horrible acts like premeditated murder."

Dad stands there, thinking. Then he says, "I've been a cop for more than twenty years. Before that I fought a war in a desert. When it comes to violence, I've seen it all. Nothing surprises me anymore. Most people are good, but to answer your question, yes, I do believe in evil, but I'm not saying all murderers are evil. I've worked plenty of murder cases where, deep down, I felt the victim deserved to die." He pauses, Dad surely wondering how much detail I can handle. "But I've met way too many murderers who *are* evil. They kill because they enjoy it. I don't know how their minds work. I've never understood how one human being can derive pleasure from killing one of their own for no reason."

"What do you think makes somebody that evil?" I say, thinking back to Vagabond's demonic possession theory. "For example, are serial killers born or made?"

"That's the billion-dollar question, isn't it?" Dad shrugs. "I don't think there's one single cause of evil, Alix. I think evil emerges in a person through a combination of societal, environmental, and emotional factors." He rubs his eyes, Dad looking exhausted. "But imagine if there was a single cause of evil. If we knew what caused evil, we could probably figure out a way to eliminate evil."

"And then you'd be out of a job."

"I would have no problem with that." He winks. "It's late, Alix. Get some sleep."

"I'm almost there," I say. "But, Dad?"

"What is it, honey?"

"How come you never told me about the boy who died in this house? William Weed. It's still a story at school, especially with kids who know where we live."

Dad stares at me from the open doorway, focused thought going on behind those eyes.

"I figured you'd find out about him sooner or later," he says, leaning against the door frame. "I guess . . . I don't know. I should have told you, but I didn't want your mind distracted with another death, especially a teenager's suicide."

Oh, Dad, if you only knew what I was dealing with right now.

"It happened in this room," I say. "I think you should've told me that."

"I know. I'm sorry. Look, I don't know anything about the kid. All I know is that his parents moved out of state after it happened, and this house sat on the market for almost two years." He shrugs. "I couldn't pass up the deal, Alix."

"My history teacher was murdered and some kid died in my own bedroom," I say. "Welcome to Beaconsfield, Michigan. Why are rich suburbs so strange?"

"I agree with you on that. Look, you can switch bedrooms if it bothers you that much. We have three empty ones to choose from."

"No." I wave a dismissive hand. "I'll be fine. It's just a weird thing, knowing somebody my age died in this room."

I decide to see if Dad knows anything about William's case. "Some budding conspiracy theorists at school say William was murdered and that the killer staged it to look like a suicide."

Dad ponders that. "I wouldn't know anything about it. It wasn't in my jurisdiction. But as a law-enforcement official, I can tell you that the cops usually get things right."

"I know." I yawn and realize that I actually am tired. "Good night, Dad."

I'm hoping he doesn't give me a hug, not with this knife in my pocket.

"Sleep tight, Alix," he says, remaining in the doorway. "And good luck with this Lewis kid. He's an idiot if he doesn't see how lucky he is to have you interested in him."

"Thank you," I say, blushing and rolling my eyes.

He smiles and closes the door.

CHAPTER 22

Thursday, September 6

I emerge from a deep, dreamless sleep, enjoying the few minutes I experience in that foggy state between sleep and wakefulness. It's a safe and peaceful time during which I forget about everything I've been through since Tuesday morning. I sense the early morning light penetrating through the window and hear birds singing to start their day. My lips curl into a smile as I imagine Mom and Dad together on a well-deserved vacation somewhere far away from Beaconsfield. My smile widens. I picture myself graduating valedictorian in June and looking forward to a summer job at a children's camp somewhere on the East Coast. Things get really interesting when I imagine Lewis and me lying together on a Lake Michigan beach, the two of us enjoying a brilliant orange sunset, Lewis leaning over and pressing his lips against my neck as I try to maintain control over myself.

Normal things. Parents having fun together. A hardworking student achieving a lifelong goal. A summer job with kids. Kisses on the beach from the teenaged boy of your dreams. I think about normal things and the happiness they bring. I find it all so odd. Why am I so happy with such normal thoughts?

That's when my smile fades and I emerge from my drowsy state, feeling refreshed but depressed at the realization that normalcy might be out of my grasp for the rest of my life. Normalcy is becoming increasingly foreign to me, which is why I crave it so badly.

Lying on my back, I open my eyes and stare at the white ceiling as a word cloud slices through my head, the bold black letters settling in against the white background. Two words I know well:

Lewis Wilde.

The vision ends. I sit up in bed still wearing the same outfit from last night. I remember Dad telling me to sleep tight. Then he left the room. I washed my face, brushed and flossed my teeth, and told myself I would lie down for a few minutes before changing my clothes. Well, I never made it to the pajama part.

I rub sleep from my eyes, reach for my glasses, and check the time: 5:30 a.m. Okay. I haven't overslept, but it is time to get rolling, so I set my feet on the floor and realize my neck is sore. More importantly, the silver knife isn't in my back pocket. It's surely a good thing that I didn't fall asleep with it back there, but panic sets in at the thought of where my trusty weapon might be, especially if I left it in the bathroom, and Dad came across it.

Damn. Where did I put it? And why is my neck so sore?

I stand and rub my face with my palms. Despite getting less than six hours of sleep, I feel energized, but where the hell is Blade?

I check the bed and desk but find no sign of the knife. Part of me still secretly hopes the past two days never happened and that today is Tuesday, the first day of school, but that wish explodes in my face when it occurs to me why my neck is so sore. Whiplash from the truck accident with Lewis.

I wonder how Lewis feels. My heart dances at the thought of seeing him this morning, but right now I'm on the brink of a panic attack. I have to find that knife. I'm all over the room now, checking the closet, under the bed, every drawer in the room. Nothing.

"Blade," I whisper. "Where are you?"

I stare at the mattress and smile as a wave of relief washes over me. Now I remember. I walk over and lift the mattress, happy to see the shimmering silver knife resting exactly where I put it just before lying down last night. I drop the mattress back into place, leaving Blade tucked away until I have to leave for school.

Next I check my phone, hoping for a message from Lewis but not finding one.

Lewis. The word cloud with his name. What was that all about? It had to be some kind of message.

Come on, Alix. Think.

I figure a hot shower will clear my head and help soothe my aching neck, and I'm walking toward my bedroom door when I glance at my desk and see my tablet. There's nothing unusual about where it is. In fact, it's exactly where I left it last night. But that's when I remember what I was doing just before the Heater attacked me. I was ready to search for information about the symbols on the handle.

I don't have time for that right now, but I do feel a strong urge to search for anything related to Lewis Wilde. Thinking back to when he dropped me off last night, I knew he was irritated when I asked him for his grandparents' address. But what scared me was the troubling vision during our second kiss. Lewis's white light changed to a wall of fire. That's happened twice. Once with the homeless man in Oval City, who I *knew* was evil. The second time it happened with Lewis, who *isn't* evil. There's no way he's a bad person. It's just something I know in my heart. Last night I took the strange vision as a possible sign that I was already losing my abilities. Well, now I know that's not the case, so why would I read Lewis as a wall of fire?

According to Vagabond, Light is good and Fire is evil. It's that simple.

But I must be missing something because I love Lewis Wilde, and I doubt a demon slayer would fall in love with a demon.

I mean, there's no way, right?

I sit at the desk and use my tablet to search the words "Lewis Wilde, Eastland, Michigan," nervously picking my nails as I scan any results connected to Lewis and the neighboring city he claims to hail from. There's nothing remotely related to the Lewis Wilde I know, but I'm not too worried about that. I'm guessing most high school kids don't show up in Internet searches unless they've either been in serious trouble with the law or excelled in certain areas of high school life, especially sports. Despite his incredible body, Lewis is no jock, which is yet another reason I'm so attracted to him.

Next I think about the address he gave me for his grandparents' house. I remember it being over on Bloomfield Street, but the numbers escape me, so I search "Wilde, Bloomfield Street, Beaconsfield, Michigan," making the assumption he's living with his paternal grandparents.

I must be wrong on that assumption, because once again I get nothing related to what I'm looking for.

What was the exact address? It takes a few moments, but the four numbers come to me when I remember that they totaled eleven: 3116. I rub my hands together, take a deep breath, and type "3116 Bloomfield Street, Beaconsfield, Michigan" into the search bar.

There's no match, just page after page of unrelated results containing some or all of the search string.

"Beaconsfield Middle School."

Nope.

The three nearby and wealthy Bloomfield communities: "Bloomfield Hills," "Bloomfield Township," and "West Bloomfield."

Nope.

And no direct map link to Lewis's grandparents' specific address, not even after I add our zip code to the search and try again.

My stomach begins flipping and my throat goes dry. I'm rubbing my chin in frustration, wondering why Lewis would lie about where he's living. Maybe I typed in the wrong street number. I consider that, but no, I remember specifically chunking the 3116 in order and noting that the numbers totaled eleven. I know he said Bloomfield Street, and Bloomfield is indeed a Beaconsfield street. In fact, it's two streets down from ours.

Back in middle school we used to have fun finding our houses on Google Earth. Of course, all you have to do now is Google a specific address, and the street-view option automatically appears at the top of the results page. According to my search, Lewis Wilde's grandparents' house doesn't exist, so I make a decision to take a little detour down Bloomfield Street on my way to school this morning.

CHAPTER 23

Dad's already gone when I leave the house at six thirty. It's another beautiful morning in Beaconsfield. Driving down Maple Grove in the Explorer, I roll down the windows and enjoy the cool breeze, cloudless sky, and bright sunshine, nearly forgetting the fact that Lewis popped into my life out of nowhere almost exactly forty-eight hours ago.

I nervously run a hand through my hair as I approach Bloomfield Street and glance at the glove compartment, where Blade rests inside. Turning onto the 1000 block of Bloomfield, my nerves build. I pay attention to the even-numbered addresses on my right. Some of the largest, most expensive Beaconsfield homes are on Bloomfield, and my jaw drops at the sight of such wealth and luxury. All of these multistory homes have huge expanses of lawn and rest atop natural rises, making them more impressive from street level. I have to crane my head over the passenger seat just to see the roofs of some of these beasts.

I pass through a quiet intersection and coast into the 3000 block, part of me expecting Lewis to show up in the middle of the street like he did two days ago. As much as I would love for that to happen, it doesn't. Instead, a couple of old men drive by in the opposite direction, one in a Lexus and the other in a Mercedes, and the next thing I know I'm driving past 3100 Bloomfield, followed by 3110 Bloomfield, both huge, stately homes that look far more expensive than something even a lifelong automotive engineer in suburban Detroit could afford.

It's official. Lewis lied about where he lives.

That's all I can think about. My heart rate spikes, so I pull over to the side of the road and park beneath a giant, leafy maple tree to think. Why would Lewis lie to me? Does he just not want me to know where his grandparents really live? Part of me actually gets that. After all, it's only been two days. But somehow I know that's not the reason. Does he even have grandparents in Beaconsfield? Is he even living in this city? Yes, Lewis has to live here, because the school district has strict residency requirements that help maintain its stellar national reputation. You have to live in Beaconsfield to attend its public schools.

I grab my phone from the middle console. No messages. I think about firing off an angry text to Lewis, but the investigator in me knows I need more information. I'm giving Lewis the benefit of the doubt for now, but if he's lying about where he lives, there's a good chance he's lying about other things.

Ugh. It's like I can feel my heart breaking. Just when you think you've met Mr. Right, you learn something that makes you realize he might be Mr. Ass.

So I'm sitting here curbside, trying to stay strong and not cry, when I glance in the rearview mirror and spot a white Beaconsfield Police car creeping up alongside me.

Great. My heart seems ready to fly out of my mouth. If I get a ticket for something and the officer runs the plate, he'll see my dad's name, and it's like every cop in Michigan knows who my dad is, meaning Dad will ask me what I was doing on this street and not driving straight to school.

Just relax, Alix. Breathe.

The officer stops his cruiser beside me, powers down the passenger window, and says, "Everything okay, Miss?"

"Um . . . yes, sir." I look him in the eyes and keep my hands on top of the steering wheel where he can see them, something Dad told me to do if I ever got pulled over. "I'm on my way to school."

"Beaconsfield High?"

"Yes."

"It's back that way." He jabs a thumb over his shoulder.

"Oh," I say. "I guess I took a wrong turn. It's only my third day. I'm not feeling great this morning."

"I see," he says, studying me. "Well, there's no parking on either side of this street. Take a look around." He's right. I'm the only car parked curbside on Bloomfield. "Can you get to school on your own? I can follow you if you want."

"No, thanks," I say, horrified at the thought of a police escort to school. "I'm fine, Officer. I know where to go now. Sorry for parking here."

"Not a problem. Have a good day at school." He pauses. "You know, if you're sick you should think about taking the day off. My wife's a teacher and always complains about students who come to school sick and end up getting other kids and teachers sick." He shrugs. "Just a thought."

He gives me a friendly wave and drives off.

I'm watching the back of the squad car when the white light blinds me and delivers another black-on-white word cloud. This one consists of a single word:

Eastland.

My vision clears. I check my phone. It's six forty-five, still forty minutes before first hour. Eastland is Beaconsfield's eastern neighbor. Of course, it's also the city where Lewis told me his parents' house is. Lewis also said he went to Eastland High through last year, meaning there should be plenty of students and teachers there who know him.

I pull into a neighboring driveway and back out to head to school, thinking about the perfect attendance record I've had since sixth grade, when I came down with the flu and missed a week of school. Prior to that I'd never been absent, and to this day I've never been tardy to a class. It's a streak I'm proud of, a streak that reflects the discipline and strong work ethic Mom and Dad drove into me over the years. Mom had several years of perfect attendance as a middle school teacher, and I don't remember the last time Dad took a day off work. Maybe he never has. I feel guilty with what I'm about to do, but I'm not exactly the same Alix Keener I was a few days ago. After all, I have to solve a murder and destroy a leader demon by the end of tomorrow night.

My plan is risky, but my life seems to have turned into one big risk over the past two days. So instead of going to Beaconsfield High this morning, I decide to skip first hour and head east, looking forward to walking the halls of Eastland High School.

∞

Traffic is light. I pull into the student lot behind Eastland High just after seven, giving me about twenty minutes to get inside and ask about Lewis. I don't have a student parking permit, but right now I could care less, and I park in the first spot I find.

Like Beaconsfield High, Eastland High School has a national reputation as one of the finest high schools in the country. Eastland was actually one of the possible cities on our short list of places to move to. In the end Dad and I chose Beaconsfield because the high school there ranks even higher than Eastland's. Of course, now I know the real reason why Dad wanted Beaconsfield. He bought the house for a steal.

Eastland definitely has money, but as I look around the student lot, I notice a slight decrease in quality between the students' cars here and those at Beaconsfield. The Eastland cars are nice overall and surely more expensive than those found in more than 99 percent of America's public high school student parking lots, but I don't see nearly as many Lexus, BMW, and Mercedes models here as I do at Beaconsfield High. There's absolutely nothing wrong with that, of course. In fact, what I realize as I approach the rear entrance of the modern school is that I would feel far more comfortable in a community like Eastland than I do in the filthy rich fantasyland known as Beaconsfield.

Damn. We should've picked Eastland, Dad.

The school is huge. The wide hallways are a welcome change from the narrow old confines of Beaconsfield High. Countless students roam the halls, most of them wearing clothing that, like their cars, reflects upper-middle-class status. I blend in far more easily here than I do at Beaconsfield, although I do draw some curious glances from kids who surely realize they've never seen me before and must think I'm a new student.

I figure the main hallway is near the front of the school, a theory that proves correct as I pass through a huge glass atrium and reach the main offices bordering the front of the building. I spot a row of classrooms on the opposite side of the hallway. A short, overweight but pleasant-looking older female teacher is standing outside one of the rooms. She's smiling behind enormous glasses and greeting passing students, a telltale sign of a teacher who actually enjoys her job.

I cut across the hallway and approach her.

"Good morning," she says. "We haven't met, have we? I'm Mrs. Leonard." She extends a plump hand. "And you are?"

"Um . . . Stephanie." I shake her warm hand. "Stephanie Flanders. It's my first day."

"Hmm. I haven't received any new student notifications for my classes today. Am I on your schedule?"

"Oh no," I say. "I wish you were, but I was wondering if you knew a friend of mine who went to school here until this year. His name is Lewis. Lewis Wilde. Do you remember him?"

"Lewis Wilde," she says, scratching the side of her head. "No. I don't recall the name. Did he have me as a teacher? I've been doing this for more than thirty years and never forget a name."

"I'm not sure. Probably not. I guess I have the wrong teacher."

"I'm afraid so," she says. "Anyway, welcome to Eastland High, Stephanie."

I thank her and move on, eventually taking a right down a narrower middle hallway packed with students and lined with lockers on both sides. I ask two younger male teachers talking together near a bank of lockers if they either know or have ever heard of Lewis Wilde. They haven't.

The ten-minute warning bell wails. I need to ask some students about Lewis, preferably seniors, so I remind the male teachers that it's my first day and ask if there's a senior locker section anywhere in the school. There is, and it's located in the neighboring hallway. I thank them and rush off.

I draw plenty of stares in "senior row," and for some reason I find it difficult to decide who to ask about Lewis, so I stay in the middle of the hall, moving forward with the masses and glancing at the students huddled around their lockers, trying to find a candidate who appears kind and helpful.

I quickly find two, a girl and a guy, and it's their hair that catches my interest. Well, that and the fact they won't stop staring at me, especially the guy. It's as if he's expecting me. He looks familiar. I know him from somewhere, but I can't remember exactly where. The girl is drop-dead gorgeous. She has shoulder-length, shiny, and straight jet-black hair with stunning purple streaks that make her look like a rock star. The guy is clearly her boyfriend, but I find that a bit strange. He's tall and skinny, with curly brown hair and geeky glasses. Still, there's something about him that draws me in.

"Hi," I say, sliding out of the cattle herd.

"Hey," the girl says. "You're new here, aren't you?"

"Yeah. I was wondering if you could help me with something."

"Sure," she says. "It's a big school. What do you need?"

She exchanges glances with her boyfriend, who keeps staring at me but hasn't uttered a word.

"I was wondering if you know my friend," I say. "Lewis Wilde. He's a senior over at Beaconsfield this year, but he went here through junior year."

They look at each other again, shrug, and shake their heads.

"I'm sorry," she says. "I've never heard of him, and I know who everybody in our senior class is." She makes an apologetic face. "I'm Brooke, by the way. Brooke Sparks."

"Stephanie." I shake her hand. "Stephanie Flanders."

For some reason the guy stifles a laugh at my name, but when he introduces himself I understand why.

"Hi . . . Stephanie, is it?" he says, smiling. "I'm Roman. Roman King."

My stomach drops a mile. Roman King. The guy Vagabond mentioned as being a recent addition to his team. Vagabond said we would meet soon. And now I remember why the name Roman King sounded familiar when Vagabond mentioned it.

"Roman King," I say. "You're the guy who stopped that kid from shooting people at a football game last year, aren't you?"

"That's me." He raises an index finger in front of his nose to quiet me. "But that was a year ago. No offense, but I don't like talking about it."

"I get it," I say, noticing a shiny silver band on his right ring finger. There are a lot of silver rings in the world, but this one is simple in design and looks identical to the one London Steel had on at Zeppelin Coffee. Also, like London's ring, I sense something special about Roman's silver band.

"Anyway, it's nice to meet you . . . Stephanie," he says, again smiling at the sound of my pseudonym.

He extends his right hand. I seize the opportunity to shake it, hoping his ring gives off the same special warmth as London's.

It does, and I think Roman can sense it, because as the pleasant warmth of his ring spreads through my hand, a flash of beautiful white light fills my head, followed by a vision of Roman fighting alongside London Steel. They're in a dark space full of fire, the two of them covered in yellow demon ooze as they battle a large demonic beast that looks like a spider the size of an elephant. Unfortunately, another disturbing wall of searing orange and red flames fills my field of vision and blocks out everything. Then Roman releases my hand, ending the brief but revealing reading.

I've confirmed that Roman is indeed a warrior. Vagabond's warrior. Roman King has slayed demons with London Steel.

"Are you okay, Stephanie?" Brooke asks, looking at me and then at Roman.

"I'm fine, thanks." I adjust my glasses and catch my breath.

"Listen," Brooke says. "I'm almost positive there was no Lewis Wilde here last year, but if you want to know for sure, just ask somebody in the attendance office to search his name on the computer."

"Great idea," I say, wondering if I should say anything to Roman about the things we have in common. "Thanks, you guys."

Another obnoxious bell blares through the school. Frantic students scatter in all directions. The tinny, high-pitched sound nearly makes me cover my ears.

"That's the two-minute bell," Brooke says, scrunching her nose at the sound and closing her locker. "Who do you have first hour, Stephanie?"

Her question catches me off guard. I have no answer, so I stand there like a stunned animal.

"She doesn't go to school here," Roman says. "Do you, Stephanie?"

"What?" Brooke says, giving him a look. "How do you know that?"

"Vagabond," I say. It's the first word that comes to mind. Roman smiles. That's all the answer I need. "Nice ring, by the way."

"Oh," Brooke says, rolling her eyes. "Are you in the Group, Stephanie? I hope not, because Vagabond promised Roman he was on vacation for a while."

"She's not in the Group," Roman says. "Not yet."

"How do you know all of this?" I say.

"Think about it."

"London." I nod at the obvious answer. "You know my real name then?"

"Yes." Roman hoists his backpack over his shoulder. "Good luck with Vagabond's test, Alix. From what I've heard, you're doing great."

"I have a feeling the hardest part is still to come."

"It is," Roman says. "See you at lunch, Brooke." He gives her hand a squeeze and rushes off to class, leaving Brooke and me alone.

"I have to go too," Brooke says. "It was nice meeting you, Alix. I don't have any special abilities, but I have a feeling we'll see each other again soon."

"One question, Brooke. If you don't have powers, how do you know about us? How do you know about Vagabond and the Group?"

"It's complicated, but it has everything to do with the power of love." She leans in close and whispers, "Demons fear love, Alix. Remember that."

She smiles and hustles down the emptying hallway.

∞

The tardy bell rings as I push open the door to the attendance office. It's a small, windowless room connected to a much larger main office. The attendance secretary doesn't bother looking up from her cluttered desk, her face glued to the computer monitor. The office smells like stale coffee, cigarette smoke, and cheap air freshener. The frumpy, overweight woman in front of me is a prime candidate for one of those professional style-makeover shows. She could be pretty if she tried, but she strikes me as a woman over fifty who has given up on ever meeting somebody special. The absence of a wedding ring reinforces my theory.

"Um . . . excuse me," I say. "I was wondering if you could—"

"Shouldn't you be in class right now?" she interrupts, eyes still pasted to her computer.

"I suppose."

"Do you have a pass to be here?"

"No, but—"

"Then you need to leave," she says. "You're late for class."

Her lack of eye contact and awful attitude is pissing me off. I only have a few minutes before I need to leave. My mind is a wreck right now, and the guy I'm in love with is lying about where he's from, so maybe it's no surprise that I feel like I'm about to snap at this woman.

I force myself to take a breath and stay calm, knowing that anger won't get me anywhere with somebody like this. Her desk looks like a tornado roared through it, but I do spot three framed photos of an adorable chocolate Labrador retriever.

"Your dog is beautiful," I say. "Is it male or female?"

That gets her attention. She looks at me. A smile crosses her face. She shifts her gaze between the pictures and me. I have a feeling I'm the first person who has spoken with her this morning.

"That's my Oscar," she says, beaming. "He turns seven next week."

"That's great. I love dogs, but my dad says we're too busy to care for one. My mom used to say the same thing. I guess they're right.

Our house is empty most of the time. But I hear Labs are great with kids. Do you have children?"

"Me?" she says, laughing. "Oh no. I guess you could say Oscar's my only child. He does love kids, though. That's why I take him to the park so much. Oscar worships people." She gives me a blank stare. "I'm sorry, honey, but why are you here again?"

"Oh right," I say. "I was just talking with Roman King and Brooke Sparks—"

"Roman and Brooke? I just love those two. Aren't they wonderful together?"

"Um, yes," I say, happy the name-dropping paid off. "They're an amazing couple. So, I know this guy who went to school here until the end of last year. He's a senior this year, but he never told me he was moving. We've lost touch. I don't even have a working phone number or e-mail address for him. It's like he just vanished. Brooke said you were awesome and suggested I ask you where he might be going to school this year."

"Brooke Sparks said I was awesome?"

"Yes. She also said you had the cutest dog on the planet."

"Oh, bless her." She rests her fingers on the keyboard and looks at the monitor. "Okay. What's his name?"

"Lewis Wilde."

I spell his entire name out for her. She types and waits. A concerned look eventually crosses her face.

"Are you sure you spelled his name right?"

"Yes." Again, I spell out his complete first and last names. "I'm positive that's correct."

She types again. My heart hammers away with every keystroke.

"Honey, I'm sorry." She shakes her head. "There's no record of a Lewis Wilde attending school here or anywhere else in Eastland, and these records go back twenty years. You must have the spelling wrong."

She stares at me. I feel my jaw dropping. Lewis Wilde is turning out to be one big lie.

"What's wrong?" she says. "You look like you're about to cry. What's your name, anyway?"

"Thank you. You've been a great help." I'm barely able to get the words out as I turn and push through the door.

"Wait," she says. "I'll write you a late pass."

The door closes with a dull thud. The hallway is deserted, and that's exactly how I feel right now. Deserted. I also feel cheated and used. A whirlwind of emotions rolls through me as my rapid footsteps echo through the halls. I want William and Lewis to switch places. I want William to be real and Lewis to be the ghost. William wouldn't lie to me like this. Part of me wants to break down and cry. Another part of me wants to find Lewis and beat his ass.

Why is Lewis lying? I still can't figure it out. And this isn't just some little lie. If he's not from Eastland, where is he from? Are his parents really working in China? Does he even have grandparents in Beaconsfield? Perhaps most troubling of all, where exactly has he been staying the past few days?

My sadness and hurt turn to anger as I approach the back of the school. I can't imagine sitting next to Lewis in history class today. I'm afraid I'll punch him if I see him. What does he want from me? What is he using me for? Is Lewis Wilde a demon? Is he Fire?

So many questions, but I do know one thing: I'm not one of those weak and passive females who allow guys to walk all over them. How dare that bastard lie to me and actually think he can get away with it. I don't care how beautiful Lewis is; lying just made him ugly.

I push open the double doors of the school and step into the blinding morning sunlight. My walk turns into a jog, which quickly becomes a full sprint to my Explorer, where I again think of London and Vagabond's words of wisdom.

London: *Trust your abilities, but don't trust anything or anybody else.*

Vagabond: *My advice is to not trust anything or anybody except your abilities.*

I slam the door and pull out of the student parking lot so fast that I squawk the tires. I should go directly to school, but there's no way I'm going to Beaconsfield High today, not until I know who Lewis Wilde really is.

CHAPTER 24

The word cloud hits as I cross the border from Eastland into Beaconsfield. The name Marc Watkins flashes through my mind in brilliant black letters against a crisp white background. The word clouds are getting clearer with each occurrence. My first one with London Steel yesterday was a fuzzy mess compared to this one. It's like my mind's-eye vision is improving. My abilities are getting stronger. I'm understanding them better and not fighting them.

"Okay," I say, focusing on the road and traffic in front of me. "What about him? What about Mr. Watkins?"

Nothing happens for about a minute, but when I glance at my phone in the cup holder, I somehow know exactly what to do.

I pull into the Trader Joe's parking lot, where I manage to fight off a wicked craving for more vegetarian kimchi topped with a fried egg. Using my Google app, I search the words "Marc Watkins Michigan address." WhitePages.com has four matches, but only two of them have the correct "Marc" spelling. The other two spell the name the traditional way with a *k*. Of the two Marcs, I see the one I'm looking for right away. Marc Watkins. Age 35–40. 2120 Cranbrook. Beaconsfield. Oakland County.

I honestly don't know how people accomplished anything before the Internet, especially detectives.

What surprises me is the Beaconsfield address. I'm not sure how much public school teachers get paid around here, but there's no way it's enough to maintain a Beaconsfield lifestyle. Then again, my dad's a cop and we live here, so there must be plenty of cash somewhere in the Watkins family tree.

∞

Unlike Bloomfield Street, you're allowed to park on Cranbrook, so I pull curbside in front of the generous white colonial at 2120 and sit there, wondering what to do next. It's 7:45 a.m. The driveway is empty, the doors and windows all closed, blinds and curtains drawn, and the garage is shut. There aren't even any media or law-enforcement types around, so I figure the grieving widow Mrs. Watkins has taken the kids and gone to stay with somebody. I know the feeling. Dad and I never felt comfortable in the Wayne house after Mom died.

The Watkins house has a long, tall privacy hedge on both sides, screening the residence from neighbors. I look around. Still not seeing a soul, I silence my phone and get out of the Explorer. Seconds later I'm halfway up the Watkins's driveway, fully aware that I'm trespassing on a dead man's property and that Dad will probably kick me out of the house if he finds out I'm ditching school and nosing around here.

An immaculate Asian-style wooden fence rests between the house and the detached garage, concealing the backyard from view. I'm sure the ornate gate will be locked, so I'm surprised when I turn the metal handle and it opens slowly toward me.

I see her the moment I step into the beautifully landscaped back-yard. She's about thirty feet away, sitting on a stone bench beside a pond that looks as if it's straight out of some Zen garden in Japan. Her back is facing me. She's looking at the pond. If she heard me open the gate, she doesn't seem to care.

I'm not sure what to do. The woman is dressed in black, so I'm fairly certain it's Mrs. Watkins. I take a moment and debate whether to continue forward or retreat and leave this poor woman alone.

The backyard. Wait. It *is* a Zen garden. That's the intention, and somebody pulled it off with stunning success. Japanese maple trees and other Asian-looking trees and shrubs fill the space, all of them placed perfectly and displaying a lovely combination of green, red, and purple foliage. It's incredible. I see some stone paths and hear a gentle waterfall near the pond. There's even one of those large, reddish-orange Japanese-shrine gates in the back of the garden.

I take a deep breath and continue forward along a pea gravel path, desperately wondering what I should say to her. This feels right, though. The Marc Watkins word cloud led me here for a reason.

She hears my feet crunching the gravel and turns, revealing one of the saddest faces I've ever seen. She's a pretty woman, but thin and pale, her eyes red and swollen from crying. I remember my eyes looking that way when Mom died.

Mrs. Watkins's stylish long-sleeved black shirt and pants are in stark contrast to her long blond hair and pearly skin, giving her an almost ghostlike appearance. I stop on the path ten feet away from her.

"Who are you?" she says, standing and sliding on a pair of black sunglasses. "And what are you doing here? You need to leave, or I'll call the police." She shows me her phone. "Do you understand?"

"I'm sorry, Mrs. Watkins. My name is Alix Keener. I'm a new senior at Beaconsfield. I picked the school because of your husband's reputation as a teacher. I just wanted to say in person how sorry I am for your loss."

"Keener," she says. "Are you the policeman's daughter? The one who lives on Maple Grove?"

"Yes, that's me," I say, wondering if I just got myself into big-time trouble. "My dad's doing everything he can to find out who's responsible for your husband's death."

"What you just did. It takes a lot of nerve to walk into somebody's backyard like that, especially under these circumstances."

I shrug. "I guess I have my father's law-enforcement instincts."

"Nobody knows I'm here," she says. "Please keep it that way. A neighbor helped me get back here undetected. I can't stay long. I have to get back to my boys, but I just had to spend some time alone in the garden. It's probably the last time I'll see it."

"I understand. It's an amazing space."

"It was a mess when we moved in two years ago," she says, smiling at a pleasant memory. "Marc revived the whole thing." She shakes her head and looks around. "He was an incredible gardener. He used his chemistry background to create all sorts of organic pesticides and fertilizers. They all worked too. He planned on opening an organic gardening center after he retired from teaching."

"I'm sorry I never met him. The whole school is devastated. Students. Staff. They loved him, Mrs. Watkins. I'm not sure if that helps, but I wanted you to know."

"Thank you. My name is Mary, by the way." She wipes tears away. "I'm sorry about your mother. From what I've read and heard, she was very well loved too."

"Yes," I say. "Thank you. She was."

Mrs. Mary Watkins stays silent for several moments, surely staring at me behind those big black lenses. A cool but light breeze blows through her straight blond hair and rustles the Japanese maples, sending several dead leaves to the ground. Watching her, I sense she's a kind but lonely and shy woman, a wonderful mother who doesn't have many close friends. There are things she wants to talk about but for some reason can't. I need to shake her hand or hug her. I need physical contact to get a better reading.

"It's still difficult for you, isn't it?" she says. "Dealing with the loss."

"I struggle every day."

"Has it gotten any easier? I can't imagine feeling this hollow and empty for the rest of my life."

"You learn to function," I say. "That's about all I can say."

She gestures toward the bench. "Would you like to sit down?"

"Sure." I walk toward her. "I'd like that."

We sit beside each other and stare at the pond, which is stocked with the most beautifully colored Japanese koi fish I've ever seen. Dozens of them swim near the surface, their large, brightly colored bodies showing a variety of orange, yellow, black, and white patterns. It's hard to believe there can be such sadness amidst such a peaceful and gorgeous setting.

Mary opens up quickly. I suppose it's our shared bond of loss that makes her feel comfortable with me. I listen to every word. She talks about her six- and eight-year-old sons, Joshua and Ethan, who keep asking when Daddy will be home. She talks about the lack of respect the media has had around her. I tell her I can relate to that one. She understands that the police are simply doing their jobs, but she doesn't see why they have to ask her so many questions. I like her more with every passing second, and it occurs to me that I haven't had such a meaningful conversation with an adult woman since Mom died.

"Alix?" she says. "Why are you crying?"

Her question surprises me. I'm staring at the fish, unaware of the tears rolling down my cheeks. I wipe my face and take a deep breath.

"I'm not sure," I say. "Maybe it's because I don't know why good people have to experience so many horrible things. Maybe these experiences make us stronger in the long run, but it sure seems like a high price to pay."

"That's a wise statement for a girl your age. Then again, you've been through a lot."

"You have no idea. No idea at all."

"What do you mean by that?"

"Let's just say this goes way beyond my mom," I say. "My life changed forever two days ago. Sometimes I feel like I know what I'm doing. Other times I feel like a lost child."

"Welcome to adulthood," she says.

She takes my hand and squeezes it. I'm surprised with how easily we both break down. My tears return like a waterfall. Mrs. Watkins hugs me. I soon feel her shaking and crying, so I hug her. We're both a total mess for a minute or two, but I could care less. I feel the emotional weight of the past few days melting away with every tear. I don't have a mother. Mrs. Watkins doesn't have a daughter. We're simply two women in the right place at the right time, but for all the wrong reasons.

The vision comes near the end of the hug. White light floods my mind. I see them arguing in their kitchen, Marc and Mary Watkins fighting about money. They're trying to keep their voices down so the boys can't hear them. She wants to know how much money he has, but he won't tell her. He's afraid of something or someone. There's something else related to cash, but I can't figure it out. All I know is that they were not getting along well in the weeks before he died, and it had something to do with money and fear.

The vision ends without any hint of fire, just another flare of white. I'm back in the moment, still in Mary's arms. This is good. The lack of fire must mean Mary Watkins is innocent of any involvement in her husband's death and that she has no clue about the worlds of Fire and Light. She's a normal human. Despite her current circumstances, I envy her for that.

"Mrs. Watkins, what happened?" I ask, finally getting myself together. "What do you think really happened?"

She looks at the pond and places her palms on her thighs, thinking. "My husband was a brilliant man and a master teacher," she says. "His brain was a sponge for knowledge. Chemistry and history. He couldn't get enough of it. Marc read more books than anybody I know. Money wasn't important to him. All he cared about was educating young people. You don't become a teacher with the idea of getting rich from it. For years we lived in a small but nice bungalow in Royal Oak." She pauses. "But something happened to him about six years ago, right around the time Joshua was born. There was a shift in his thinking. Marc suddenly wanted to do more than just teach in Beaconsfield. He wanted to be Beaconsfield. He wanted . . ." She gestures toward the house and garden. "He wanted all of *this*."

"Which is impossible on a teacher's salary."

"Exactly," she says. "Neither of us comes from a wealthy background either. He talked about switching careers. I even volunteered to work outside of the home, but he said that was out of the question. Marc was a firm believer that being a stay-at-home mom is the hardest but most important job on the planet." She smiles at that. "Anyway, a few years went by, but nothing really changed. He felt stuck and was becoming increasingly unhappy. I thought he wanted a divorce, but he insisted his frustrations had nothing to do with our marriage." She shrugs and looks at me. "I don't know what to say other than Marc was angry at not being rich. He wasn't arrogant. He just believed he had the intelligence to make a lot of money."

"And he eventually did," I say. "So what was the problem?"

Mary Watkins looks away and doesn't say anything.

"I'm sorry," I say, feeling like an idiot for getting so personal. "It was the wrong question. I apologize, Mrs. Watkins. I should probably get going."

I'm getting ready to stand when she grabs my shoulder.

"Wait, Alix." I nod and sit. "It's okay," she says. "You don't need to apologize. I've already told your father and other law-enforcement people all of this, so it's not like I'm revealing anything new to you."

She removes her hand from my shoulder. I feel my pulse quicken. Regardless of what she just said, she's about to reveal things she hadn't planned on revealing to a seventeen-year-old stranger.

"About three years ago," she continues, "Marc got mixed up with the wrong people. He kept it hidden from me for about a year, but I knew something was going on. He was coming home from school later than usual, and during the summer he was gone for hours at a time during the day. He always said he was at the gym, but I knew he was lying. I thought he was having an affair, but then one day two years ago he came home happier than I'd seen him in years. He told me he'd invested well and had saved enough money to move us to Beaconsfield." She shakes her head. "Marc always took care of the finances. I didn't know anything about money we did or didn't have." She pauses. "But I knew his so-called saved money was dirty, Alix, and I knew it came as a direct result of whatever he was up to on the side." She removes her sunglasses, rubs her swollen eyelids, and slides the glasses back on. "What I regret more than anything is not confronting him about it that very first day. I never asked about the money, because I was so happy to finally see *him* happy." She starts crying again. "Does that make me a bad person?"

"Not at all," I say, thinking back to the vision of their kitchen argument. "Because you finally did ask about the money, right?"

"Not until it was too late."

"What do you mean?"

She wipes tears from her face. "Alix, do you know what Perennial is?"

A wave of nausea overcomes me. It's as if I can feel my blood draining from my body.

There's no way. There's just no way Mr. Watkins was involved.

"Alix, are you okay?" she says. "You don't look so good."

"I'm fine," I say, forcing myself to keep my emotions in check. "Yes, I know what Perennial is. It's a highly addictive drug."

"It is," she says. "Marc was working with federal law-enforcement agents in an attempt to bust up the Perennial drug ring."

"As a teacher?" I say. "Was he keeping tabs on students who might be Perennial dealers or users?"

"I'm afraid not," she says. "Alix, Perennial was the *source* of Marc's dirty money."

There's a long silence. I place a hand over my mouth, trying to make sense of what she's telling me.

"Mr. Watkins was selling Perennial to students?" I ask, lowering my hand.

"No." Mary places a hand on my shoulder as if to prepare me for something big. Then she looks at me and says, "Alix, my husband created Perennial."

Everything starts spinning. I put my face in my hands to keep from throwing up. Mrs. Watkins wraps her arms around me and tells me to look at her, which I force myself to do. She's removed her sunglasses again, Mary Watkins staring at me with blue eyes that match the color of the clear morning sky above us.

"His chemistry background," I say. She nods. "But *why*?" I ask. "Why would a man who devoted his life to teaching kids create something that has devastated the lives of God knows how many young people?"

"I don't know, Alix. I honestly don't know. That secret died with him. The only thing I know is that Marc was afraid of somebody who had muscled his way in and taken over the Perennial operation from him. Marc was so terrified of this person that he turned himself in to federal authorities and cut a deal." She pauses. "In exchange for immunity from prosecution, Marc gave the Feds the names of all of his dealers, as well as the name of the violent kingpin who threatened to kill him."

"Face," I whisper, staring at the pond. "Mary, did your husband ever mention somebody named Face?"

She thinks about it. "No," she says, shaking her head. "Marc refused to talk about any of it with me. That's why we fought so much toward the end. I suppose he was trying to protect the boys and me."

She squeezes my shoulder gently. "Everything I just told you came to me through the federal agents. When I came home with the boys from my parents' house on Sunday evening, Marc was gone, and somehow I knew he wasn't coming home. He was dead. Murdered. Deep down I knew the man he was afraid of had killed him." She sniffles and bites her lower lip. "The poison Marc created ended up destroying him."

She watches the colorful koi. I do the same, trying to make sense of everything and nearly forgetting about the fact that I still have no idea who Lewis Wilde really is.

"Mrs. Watkins?"

"Mary," she says. "Please, Alix. Call me Mary. Watkins disgusts me at the moment."

"Mary," I say. "I appreciate your honesty and candidness, but I don't know why you just told me all of this. I just learned more from you than my father would ever tell me. I know you know that, so why? Why do you want me to know this?"

She turns to me. "Because you're a student at his school, Alix. You might think I want his reputation saved, but I don't. Marc invented a horrible drug that kills people and, as you said, has devastated countless lives. The son of a bitch didn't even look for a way out until he was afraid for his own life. He would've kept on going too. He wasn't addicted to Perennial as a drug. He was addicted to the power and money that came with Perennial." She lightly smacks the side of her head with an open palm. "And I was too passive to ever challenge him on it. How do you think that makes me feel?"

I don't respond.

"Besides," she says, "you're looking for answers too, Alix. I saw it the moment you introduced yourself, when I realized you were Clint's daughter. There's something special about you, something different. I don't know what it is, but I feel it."

"Maybe," I say, dusting off my thighs and standing. "Maybe I am different, and maybe I am looking for answers." She joins me and stands. We look toward the pond and the red shrine gate beyond. "Mary, will you do me a favor and not mention to anybody that I was here today, especially my dad?"

"Of course. Listen, everything I told you will become public sooner or later. I might even talk to reporters about it as soon as I get the okay from the Feds."

"What about your sons? How will you tell them?"

"I'll tell them the truth when they're ready for it. Lying doesn't do any good. And all of this," she says, indicating the house and the garden. "All of this is gone, seized by the federal government, which will sell it to the highest bidder, I suppose." She shrugs and slides her sunglasses on. "I'm planning on changing our last name and moving somewhere out of state. I never want to see Beaconsfield again."

"I understand. Thank you, Mary. Not just for the information, but for talking to me about my mom. I hope we can stay in touch."

"I'd like that." She gives me a warm hug and says into my ear, "I hope you find whatever it is you're looking for."

"Me too," I say. "Me too."

We exchange smiles as she sits down on the stone bench. I turn and head down the pea gravel path toward the backyard gate. A million thoughts race through my mind. If Face killed Mr. Watkins, then he surely murdered William as well. As for Lewis, I still don't know what to do about him. I love him and hate him at the same time.

"Alix?" Mary says from the bench.

"Yes?" I stop and turn.

Mary looks over her shoulder and says, "Can I tell you the real reason I came to the garden this morning?"

"Sure," I say. "If you want to."

"I came here because this garden is a reminder of what Marc was capable of as opposed to what he actually became."

She turns toward the koi pond.

I continue walking, listening to the falling water behind me and the sound of the pea gravel beneath my feet, but most of all realizing that I'm now on the road to possibly solving two related murders instead of a single isolated one.

CHAPTER 25

What do you do when it seems as if the world is crashing down upon you?

That's what I'm thinking as I spend the next few hours driving in a continuous loop around Beaconsfield, looking for answers I can't find. It feels as if fantasy has become reality and reality has become fantasy. I own a magical knife that has destroyed two demonic beasts, my boyfriend doesn't seem to have a place of residence, and the city's most beloved teacher created a sinister drug that is now in the hands of a demon who potentially plans on using it to possess people worldwide.

And it's up to me to stop it all by the end of tomorrow night, which means going back to Oval City and doing so alone. Impossible. That's what I keep saying to myself. Based upon what I saw in Oval City, there's no way I can saunter in there alone and expect to find the violent and elusive Face. Besides, Dad saw me there last night, and it took one huge lie and an Oscar-worthy performance to convince him that it wasn't me in the truck. Thanks to Mary Watkins, I now

have confirmation that Dad is working closely on the Perennial case
and knows all about Mr. Watkins's secret life, meaning Dad will more
than likely be undercover in Oval City for the next several nights. So,
if I'm going to destroy Face and Oval City, I'll have the added difficulty of dodging my dad while doing so.

Good luck, Alix.

I'm famished and exhausted well before noon, so I hit the Taco
Bell drive-thru and head to a nearby park, where I park the Explorer
in a secluded, wooded spot next to a stream and eat the greatest fast
food ever created. I nervously check the glove compartment twice
to make sure Blade is safe and sound. Watching the stream flow, I
try to temporarily forget about my problem with Lewis and what I
now know about Mr. Watkins, so I think about William instead and
smile at how helpless I felt in his presence during the three dreams,
especially the last one. I know we won't make dream contact again,
but I hope he can see me right now. As much as part of me wants
to summon Vagabond, hand him the silver knife, and tell him that
I quit, I just can't bring myself to abandon William. William is the
reason this all began.

I imagine William Weed sitting next to me in the Explorer right
now, William in his backwards baseball cap, sunglasses, and cargo
shorts. I imagine kissing him and running my hands over his dragon
tattoos. Then I imagine what might happen if we decided to move
things further . . .

. . . And the next thing I know, I'm gasping and opening my
eyes in the driver's seat as Taco Bell wrappers fall to the floor mat
below me. I must have fallen asleep after eating and thinking about
William.

A panicky feeling sets in. What time is it? I dig my phone from
my pocket. It's almost 2:00 p.m. I was out for more than two hours!

I look out the windows in all directions. There's nobody in this
part of the park, just an endless expanse of green and the relax-
ing sounds of birds and the flowing stream. School ends in twenty

minutes. I feel slightly depressed and guilty as I think about the end of my attendance streak. Part of me wonders if the attendance office contacted Dad. I check my phone again. There are no texts, voice mails, or missed calls, so I doubt he has any clue that I ditched. Hopefully it stays that way.

I take a deep breath and start the Explorer. My stomach rumbles. I figure it's the Taco Bell digesting, but then I realize it's a bad case of nerves from knowing that I have about thirty-four hours to destroy Face and a demonic lair that encompasses an entire city block in the most dangerous part of Detroit.

∞

I pull into my driveway twenty minutes later to the sight of Lewis Wilde sitting on my porch. I almost throw the Explorer into reverse and take off, but all that will do is prolong the inevitable confrontation between us.

I park and kill the ignition, but I don't get out. There's something different about Lewis today. Less than twenty feet separates us. He's as gorgeous as ever, his pale skin, wavy black hair, and green eyes irresistible to look at, but as we stare at each other through the Explorer's windshield, I'm surprised with the emotionless look on his face. It's as if he's the world's most beautiful zombie. I'm worried he might be high, but his eyes don't look red or glossy from here.

He's just staring at me, Lewis wearing a pair of perfect-fitting black jeans and a long-sleeved black crew-neck tee that sticks to his chest, shoulders, and arms like a second skin. It's like he knows I'm angry with him, and he's simply waiting for me to get out and start the fight.

"Fine," I say, opening the door and hoping he can read my lips. "If this is how you want to do it, this is how we'll do it." I open the glove compartment and grab Blade. The knife isn't moving, meaning I'm fairly confident Lewis isn't a demon. Still, I sheathe the shimmering weapon in my back pocket just in case things get weird. "So many lies," I whisper, stepping out of the Explorer and slamming the door. "So many lies."

He stands and folds his arms across his chest, Lewis looking me dead in the eyes and not blinking as I walk up the concrete path leading to the porch and stop a few feet away from him. I feel like screaming, but that's the old, fly-off-the-handle Alix. That's the Alix Mom and Dad worked so hard to fix.

Well, Mom and Dad, it finally worked, because I've seen things called Brawlers and Heaters that can get you killed if you overreact to them, and after learning about the real Mr. Watkins this morning, I can't imagine discovering anything else that could possibly come close to sending me over the emotional cliff.

I adjust my glasses and glare at Lewis, waiting for him to say something.

He won't speak, so I roll my eyes and say, "Okay, you want me to start?" There's no response, just that cold, unblinking stare. The only good news is that he doesn't look stoned. "Here we go then," I say. "You're probably wondering why I wasn't in school today. Well, I took a little field trip. First of all, you don't have grandparents on Bloomfield Street. The address you gave me doesn't even exist. Second, you never went to Eastland High. I know because I went there and had a secretary search your name. In fact, there's no history of you ever attending *any* school in Eastland."

I pause and wait for a reaction from him that doesn't come.

"Jesus, Lewis, say something, okay?" He doesn't, and he still hasn't blinked. "How can you just lie to me like that? And how dare you take advantage of me like you did yesterday. I told you how I felt about you. I said it was all new for me, and that I didn't want any games." I jab a finger toward his chest. "I don't know about any of the other girls you've been with, but I'm not somebody you can just use and lie to, you idiot." I throw my hands in the air. "I mean, who are you anyway? And what's your role in this whole William thing?

Because I know you're involved, Lewis." I groan and look skyward. "Please, just say something before I punch you in the face." Silence. I exhale deeply, look him in the eyes, and say, "Last chance. Have you told me the truth about *anything* since I met you?"

He stands there like a statue, arms still folded in front of him. I reach out and plow my hands into his powerful chest. He barely moves, just a slight backwards tilt as he continues to hold my gaze.

"Talk," I say, giving him another shove that accomplishes nothing. "Why are you being like this? Come with me right now and show me where your grandparents live, because I know you have to live in Beaconsfield to go to school here."

I grab his arms and pull, but he won't move. He's like a stubborn dog.

"Screw you, Lewis!" I ram the bottom of my fist down onto his forearm. "I hate you!" I reach up, grab his shoulders, and start shaking him as if he's a stuffed animal. "I hate you! I hate you! I hate you!"

He continues staring at me as I jolt him back and forth. As much as I want to burst into tears from all the pain and hurt his silence is causing me, I manage to hold back.

Exhausted, I finally stop shaking him. Then I drop my head and slowly run my hands down his sleeves before finally letting go once I reach his wrists.

It's the blue I see first, just a hint of it along his left wrist. His arms are still folded. The rest of the colorful mouth appears as I push the cuff of Lewis's sleeve above his wrist and past his forearm. I feel my own mouth drop open at the sight of the dragon's green eyes and purple, red, and orange head.

"What the . . . ?" I swallow hard, my mouth going dry.

I glance at Lewis. He finally blinks. He looks more at peace and far more comfortable now. I pull his left arm toward me with both hands. Lewis doesn't fight it and fully extends his arm. The rest of the brilliant dragon tattoo emerges as I force the sleeve up past his large, toned bicep, stopping only when I reach his shoulder and can't move the fabric any further.

The dragon is identical to those William had on his arms. The ink looks brand new, the tattoo an intricate full-color work of art. There's a moment where I think Lewis must have arrived here directly from the tattoo artist, but an ornate, full-arm design like this must take numerous sessions to complete.

"Your shirts," I say. "I've never seen you in anything but long sleeves." I run my fingers along the length of the dragon. "It's the same as Will . . ." I trail off, remembering that Lewis has no idea I've had contact with William's ghost.

A slight smile crosses Lewis's face. I feel like he's reading my mind.

"What's going on?" I whisper.

He glances at his opposite arm and extends it toward me. The long sleeve still covers his skin like a magician's secret curtain.

Heart thumping, I begin pushing up the sleeve on Lewis's right arm, feeling dizzy as I once again see a colorful open mouth followed by the incredible combinations of green, blue, orange, and purple that comprise the remainder of the arm-length Japanese dragon.

They have identical tattoos, I say to myself. *I don't understand why, but William and Lewis have the exact same tattoos.*

That's the thought that keeps looping through my mind as I gently lower Lewis's bare arms to his sides. I'm feeling dizzier now, but I do notice that Lewis's arms are even more muscular than I imagined. In fact, he's just as muscular as . . .

As if sensing my growing loss of balance, Lewis extends his dragon-covered arms again, this time placing his strong hands around my waist. I can't make sense of what's happening. Things are spinning. I'm angry, curious, excited, and fascinated.

I manage a deep breath and feel a touch of stability returning as he holds me in place.

"Who are you, Lewis?" I say, the words barely audible through my dry mouth. "I need to know, because I don't have much time."

Lewis looks so peaceful, almost childlike as he takes a step back and removes his hands from my waist. He raises his arms and turns his palms so that they're facing up. As he does so, I notice how the matching dragons seem to follow his movements and wrap around his arms.

I'm not sure what he wants me to do. We stare at each other. His palms continue facing skyward. Then he gives me a slight nod, and I realize what's happening.

"You *know*," I say, fighting the dizziness again. "You know what I can do, don't you?" His lips curl into a smile. "You want me to read you?" He continues smiling. I think about Blade, still motionless in my back pocket. That's good.

Gazing into Lewis's wonderful eyes, I say it again, knowing this will be the final time I need to ask.

"Who are you, Lewis Wilde?"

He glances at his tattoos before looking into my eyes.

Then he says, "It's all in the name, Alix."

I take his hands and squeeze.

The flash of white light is so powerful this time that it jerks me forward several inches and forces me to close my eyes. I feel Lewis stabilizing me as the clearest word cloud yet flashes through my head. This is what it says:

LEWIS WILDE = WILLIS WEED

Confusion sets in. I've yet to see a word cloud like this one, so I have to analyze it in my mind's eye for a few moments. And when I finally see the obvious anagram, I feel like everything around me is falling.

Ten letters in each name. The *same* ten letters. And the same ten letters create the same two names.

Silence. Then:

Lewis Wilde *is* Willis Weed.

White light flares, taking the word cloud with it.

I gasp and open my eyes. He's still here. I'm wobbly. I grip his hands tighter.

"William?"

"Hello, Alix. I'm sorry it had to take this long."

"William?" I say it again, unable to believe what I'm seeing and hearing.

"It's me." He finally shows those perfect teeth. "But I really do prefer Willis."

"William?"

"Yes?" he says. "Are you okay, Alix?"

"Oh God," I say, losing all sense of balance. "Catch me, William."

The last thing I see is a pair of brilliant dragons coming closer to my face. Then I pass out in the muscular arms of the living ghost of William "Willis" Weed, my Dream Guy in the flesh.

CHAPTER 26

My world has gone black, but I feel two large, powerful hands—one holding up the back of my head, the other gently massaging the length of my left arm. I'm lying down somewhere. If this is a bed, it has the world's most uncomfortable mattress.

But it's not a bed. It's the porch.

Lewis Wilde. William Weed. One and the same. A living ghost.

At first I feel relief at the realization that I can toss all of those conflicting emotions about Lewis and William out the window. He's real! William is real! I no longer have to feel guilty about simultaneously falling in love with a ghost and an actual person.

But an overwhelming fury soon smothers the relief. William tricked me for three days. And how about all that time I spent feeling guilty about the conflicting feelings? How could I not realize it myself? All of the clues were right under my nose.

I think back to "Lewis's" sudden appearance and disappearance in the middle of the street Tuesday morning. I mean, how weird was that? And what about all of "Lewis's" stories about his friendship with William? Lies. Lies. Lies.

I open my eyes and sit up, instinctively pushing William's hands away and scrambling to my feet. William stands as well, the two of us studying each other on the porch now, a few feet separating us. I reach behind me and feel Blade, secure and motionless in my back pocket.

"It's okay, Alix," he says, making a calming gesture with his hands. "It's me. It's William. I know you're angry. I would be too."

"You have no idea," I say. "What about Lewis? Was there ever a Lewis, or has it been you since Tuesday morning?"

"What do you think?" He shrugs.

I look out toward the pristine lawn and a quiet Maple Grove Street.

"Did he ever exist?" I say. "The whole story about the alternative academy and Lewis getting clean and trying to help you? Was there ever a Lewis?" I rub my forehead. "And everything else, like the whole Aruna thing." I pause. "God, there's so much more, and you made it all up, didn't you? You're one big lie."

"I had to," he says, watching the street as if he's waiting for somebody.

"What are you talking about? You had to? What does that even mean?"

"Alix, I'm almost positive Vagabond doesn't know I crossed over," he says, looking at me. "If he knew, he would've pulled me back by now."

"What?" I squint. "Jesus. You need to leave, William. I have no idea what you're up to, but you don't mess with Vagabond. You know who and what he is. He'll crush you, and I don't want any part of it. I might not like Vagabond, but right now he's my boss." I point toward the sidewalk. "Leave. I mean it. Go away and never come back. I'll solve your murder, but I'll do it on my own. I can't have you around if I expect to pass this test."

William stands there, determined and not showing any sign of leaving.

"Damn you, William. Vagabond promised me my mom, okay? That's what I get out of this. I get to see my mom, and I won't let you or anybody else jeopardize that, so turn around and stay out of my life forever!"

"You don't understand," William says. "Vagabond's rules still apply. I know what this means to you, and I know what it means to me. I took a huge risk in doing this, but I didn't do it to interfere with your test."

I roll my eyes and put my hands on my hips. "Then why did you do it? Why are you here?"

"I didn't cross over to *help* you, Alix. I crossed over because I *love* you." His green eyes seem to stare clear through to my soul. "I'm in love with you, okay? I knew it from the moment we first made contact Monday night. I crossed over Tuesday morning. There's a reason you almost ran me over that day. That's the moment I showed up. If it seemed like I appeared out of nowhere, it's because I did."

I shake my head and look away. All of the hints and connections about his true identity continue running through my mind.

"You were gone when I looked in my rearview mirror," I say. "You said you took some shortcut your grandpa told you about. I knew you were lying, but I didn't expect this." I exhale deeply and stare at him. "You really did just disappear, didn't you?"

He nods.

"And what about school? How did you register at Beaconsfield if you don't even exist?"

"Here's the thing," he says. "I'm *not* registered. I figured I'd get away with it for a day, and I did, but I was surprised when nobody said anything to me yesterday. I guess it's because every adult in the building is so rattled about Mr. Watkins. Two teachers finally asked me for my name today when they realized I wasn't on their rosters. Mr. Dobbins was one of them. Actually, Dobbins told me I wasn't even in the attendance system." William shrugs. "I played dumb and said it must have something to do with me being a new student. It worked, but they'll know something's up tomorrow." He pauses and looks away. "It doesn't matter. Tomorrow's my last day anyway."

"Last day *here*," I say, indicating everything around us. "As you are now, you mean. As William."

"I'm a ghost with a deadline," he says, looking back at me. "The same deadline as you. I'm gone at the end of tomorrow, whether you solve my murder or not."

There's a silence during which I remember something important about my conversation with Vagabond.

"You're right," I say. "Vagabond doesn't know you're here."

"What makes you so sure?"

"Yesterday I told him a guy at school named Lewis Wilde told me what Perennial was. Vagabond had no idea who Lewis was."

"Well, that's good then," William says, nodding. "That's excellent actually."

"I need to know how you did it. Because at this point I don't trust anybody or anything except my own abilities and a certain silver friend in my back pocket." I fold my arms in front of my chest and give him a look. "I hate liars, William, and right now I don't know whether I should punch you or kiss you."

William says, "I'll tell you how I pulled it off, but first let me just say that I honestly thought you would figure out the Lewis Wilde anagram sooner. And yes, I've told a lot of lies, but I had to in order to keep Vagabond off my trail. I never lied to deceive you. I was being honest when I told you time and distance had lessened my feelings for Aruna. I don't love Aruna, Alix. There was a time when I did, but that was long ago."

As angry as I am, I can't help but like that statement. Unfortunately, the joy I feel disappears when Blade suddenly begins vibrating in my back pocket.

"Tell me how you did it." My muscles tense involuntarily. It's as if my body is preparing for a fight before my brain even knows one is coming. "And you better make it quick."

"I cut a deal," he says, unable to hold my gaze.

"With who?"

"You won't like it."

"Who did you make a deal with, William?"

Blade's movements intensify.

"I made a deal with the Army of Fire," he says.

I reach behind me with incredible speed and grasp Blade's handle.

"Alix, no!" William raises his hands to the point where they look like stop signs. "I know what you can do with the knife, so just stop and hear me out, okay?"

"You made a deal with *demons*?" I say, glaring at his dragon tattoos as I release the handle and bring my hand back in front of me. Blade protests and goes wild in my pocket. "You made a deal with *evil*? How could you, William?"

"I'm trying to tell you, but I need you to listen."

"My knife is telling me to do otherwise."

"Think back to Monday night and the first dream," he says. "Vagabond used me as a guinea pig to see if we could make contact. It worked, but doing something like that doesn't come without risks for him. By making me active in the Light world, he also made my presence known to the Fire world. The moment I saw you, I knew I had to find a way to be with you. Fire must have sensed this, because one of their messengers offered me the deal right after the first dream ended."

"What exactly did you agree to?" I say, relieved that Blade is settling down, meaning William must be telling the truth now.

"Fire said I could use a portal to cross over and be with you until Vagabond's deadline. I agreed. I didn't care what they wanted."

"Where's the portal?"

"You know where it is."

"Oval City?" I say. William nods. "What did they want, William? What does Fire get out of this?"

William takes a deep breath. "I agreed that if you fail to solve my murder, Fire can have my soul." He pauses. "Forever."

I stand there in stunned silence, my mouth hanging open in disbelief. I suddenly understand why Blade wanted me to attack William just now and why I saw fire after the light during my reading on "Lewis" when we shared our second kiss in his truck.

Fire has tainted William.

"You're telling me that if I can't pull this off, not only will I not see my mom again but I'll probably die, and your soul will be possessed permanently by the Army of Fire?" I don't wait for an answer. "William, how could you *do* this to me?"

He steps closer. Blade has stopped moving, so I don't protest William's advance. I want to drop to my knees and give up, but I can't show any sign of weakness. I love William Weed, but what do you do when your true love is a lying ghost whom you can't trust?

"I know it sounds selfish," he says. "And maybe it is, but it also shows how much faith I have in you. Vagabond's not the only one who sensed how special you are. Fire offered me the opportunity to physically be with you for four days. I jumped at it, regardless of the personal risks." He pauses. "I know you'll solve my murder and destroy Oval City. I'm not worried about that. If getting the chance to be with you for four days means risking where my soul might end up for eternity, I'll take it. I'm already dead, and trust me when I tell you that most dead people never get an opportunity to do something like this." He gently grabs my left hand. "You don't have to trust me, but I know how we feel about each other. We have a little more than twenty-four hours left together. I think we should make the most of it."

"But what happens if Vagabond finds out?" I say, succumbing to an overwhelming urge and running my right hand along the dragon on his arm. I can't resist. He's too beautiful and my feelings are too strong for him.

"He won't find out," William says. "But even if he does, it's between him and me. I'm here to be *with* you, not to *interfere* with you."

"Meaning what exactly?"

"Like I said, Vagabond's challenge rules still apply." He takes my right hand in his left, clasps our fingers together, and kisses the top of my wrist. "I might be physically present, but I can't help you with anything related to my murder." He smiles. "We can do a lot of other things, though."

He leans in and starts kissing my neck. I close my eyes and feel like I'm melting.

"Wait," I say, somehow managing to pull away and open my eyes. "What about everything you've already done to help me? As Lewis, I mean. You told me about Perennial. You took me to Oval City. What if you've already ruined everything?"

"I haven't told you anything you didn't learn on your own," he says. "Think about it. You basically forced me to take you to Oval City. And yes, I told you what Perennial was, but only after you already had it in your hands. Deep down you knew the purple powder was some type of drug." William smiles. "And even if I did steer you in certain directions or let certain things slip, Vagabond never said anything against a guy named Lewis Wilde helping you out a little."

"What about the *Vagabond's Warrior* blog post?" I say. "And the list of words in the first dream? That's what started all of this."

"Vagabond set all of that up and told me what to do," William says. "Vagabond put you on the scent of Perennial. You took over from there."

I'm silent as I take it all in. I think back to the evil homeless man in Oval City and how he claimed he'd seen "Lewis" the previous night. That was true, I realize. If William crossed over via the Oval City portal, it only makes sense that he's spending time in Oval City.

Again, more lies. Still, I want to trust him. If William crossed over for my love, I have to give him a chance.

"Oh, William, I don't know about this," I say, putting my face in my hands and groaning. "I sure hope you're right."

"Hey, listen to me," he says, taking my hands and lowering them. "Don't you think Vagabond would have already called things off if he thought you had broken any major rules? Alix, you're developing into a badass two-way psychic demon slayer. That's exactly what the Army of Light was hoping for. I'm here until the end of tomorrow. There's nothing you can do to change that. I can't help you in any way, especially now, but you're at the point where you don't need help from me or anybody else. Just do what you have to do and end this thing."

"Thanks for the pep talk," I say. "But the last thing I need is the future of your soul on my already overloaded plate."

"Forget my soul," William says, grinning now. "I'm right here in front of you. Right here. Right now."

"You're awfully happy for a guy who's literally playing with Fire."

William scans the street and yard. There's nobody around.

"Close your eyes until I tell you to open them," he says.

"What?" I give him a look. "Why?"

"Just do it. I want to show you something I think you'll like."

"Fine." I fold my arms in front of my chest and close my eyes. "But don't take forever."

I hear what sounds like something brushing against his jeans. Seconds later, William clears his throat, stifles a laugh, and says, "Okay. Open your eyes."

I open my eyes. "Oh my God," I say, trying but failing to muffle a laugh of my own. "Now I see how you pulled it off."

William Weed has just become the "William" of my dreams. He's wearing his black baseball cap backwards on his head, all of "Lewis's" dark, wavy hair tucked up inside, his dark sunglasses concealing the "Lewis" aqua-green eyes. Although the black cargo shorts are

missing and he isn't quite shirtless, I instantly understand the lengths
to which he went to conceal his identity when he crossed over.

"Told you you'd like it," he says, smiling.

"Was your hair that long when . . . ?"

"When I died?" he says. "Yeah, but I always wore it tucked into
this hat."

"Why?" I say. "It's gorgeous hair."

"Thanks, but this is Beaconsfield," he says. "It's not exactly a
friendly city to long-haired guys. I've lost count of how many jocks
have given me dirty looks the past three days."

"And your eyes," I say. "They're the most beautiful color I've ever
seen. Why did you wear sunglasses all the time?"

"Think about it."

It takes a few moments, but I finally figure it out.

"The drug," I say. "Perennial makes your eyes all glossy and
bloodshot."

"Exactly," William says, inspecting his arms now. "But the dragons worried me most. Even though I never went to Beaconsfield
High when I was alive, and it's been two years since *anybody* has seen
me, I knew I had to hide the tattoos. It was too risky to show them."

"And your parents?" I say. "Where are they?"

"I lied about Eastland but not about China," he says. "My parents have been working in Shanghai since shortly after I died. They
needed to get far away from Beaconsfield."

"And the truck we took to Oval City?" I raise my eyebrows and
rub the back of my sore neck. "The truck that crashed and gave me
whiplash. If it wasn't your grandfather's, then where did you get it?"

"Right," William says, rubbing his palms together and shrugging. "I sort of borrowed it from the parking lot of a liquor store."

"You stole the truck?"

"Borrowed. I returned it after I dropped you off. Damaged, yes,
but insurance will take care of that." William clears his throat. "Look,
I've done it before, okay? It's amazing how many drivers still keep

their vehicles running when they need to make a quick stop. I look at it as teaching them a lesson." He pauses. "That's the first time I ever crashed one, by the way."

Maybe it's the stress of the past few days and the enormity of what lies ahead of me over the next thirty-plus hours, but for some reason I find the truck story trivial and funny, so I start laughing. It begins as a giggle, but I soon lose control and break into hysterical laughter. William joins in too, and before I know it I'm back in his arms, the two of us laughing and managing to put aside the harsh realities facing us. I feel wonderful, normal, and innocent for the first time in days, and I decide to preserve the mood for as long as possible.

"Take this off," I say, grabbing the hat and throwing it onto the porch. "I want to see that incredible hair for as long as possible." I run a palm across the side of his pale face and through his wavy hair. "Let's ditch these while we're at it." I reach for his sunglasses and toss them onto the baseball cap. "That's better," I say, staring into his lustrous eyes. "It should be illegal to cover eyes like yours."

"Wow," William says, planting a soft kiss on my lips. "Who's being aggressive now?"

He pulls me against him and kisses me deeply, William placing his hands on either side of my face as our mouths open. A wonderful heat floods my body. I wrap my hands around his powerful shoulders, enjoying his minty breath and soapy smell.

"I just remembered something funny," I say, pulling back.

"Funny enough to stop kissing me?" He smiles.

"Just for a second," I say. "The mint and soapy smells."

"What are you talking about?"

"When you were kissing me in the last dream, there was a moment where I figured you and Lewis must use the same soap and toothpaste." I start laughing again. "Now I know they—or, I mean, you—do." I close my eyes and shake my head. "It's still hard to believe it's you."

His lips are on mine before I can open my eyes, William's soft, moist tongue exploring my own. We press closer. I feel his strong thighs against me, his fingertips traveling lightly down my spine and settling low on my waist.

"Mmm," I whisper. "So what else can living ghosts do?"

"Maybe we should go inside and find out."

"It's tempting, but I can't risk my dad coming home."

"There might be a way around that." He kisses my neck. "Can I show you something else I think you'll like?"

"Anything," I say. "As long as you promise to keep kissing me when you're done."

"Deal." He steps back and takes my hands. "Close your eyes again."

I smile and close my eyes, but as soon as I do so, I realize my hands are free. Then I hear William say, "Now open them. Fast."

I open my eyes and look around. William is gone. Vanished. The porch is empty, just his baseball cap and sunglasses lying on the concrete.

"William, where are you?" I say, holding a hand over my mouth to muffle my laughter. "How did you do that?"

"Look across the street, Alix."

It's definitely William's voice, and he sounds like he's right next to me, but there's still no William in sight. Scratching my head, I look toward the other side of Maple Grove and spot him on the lawn across the street, William standing there and waving at me with an irresistible grin on his perfect face.

"William!" I whisper. "Can you hear me?"

"Loud and clear."

The proximity of his voice makes me flinch.

"Get back here before the neighbors see you."

"Okay," he says. "Are you looking at me right now?"

"Yes. Of course."

"Cool. Check this out."

He's gone again. Poof, William disappearing right in front of my eyes, leaving me staring at the finely manicured lawn.

"Hey, stop it," I whisper, my head on a swivel as I search for him. "Where are you now?"

His voice: "You know that old belief about ghosts being invisible and able to travel through walls and all that?"

"Yes," I whisper. "Stop it. Where are you?"

"Well," he says, laughing. "It's true!"

"William!" I spin around, looking but knowing I won't see him until he decides to become visible. "If anybody saw what you just did, you'll have a lot of explaining to do. Stop showing off and get back here."

Three loud knocks from the closed front door startle me. I step back off the porch and stare at the door.

"William, are you inside my—?"

"House?" he says. "I might be."

He delivers three more quick knocks, which are followed by the sound of the deadbolt coming unlocked and then his adorable laughter flooding my ears. I shake my head and groan, but I'm having the time of my life, and William knows it. I open the door and enter an empty foyer and living room.

"Okay, William," I say, hands on my hips as I look around. "I'm inside. Where are you?"

His voice is in my ear, but he's nowhere in sight.

"Take a guess."

I glance toward the kitchen, but then I hear a footstep above me. I look up and smile.

"Are you in my bedroom?"

"No, Alix. I'm in *my* bedroom." He laughs.

"Good one," I say, my heart bouncing as I walk toward the staircase. "But technically it's *my* bedroom now."

"True," he says. "How about a compromise?"

I ascend a few steps. "I'm listening."

"Why don't we call it *our* bedroom," he says. "At least until the end of tomorrow."

"Hmm." I smile. "I think I like the sound of that."

I reach the top of the stairs and walk down the hallway.

"It does have a nice ring to it, doesn't it?" he says. "*Our* bedroom. Alix and William's bedroom."

I open the bedroom door. William is in my bed, lying on his side and facing me, with a gentle smile on his face. He has no shirt or shoes on, just his pants. He's the most beautiful thing I've ever seen.

"Hi," I say, grinning as I walk toward him. A nervous excitement rockets through me. "It's nice to see you again."

"Likewise." He moves over to make room for me. "For the record, this bed is ten times more comfortable than mine ever was."

I sit beside him and run my palms over his dragons. My heart feels like it might explode.

"Now it's *twenty* times more comfortable," he says.

"William?"

"Yes?"

I bring my legs up onto the mattress and lie beside him.

"Do me a favor and don't disappear for at least the next hour, okay?"

"That sounds promising." He kisses me softly. "Alix?"

"What?"

"You might want to put the knife on the floor."

"Shh," I say. "Stop talking."

I close my eyes and let William take the lead.

CHAPTER 27

William stays for three hours. We do many things. Not *everything*, but let's just say that I learn a lot and can't imagine being that close with anybody else. I manage to set all of my troubles aside for the first two hours and focus my attention on him, amazed with his beauty, gentleness, and uncanny ability to do everything just right. But reality keeps creeping in during the third and final hour, and I struggle with the harsh fact that the ghost I love will vanish forever tomorrow night.

"I have to leave now," he finally says.

We're lying on our backs in bed. *Our* bed. A slight sheen of sweat covers our bodies. I prop myself onto my side and let my fingers explore his chest and stomach.

"Why now?" I say. "My dad will probably work late again, and you know how to make a fast getaway even if he does walk in."

Staring at the ceiling, William says, "We both have deadlines. There are things I have to do. Important things I can't tell you about."

"Because they'll break Vagabond's rules?"

He doesn't say anything, so I interpret his silence as a yes.

"Let me ask you a question," I say. "You crossed over through a Fire portal in Oval City. Do you have to go back through it *before* I figure out how to destroy it?"

"No," William says, leaning on his elbow and looking at me. "My energy simply disappears. I'll vanish tomorrow at midnight." He pauses. "Hopefully I'll know who murdered me, and my soul will be with Light forever." I watch his Adam's apple rise and fall as he swallows. "I'd rather not think about the other possible outcome."

"Ugh," I say, knocking the back of my head against my pillow. "Why'd you have to bring that up? Seriously, what if I fail? Let's talk about that. How am I supposed to keep on living if I fail this test, knowing you'll basically end up in hell for eternity, Face will win and get away with double murder, and Perennial will continue to ruin lives and gain souls for the Army of Fire?"

"Double murder?" he says. "And what do you mean by Perennial gaining souls for Fire?"

"You don't know?"

He shakes his head, William giving me a serious look now, so I tell him about my visit with Mary Watkins and my belief that Face murdered Mr. Watkins to avoid getting busted by the Feds. I also tell him about Vagabond's theory that Face's ultimate goal with Perennial is to possess as many human souls as possible.

"Unbelievable," William says, rubbing his temples as if he has a headache. "This is way bigger than I imagined." He crawls over me, gets out of bed, and slides his shirt on. "Try not to think about where I'll end up," he says. "I'm the one who made the deal, not you."

"Easy for you to say." I stand and grab his shoulders. "I'm in love with you, William. I always think about you and always will."

He pulls me close and kisses the top of my head, William saying, "I love you too, Alix. Please don't doubt yourself. You have incredible gifts. Use them." He kisses my forehead. "I have to go."

"I know," I say, lost in his eyes. "When will I see you next?"

"Are you going to Oval City tonight?"

"No. Tomorrow's when it will happen. Friday. It's just something I feel. Why do you ask?"

"Because you're not going back there without me."

"But you're not allowed to help me with—"

"I know the rules," he says. "It's okay. I can be with you as long as I don't help you." He smiles. "Besides, I really want to borrow another truck. Or maybe a sports car this time."

I roll my eyes. "I'll see you tomorrow then?"

"I wouldn't miss it for the world."

"I'm scared, William. *Really* scared."

"I know." He looks over my shoulder, William thinking hard about something. "Try this. When you're afraid, imagine your mom and how incredible it's going to feel to see and talk with her again."

I stare at him and smile. "Thank you," I say. "That helps. You're pretty incredible yourself."

We share a long kiss that makes me want to get back in bed with him.

Seconds later I feel neither his lips nor the light pressure of his powerful body against my chest and legs. I open my eyes. The bedroom is empty. The only traces of William are the slight smells of soap and mint.

∞

Whoever or whatever created Blade used an ancient form of writing called cuneiform on the shimmering handle. It takes less than two minutes for me to find an image match online via the search phrase "ancient writing." Scrolling the image results, I see dozens of ancient Egyptian hieroglyphs before coming across several clay tablets full of the familiar golf tee–like symbols.

I learn that cuneiform is one of the world's earliest writing systems, dating back about five thousand years to Sumer, the first

Mesopotamian city-state, in present-day Iraq. Cuneiform means "wedge-shaped," which is a perfect description of the triangular symbols and their accompanying straight lines. Sumerian scribes wrote on wet clay tablets using a reed stylus, then placed the tablets in the desert sun to dry. The hot, dry climate acted as a great preserver, which is why so many cuneiform tablets have survived. Of course, this knife is made of silver and steel, so there's no way Blade is anywhere near five thousand years old, but I need to know what the cuneiform means, so I search "Sumerian cuneiform alphabet" and quickly find a translation guide.

There are dozens of symbols on Blade. The alphabet-translation image on the screen isn't exactly perfect, so it takes time and a lot of squinting to match the lines and triangles with their correct letters. I jot the letters down but get nothing but nonsensical garbage on my first two translation attempts:

AMJOTNEIRR
AMIVXEERIR

Frustrated, I take a break and rub my eyes.

"Come on," I say to Blade, which is lying on the desk in front of me. "If you refuse to show up in pictures, at least let me figure out what it says on your handle."

I stare at the two meaningless strands of letters and begin shifting my gaze between them and Blade. I decide to focus on the letters I'm most confident I translated correctly. There's no doubt about the first letter, *A*. I definitely nailed that one. The next several are difficult, though, but I feel good about the last letter, *R*.

It's at that point that my mouth feels like it hits the floor.

"No way," I say. "There's no way."

Heart racing, I look at the second letter. I thought it was *M* on both translations, but now I see that I overlooked one of the horizontal lines. It's not *M*. It's *L*.

It doesn't take long from there. It's like being on a real-life version of *Wheel of Fortune.*

"Pat, I'd like to solve the puzzle," I say, smiling at the thought of Mom's all-time favorite TV show.

Letter three is definitely the *I* and not the *J* I'd guessed in round one.

ALI _ _ _ _ _ R

The *O* and *V* I wrote as the fourth letter are similar to each other in cuneiform, but now I notice that the fourth letter on Blade's handle is actually a cuneiform *X*.

ALIX

I don't bother looking back at my remaining original written guesses. Using only Blade's handle and the translation guide, I confirm that the final six symbols match perfectly with "Keener."

ALIX KEENER

The knife was made for me.

"Unbelievable," I say, grabbing it and holding it in front of me. "No wonder you're a perfect fit for my hand. Now I see why Vagabond wanted *me* to decipher the symbols." Then I have a troubling thought: "But if you were made for me, how did Face ever come into possession of you?"

I don't have time to think about an answer to that question, because the sound of breaking glass from somewhere on the first floor instantly puts my senses on high alert. I stand and listen, hearing nothing further. Still, I'm not crazy. Something broke below me, and I know I'm in for a fight when Blade begins spinning clockwise on my desk and stops when the handle faces me.

"Here we go again, my friend," I say, grinding my teeth and preparing for battle. "Here we go again."

I extend my arm toward Blade. The knife flies three feet under its own power, the handle landing in my hand as softly as a butterfly. I smile, unworried by the fact I'm starting to enjoy demon slaying. Then I saunter out of my bedroom and down the hallway toward the stairs.

CHAPTER 28

I'm moving ninja-like through the living room, listening to little noises coming from the vicinity of Dad's office at the western end of the house. Blade's movements in my hand confirm that I'm heading in the correct direction, so I continue silently past the kitchen and down the long hallway that ends at the closed office door.

Dad has a large safe in the office. He keeps the door to the room unlocked, because the emergency gun is located in the top corner of the office closet. Knowing an intruder is in the "gun room," the old Alix would've gotten out of the house as fast as possible and called 911, but the customized silver knife in my hand is all the protection I need. It's silent again, but there's something behind the door, something made of Fire and up to no good.

I don't see any light showing in the narrow gap between the floor and the bottom of the door, so I stand there for a few moments, thinking about the demonic cat-beast I destroyed in the living room yesterday. Vagabond called it a Brawler. I scored my first Fire off it when I stabbed its grotesque tongue and pinned it to the floor. I smile at the memory. Then there was that nasty flying Heater, which despite its compact size was scarier and more difficult to deal with than the Brawler. I destroyed the Heater by sending Blade through one of its freaky red eyes. Vagabond also mentioned beasts known as Crawlers, and something tells me one of those awaits me in Dad's office.

I place my palm on the door. The wood is eerily warm. White light blasts inside my head.

The word cloud:

Crawler.

I open the door and flick on the light, Blade raised in front of my chest and locked into my hand like a permanent seal. *Quick. There's not much time to think. Just observe and react.* My mouth tastes like pennies. Adrenaline.

I scan the room. Nothing. The desk and safe on the far side of the room appear untouched. The closet is closed. Good. The paper blinds are drawn.

Wait.

One of the blinds is moving—the one nearest the desk and safe. There's a broken window behind the blind, and the breeze is gently blowing the thin paper. That's how the Crawler got in.

Then there's a noise from behind the desk.

"Get up," I say, staying close to the open door. "Show yourself."

A deep, guttural laugh comes from somewhere near the desk. It's an awful sound—evil, wild, and otherworldly. I feel the hair on my arms and the back of my neck stand on end.

"Who are you?" I say, standing my ground. "What do you want in here?"

There's a sickening crunching sound as a large figure with that same creepy, slimy black skin the Brawler had rises and stands behind the desk. It was dark when I fought the Brawler, but tonight the brightly lit office gives me a clear view of my latest enemy. This one is taller than the first—at least seven feet tall—with a wide, muscular body, demonic black eyes, and a large mouth dripping with yellow demon ooze. I know it's about to shape-shift into a Crawler, so I decide to see if I can get any information out of it.

"Face sent you," I say, stepping closer and slowly waving the knife back and forth in front of me. "Where can I find him? He's a coward for sending scouts and not fighting his own battles."

The creature makes a pained face and returns to that awful laughing that seems to dig into my brain. As it convulses with laughter, I hear what sound like bones snapping inside of its body.

"You're so wrong, Alix," it says, the voice low and gravelly. "Face is everywhere." It laughs again. "You can make all of this go away if you just give me the knife."

I glance at Blade and then back at the creature. "I'm afraid I can't do that. This knife was made for me." I flash a smile of my own. "If you want the knife, you'll have to come and take it, but that didn't work out so well for Mr. Brawler and Mr. Heater." The beast glances at the safe and then at the flapping blind in front of the broken window. "Wait a second," I say. "If all you want is the knife, what are you doing behind that desk?" I adjust my glasses. "You want something else, don't you?"

"I gave you a chance, Alix," it says in its hellish voice. "Now it's time to dance."

The creature falls forward hard onto Dad's desk, its awful, eel-like face and black eyes looking at me as its body contorts and emits a series of cracking and popping sounds. It's transforming into something larger and changing colors during the process, the black skin turning to a pale, sickly yellow, and the black eyes changing to a hypnotic, swirling, lavalike red. The eyes draw me in like magnets. I remember the Heater's red eyes doing the same. I force myself to look away, knowing the pulsating eyes are part of its arsenal and have a power all their own.

I back off a few feet, fascinated with what's happening and actually looking forward to what the fully transformed Crawler will look like. Blade resists my retreat and tries pulling me forward. The knife wants me to take the offensive and destroy the beast before its metamorphosis is complete, but that strikes me as unfair.

A loud crunch jerks the creature sideways over the desk and onto the floor, where it lands on all fours, the Crawler literally in a crawling position now. As with the Brawler, the body arches like a cat's, the swirling red eyes now the size of small plates as they pulsate and try to draw me in.

There's an awful tearing sound as the beast's back splits open from the base of its neck to its waist. There's no blood, but a series of thick, yellowish tubelike formations slide out from both sides of the open body cavity. The moist tubes drip with yellow ooze and make sloshing sounds as the ends of them reach the carpeted floor.

"You were right, Blade," I say, wide-eyed and suddenly terrified at the creature's growing size. "We should've attacked when it was vulnerable."

I count four yellow tubes on either side of the body, each about six feet long and as thick as small tree stumps. The ends of them move and twitch slightly, as if adjusting to the feel of the carpet. The red eyes continue to swirl and sizzle, but the "human" body is nothing more than a crumpled mass below the strong, heavy tubes. A louder crunching and sucking sound as something else begins rising from the split back. An awful stench suddenly fills the room, gagging me. The eight tubes stiffen, morphing into solid forms as a new object emerges.

It's some sort of body segment, I realize—a large, wet, circular object three feet across. It looks like an enormous spherical sack, and it has the same yellow color as the tubes, which aren't tubes anymore. They're . . .

Legs. I swallow hard, frozen with dread, speechless as the Crawler comes together in front of my eyes. The legs connect to the large yellow sack. Eight legs. One body segment. I would swear it was some sort of gigantic evil spider, but the human head isn't attached.

The Crawler hisses, and the mouth of the human head suddenly opens, revealing a full set of yellow fang-like teeth that remind me of large versions of the Heater's teeth. That's when I realize the human head *is* the second body segment. The head *does* somehow attach to the yellow sack. It's one creature now, a giant spider from hell, breathing deeply as it prepares to attack.

The Crawler's eight legs creak as they rise and straighten, taking the sack and head with them. I have to crane my aching neck to look up at it. The Crawler continues to hiss, putrid yellow funk dripping from the corners if its large mouth. The human face is unrecognizable now, the same color as the rest of the beast.

The creature's red eyes swirl at dazzling speeds. It's ready.

"It's way too big," I say. "There's no way I can destroy it."

A loud splash as a waterfall of yellow fluid falls from the bottom of the Crawler and onto the remains of the now-headless human form. At first I think the creature is relieving itself, but then I see things moving around on the floor.

"No," I whisper.

They're spiders, three smaller, soccer ball–sized versions of the Crawler, their spinning red eyes the size of baseballs.

Mini-Crawlers.

And they're heading straight for my feet. Fast.

Instinct tells me to drop to my knees and attack the Minis low, but Blade wants me to move forward toward the full-size adult. It's almost as if the three Minis are designed to distract me.

I see it coming, but once again I'm too late.

An image of a large, wet, yellow web passes through my mind. Ignoring the Minis, I glance at the awful, bloated demonic spider that now fills half of my father's office and watch in horror as it spits a yellow web the size of a blanket out of its mouth with lightning speed. I try to duck and roll, but the web lands on me as I fall hard to the floor, pinning my arms to my sides and wrapping around me like a roll of carpet. The smell is grotesque and reminds me of decaying flesh. I'm helpless as numerous fist-thick strands tighten around my body and coat me with yellow demon snot, one of the strands wrapping around my face and blocking my mouth. I try screaming but nothing comes out. Blade vibrates in my right hand, but I'm unable to move my arms.

The three Minis hiss with evil delight as they crawl onto my body, their hot legs moving across my jeans and over my shirt. I don't feel any pain, just sheer terror as they crawl down my right arm and group together around my right hand.

Blade. They want Blade.

As if reading my mind, the adult Crawler's enormous eyes flare to a fiery red and pulsate with more intensity. The excited beast senses victory.

I'm lying flat on the floor, face-up and unable to see the three Minis, but I feel them now. They're making disgusting munching sounds and emitting soft but high-pitched screeches. They're eating something. I still don't feel anything, so I figure they're devouring the web to get to my hand.

A hot, searing pain hits moments later. It feels like a hundred bees stinging my hand. They're biting me. The little yellow bastards are biting my hand and fingers. Tears stream down my face, my screams nothing more than muffled grunts due to the hideous strand of web covering my mouth.

They won't stop biting. I feel my flesh ripping as razor-sharp fangs dig into my skin, the hot pain rippling up my arm and into my chest. I'll do anything to make this agony stop, but as much as I try opening my hand to voluntarily relinquish my weapon to Fire, Blade resists and seems determined to stay with me until the Mini-Crawlers gnaw my hand off.

I'm on the verge of passing out. The adult Crawler is advancing now, its body making crunching sounds with every movement, eyes throbbing as it converges on its human prey. I'm dizzy, but I notice the Crawler is too large for the room and has difficulty moving its long, slimy legs. If only I could escape this disgusting death web from hell, I could exploit that weakness.

I hear Vagabond's and London's voices in my head telling me not to trust anything or anybody except my abilities. Then I hear William's voice, William suggesting that when I'm afraid I should think about how it's going to feel to see and talk with Mom again. I think about what Brooke Sparks told me at Eastland High today—to remember that demons fear love.

I close my eyes from the pain. As consciousness escapes me and I fade toward sleep, I think about Mom, Dad, and William, and how much I love them. Then I imagine myself as the most powerful two-way psychic demon slayer in history.

Focus on love. Focus on your abilities. If this is your moment of death, then so be it.

A powerful upward and downward thrust from Blade forces my eyes open. Although the three Minis continue working on my hand and the adult Crawler now looms over me, I feel less pain and more give in my fingers and wrist.

Blade continues with fast upward-downward motions, the Minis lessening their feast on my hand with each stroke of the knife. Blade is fighting back, I realize, cutting through the web under its own power, forcing the Minis to protect themselves.

I summon every ounce of energy I have and yank my right arm upward as fast and hard as possible, hearing welcome ripping sounds as I break through several strands of weakened web. I also feel something hot and wet spray my face. More demon snot. Great.

The entire web is frail now, so I sit up and easily push my left hand through the strands, grabbing and tossing the piece of web covering my mouth off to the side. My right hand is a bloody, mangled mess. I emit the loudest scream of my life, furious for allowing myself to fall for such a trap.

The Minis are crawling away, retreating like the true cowards they are. I can't fall for the same trap and let them distract me again. This time it's *me* who catches the *adult* off guard.

An image of a yellow Crawler leg shoots through my head. At the same time, I glimpse the adult's actual right front leg coming toward me.

I roll to the left and raise the knife as I move, jabbing the weapon toward the thick, yellow leg that is now on a collision course with my neck. It's like hitting a fastball with the sweet spot on the bat. Blade severs the Crawler's leg at its midpoint with one clean slice. The lifeless half of the limb falls to the carpet, twitching for a few moments. The Crawler shrieks in agony as its gaping leg wound spews demon ooze like a volcano spewing lava. I cover my face and roll onto my stomach to shield my eyes from the spray.

"Nice try!" I yell, scrambling to my feet and keeping my distance from the weakened adult. Its red eyes fade to a dull brown and stop pulsating. The Crawler is badly injured. Still, the beast has seven legs and one awful mouth remaining, so I tell myself to keep an eye on it at all times.

I back up and lean against the far wall. The wounded adult is slumped in the middle of the room, screening my view of the desk behind it.

High-pitched screeching from somewhere close. The three Minis are up to something.

The sounds. They're coming from above.

I look at the ceiling. The awful sight of two blazing red Mini eyes triggers a fresh surge of adrenaline. My mouth feels like it might turn to copper.

A Mini drops from the ceiling with a sudden burst of speed, but I manage to lean out of its path. I sense it wanted my face. As the creature attempts to crawl away, I drop to my knees, raising Blade over my shoulder, and drive the knife hard into the Mini's right eye, which explodes into a shower of yellow that splashes my face and neck. The Mini's eye socket is now black and empty. I shield my eyes from the increased heat just before the Mini explodes into a brilliant orange-and-yellow fireball and vanishes.

I just scored my third Fire.

It's the red eyes. Just like the Heater. I have to attack the red eyes. The eyes are the power source of any red-eyed beast. The Brawler didn't have red eyes, so impaling its tongue was enough to destroy it.

The adult is still motionless and fading fast, so I wipe the yellow demon funk from my face, glance at my wounded hand, and scan the room for either of the two remaining Minis. They're crawling along the wall to my right, the small beasts headed for the open window, two yellow bodies and four red eyes moving quickly.

I see it in my head first, an image of Blade flying through the air. Knowing instantly what it means, I launch the knife toward the two Minis. Blade spins through the air, a brilliant silver blur on a line-drive course with the two creatures.

The knife plunges through the left eye of the Mini closest to the window. The creature fireballs instantly, sending a burst of orange and red light in front of its stunned partner, who turns around to avoid the heat and starts crawling back in my direction.

Unfortunately, Blade embedded itself deep into the wall near the window. *Damn.* But then another image of Blade rocketing through the air fills my head.

"Back!" I yell, the word coming out of me involuntarily as I extend my right hand toward the knife.

Blade shoots out of the wall in reverse and darts across the room, the knife-handle landing securely in my bloody palm like a boomerang returning to the hand of its thrower. The remaining Mini stops in its tracks.

"You didn't expect *that*, did you?" I smile. "Say good-bye, loser."

I launch Blade toward it with an effortless flick of my wrist. The knife buries itself in the creature's right eye so quickly that the beast doesn't have time to move. The Mini screeches as its eye bursts, its body exploding against the wall. Blade falls to the floor. I reach my right hand toward the knife, no words necessary this time. Blade knows the command and launches itself from the carpet and through the air before returning safely into my hand.

That makes five Fires for Alix Keener.

Silence now. I swallow hard and stare at the wounded adult Crawler, my chest rising and falling rapidly.

"That leaves you and me, big boy," I say, fighting through the throbbing pain in my mauled hand.

The Crawler has no energy. It's just sitting there motionless, no life in its deadened brown eyes. I almost feel bad for it, but no sooner do I think that than its eyes flare red again, making me think it's mustering every last bit of strength for one final assault.

"Bring it!" I say, furrowing my brow as I wave the knife slowly back and forth in front of my chest. "Come on, Crawler! What else do you have?"

The beast hisses and extends a front leg across the floor with surprising speed. The bottom third of the leg manages to wrap around my ankle and pull me off balance.

"Not bad," I say, falling to the floor. "But it's too little too late."

I easily break my fall with my hand and drop softly to my left knee. The Crawler tries to pull my foot toward its mouth, but the creature simply doesn't have enough strength to do so. It feels more like a toddler is playing with my leg than a demonic beast is trying to kill me.

"So long, you bloated piece of demon snot."

I raise Blade as high as possible and bring the knife down, cutting through the Crawler's leg with ease and sending yet another shower of demon ooze through the air and onto my glasses and face.

"Ugh," I say, wiping my lenses and forehead. "I hate that part!"

The Crawler now has two stumps for front legs, and its brown eyes are slowly fading to black. I don't feel the pre-Fire heat yet, and Blade continues pulling me forward, so I know what I must do.

Throwing from the hip, I sling Blade into the air with another simple wrist flick and watch the knife embed itself into the left eye of the nearly dead Crawler. Tremendous heat radiates toward me as a fountain of red and yellow liquid rockets skyward from the beast's blackened eye socket.

"Blade!" I extend my right hand toward my weapon, knowing the Fire from something the size of a Crawler will be one of epic proportions.

The sound of the explosion is deafening. The brightness of the orange and blue fireball fills the office and blinds me just as I feel Blade land safely in my palm. The force of the blast sends me airborne and backwards. My body slams into the wall, knocking the wind out of me. Then I slide down the wall and land on my butt on the carpet.

I open my eyes to a sight that no longer surprises me. The room is quiet, clean, and devoid of any evidence hinting at the violent battle that just occurred. The paper blind covering the previously broken window no longer moves. I don't have to look behind the blind to know that the glass is no longer broken. My right hand is healthy and strong. No signs of the blood and mauled flesh that existed only seconds ago. Blade rests motionless in my palm, as spotless and pristine as ever. I touch my face and feel no trace of demon ooze.

Standing, I sheathe the knife in my back pocket and stare across the room at my father's desk and safe, thinking back to the moment I realized the creature wanted something from this office besides Blade and my soul. Walking toward the desk, I whisper to myself, "What would Face and the Army of Fire want that Dad has?"

I reach the desk and lay my palms atop the dark wood. Since Dad is closely involved in both the Perennial investigation and Mr. Watkins's murder, maybe he has important information locked in the safe. My curiosity is running wild, and I seriously consider searching the desk and opening the safe, but the thought of what Dad would do to me if he found out scares me more than the image of one hundred angry Heaters flying toward my throat.

My phone vibrates in my front pocket, bringing a well-earned smile to my face at the thought of William either calling or texting me. But it isn't William. The text is from an unknown number and reads: *Come outside, Alix. We need to talk.*

I walk to a window facing the front yard and peer around the edge of the blind. A dark four-door sedan sits in the driveway, headlights on and splashing yellow light against the garage. It's not the Mercedes that picked up Aruna behind Zeppelin Coffee, but I don't care for the vibe I'm getting from this car.

I thumb back a reply: *Who r u?*

Seconds later: *Friends of Vagabond. You're safe.*

I infer from the correct spelling, grammar, and punctuation that this person is more than likely an adult, so I exit the office quickly and cut through the living room, relieved that Blade hasn't started acting up in my back pocket again.

After a few deep breaths in the foyer, I decide to step out onto the porch. I stare at the car, unable to see through the windows due to the obnoxious headlight glare. As if sensing my reluctance to come closer, the driver kills the headlights, but leaves the engine running. The passenger window powers down, revealing a man who won't look at me but does offer a nod and a friendly wave. I can't see the driver, so I leave the porch and walk toward the car, putting total faith in Blade's lack of movement as an indicator that I'm safe.

The driver turns out to be a stunning woman with long, dark hair and matching dark eyes. The man is handsome in a clean-cut, military kind of way, his brown hair closely cropped, brown eyes staring straight ahead at the garage as if he doesn't want me to see the other side of his face. They're in their late twenties or early thirties at most, the two of them wearing crisp dark suits that reinforce my hunch that they're affiliated in some way with either the US government or military. Maybe both.

"How did you get my number?" I say, crouching a few feet away from the open passenger window to see both of them.

The man still won't look at me, but the woman does, raising her eyebrows and saying, "Really, Alix? With everything you've seen and know, do you really find it surprising that we have your phone number?"

"And address," the man says, smiling but not offering eye contact.

"Fine," I say, shaking my head. "I get it. Who are you, and what do you want?"

"We're from the Group," the woman says, sporting a slight smile.

"Vagabond's Group," I say.

"Correct," she says.

"How do I know you're telling the truth?"

"Has your knife moved at all since I texted?" She smiles and exchanges a glance with her partner.

"Okay," I say, nodding. "What powers do you have?"

"I'm afraid it's not like that," she says. "We don't have the abilities that you, London, Roman, and the others possess." She pauses and looks at her partner again, who nods. It's as if she needs permission from him to reveal certain things. "We're simply two normal people, Alix," she continues. "We can't see Fire or Light, but we know about them, and we know how vital people like you are when it comes to preserving order and protecting all that's good in the world."

"Great," I say, and roll my eyes. "Why are you here? I haven't even passed the test yet."

She looks at him again. He nods.

"Vagabond suggested we stop by and say hello," she says. "He thinks very highly of you, which means we think highly of you as well. We rarely see Vagabond, but we work closely with him. We watch over the Group on this side." She shrugs. "Think of us as a big brother and big sister."

For some reason that makes me laugh.

"I don't even know your names, and you expect me to think of you as family?"

She doesn't respond.

"Why won't he look at me?" I nod toward her partner.

"Don't worry about him," she says. "He's shy."

"Right," I say. "Shy."

"She's right, Alix," he says. "I'm a teddy bear once you get to know me."

"Somehow I doubt that."

"Listen," the woman says, "we're here to show our faces and wish you good luck in Oval City tomorrow. If things go your way—"

"Which they will," he interrupts.

"Right," the woman says, giving him a look. "Which they will." She clears her throat. "Anyway, Alix, you're curious about the Group. Don't deny that. Nobody can force you to join, but trust me when I say that the Group needs you. We face more threats at the current moment than at any other time since I've been involved with the Group."

"This is true," the man says. "It's a terrifying time to be a good human."

"Fire is closing in more and more with each passing day," she says. "Think about all the evil things happening in the world right now. You know how it works. We know Vagabond told you. Demons possess. Possession triggers evil. What Vagabond didn't say is that Fire is winning. Perennial is merely one hurdle of many, but you're the Light that can extinguish Perennial and its Fire. There aren't many of you out there, which is why we recruit the hell out of you when we find you."

"Did he tell you about my mom?" I ask. "About getting to speak with her if I pass the test?"

"He should never have done that," the man says. "Stupid move on his part. By offering your mother, Vagabond drastically reduced the odds of you joining us."

"Actually," the woman says, "a semidesperate move like that shows how much he *wants* you with us." She pauses. "Let me ask you a question, Alix. You have rare powers that can save countless innocent lives and keep people safe from evil. True, your life will never be the same if you join us, but hasn't it dawned on you that fighting Fire is your true destiny?"

"Don't pretend like you know me," I say, glaring at them. "I'm not doing this to gain entry into some special little group. I never asked for any of this. Mr. Shy Guy here is correct. I only committed to the test when Vagabond offered contact with my mom. I'll solve William's murder and destroy Face and everything associated with Perennial, but I'm not doing it to prove myself to Vagabond, you, or anybody else. I'm doing it to see my mom again. Understand?"

They shrug but don't say anything, their silence only adding to my growing frustration.

"Let me ask *you* some questions," I say. "Have either of you ever pinned a Brawler's hideous tongue to the floor of your own living room and watched it explode before your eyes?" They don't say anything. "Have you ever plunged a knife through the demonic red eye of a Heater?" They remain silent. "How about something the size of a Crawler and its wicked little Mini-Crawlers? Ever destroyed either of those? Ever been sprayed with yellow demon snot, or soaked with red-eye guts?" I realize I'm yelling now. "Do you think I enjoy this?" I pull Blade out and show them the knife. "Do you think I enjoy killing things?"

"You're asking the wrong people," the man says calmly.

"You're also forgetting one important question," the woman says, her eyes twinkling.

"And what might that be?" I say, sheathing Blade and privately cursing myself for getting so emotional in front of people I don't know.

"Love," she says, smiling. "Aren't you going to ask us if we've ever been in love with somebody?"

"Love," the man says. "The first one never goes away."

"Well, unless there's some sort of deadline involved," the woman adds, giving me a wink. Then she looks away and starts the engine.

I stand there, confused and surprised. Was she referencing tomorrow night's deadline for me to solve William's murder, or does she know about William secretly crossing over to become Lewis Wilde for a few days?

As the woman slowly backs the car out of the driveway, the man finally looks at me. He's even more attractive now and reminds me of one of those older guys you see in deodorant or underwear ads.

"You might not believe this, but we didn't come here to upset you, Alix Keener," he says. "Like my partner said, we came to say hello and wish you good luck. But remember this: nobody can have it all."

I clench my fists and follow the sedan down the driveway, watching closely as it heads down a dark, quiet Maple Grove Street. The license plate is white with bold blue letters and numbers. I see "U.S. Government" centered along the top, and "For Official Use Only" centered below the plate number. There's a barely detectable light-blue American flag on the background of the plate, but seeing it gives me neither feelings of patriotism nor security. Instead, I feel fear, a rippling and intense fear at the thought of spending the rest of my life as a professional killer under the supervision of a top-secret government agency devoted to destroying demons and the hellish evil they create.

The car disappears into the blackness of the night.

A sudden chill overcomes me as I walk up the driveway. I'm exhausted and need all the rest I can get before tomorrow's grand finale in Oval City.

CHAPTER 29

I dream about Mom for the first time in months.

It's a dream, nothing more. There's no brilliant white light, no cottony mist, and no sudden crisp clearing. Unlike my dreams with William, this one possesses no deep notion of reality. That disappoints me at first, but when I finally see my mother, I want the dream to last forever.

I'm wearing a comfortable white summer dress and walking barefoot in an endless field of knee-high green grass. The cloudless sky seems too low and surrounds me like a dome. Despite the warm sun, dry grass, and blue sky, I smell rain. I also smell spring flowers—a mix of lilacs and tulips—although there isn't a blossom in sight.

Mom is fifty feet away. She's wearing an identical white cotton dress, Mom waving and smiling, her long, dark hair blowing softly in the pleasant breeze. I smile and wave as I get closer, but I have that strange feeling where you know it's a dream and won't last long, so I quicken my pace to reach her as fast as possible.

But I can't reach her. Mom remains the same distance away from me no matter how fast I walk. She doesn't seem to know this, just keeps waving and smiling as if everything is wonderful and I'll be in her arms any second. I break into a sprint, but the same thing happens. I can't gain any ground on her.

I stop, cup my hands around my mouth, and shout, "I can't get any closer, Mom."

She doesn't say anything, just continues smiling and waving in robotic fashion.

"Mom? Can you hear me, Mom?"

She still doesn't respond, so I lower my hands and place them on my hips, looking around this beautiful field of green and wondering what the point of this dream is. Is it telling me I'm not ready to see her? Am I literally chasing a dream? Or is this simply a preview of how and where we'll make contact after I take care of business in Oval City tomorrow?

I wipe sweat from my brow and continue my fruitless sprint through the tall grass. The sky seems even lower now and ready to collapse around me like an oversized swimming-pool liner. I'm breathing hard, lungs laboring as I struggle to keep the dream alive, tears streaming down my face as I watch Mom smile and wave.

Wait. I'm getting closer. *She's* getting closer.

Mom *sees* me. Her expression has changed. She lowers her hand and tilts her head slightly, squinting as if unsure of who I am.

"Mom!" I smile wide and pump my arms faster, my thighs burning from the intensity of the run. "It's me, Mom! It's Alix!"

I'm thirty feet away when she recognizes me, Mom putting her hands over her mouth and shaking her head in what must be a combination of shock and disbelief. She crouches and drops her hands to her knees, a huge smile on her face as she opens her arms wide, Mom ready to embrace me just as she did countless times when I was a little girl.

I slow down when I'm ten feet away and finally hear her beautiful voice.

"Oh, Alix," she says, standing and keeping her arms out wide. "I'm so happy you're here. I miss you so much, honey."

She's crying, which makes me bawl even harder. I reach for her, ready to hug her and tell her how beautiful she looks and how much I've missed her.

And that's when the sky turns purple and the air grows sickly hot.

There's no warning. It just happens. A thick and nasty heat chokes me, like an invisible strangler. Everything around me turns an eerie shade of purple I know too well.

Perennial. Perennial is all around me.

Perennial is far more than a drug. I realize that now. Perennial is a demonic virus hell-bent on destroying everything I love. Perennial is a plague that has shaken the foundations of all the principles I've held to be true. Perennial has changed me forever and forged my destiny, but how do you handle a destiny you're not sure you want?

I can't touch Mom. There's some sort of invisible barrier between us, and the emotional trauma it causes me is worse than any physical torture I can imagine. Mom presses her hands against the barrier. She looks terrified. Tears continue to stream down her face. I press my hands against the invisible seal, praying to God to remove it so that I can feel my dead mother's skin.

But God doesn't answer my prayer. Instead, purple raindrops pelt my skin, each one hot enough to leave a red mark the size of a penny. It's as if a swarm of angry purple hornets is attacking me. It's happening to Mom too. She's in agony, Mom unsuccessfully trying to swat the raindrops away. Screaming from the pain, I gaze skyward and watch in horror as menacing purple clouds twist and spin in the sky, the searing purple rain becoming a downpour of what now looks like an endless, pounding shower of dark paint.

My mother begins melting before my eyes, shrinking away into a shapeless glob of waxy purple material. She's no longer screaming, just staring blankly at me as her physical form deteriorates into a bubbling pool of dark liquid that drains into the now-purple grass. I'm suddenly numb to the pain of the missile-like droplets that continue to bombard me, but I emit my loudest scream yet as Mom's eyes flood with purple and close before disappearing into the poisoned earth.

The sky remains purple, but the rain finally stops. The heat is still stifling, but the invisible barrier disappears. I launch myself forward and dive into the stained grass Mom just sank into, crying like a little girl as I bury my face into the earth in a failed attempt to somehow raise her from the dead. I squeeze my eyes shut and repeatedly punch the ground, screaming at the thought of never seeing my mother again.

Dizziness quickly overwhelms me and forces me into silence. I sneeze from something inside my nose. Then my lips and skin go strangely numb. Sitting up, I open my eyes and press my palms into the ground for balance.

My skin. Oh God. No. My arms and legs have turned purple and look like a giant, gruesome bruise. The same ugly shade of purple has smothered my white dress as well. The white is no longer visible.

That's when I notice dark dust hovering everywhere, like fog.

I can barely see three feet in front of me, but for some reason I can't quite figure out, I open my mouth and breathe in the dust. I try to fight the smile slowly crossing my face, but the smile wins. My eyes feel heavy. A tingling sensation replaces the numbness and shoots through my entire body. Deep inside I know I'm supposed to refuse all of this, but I can't. It's the drug. Every droplet of stinging purple rain was a type of needle injecting me with Perennial, and the dust isn't dust at all. It's powder, the same addictive powder somebody placed inside my Explorer, and the same powder I promised I would never try.

Purple poison is racing through my cells, and a part of me doesn't care. I feel Perennial's power quickly conquering me, and despite all the horrors of the past few days, a guiltless joy spreads inside of me. I feel the drug encouraging me to do whatever it takes to get more of it. Lie. Cheat. Steal. Kill.

It doesn't matter. The overwhelming addictive quality of Perennial tears away my values and sense of morality. The high makes *any* action seem favorable as long as it results in more Perennial. No matter how dark and diabolical my thoughts turn, they don't feel disturbing or wrong in any way. My dead mother just melted into nothingness before my eyes, yet all I can think about is inhaling more powder. I feel like a happy, drug-addicted zombie, lifeless but thrilled at the thought of such a powerful drug controlling me.

That's because Perennial is more than a drug, I remind myself. Perennial is a drug that *possesses* you. Vagabond's theory is correct, I realize. Face and the Army of Fire control something the world has never seen the likes of, a drug that crushes even the strongest will. Perennial makes its victims think and do awful things that further the agenda of a growing group of organized demons committed to possessing the entire human population and using it as a weapon to defeat the Army of Light.

Despite my drug-induced haze, one terrifying realization allows me to resist the overwhelming temptation to inhale every speck of powder floating around me. The government woman said Fire was winning and that Perennial was only one hurdle of many, but the thought of a drug like this spreading worldwide and stealing the souls of people I love—people like *William*—is so sickening that I refuse to give in and let it happen. Despite a reluctance to accept my paranormal destiny, I finally commit to it once I actually experience the gripping power of Perennial.

I am Light. I will fight Fire for as long as necessary. If I was born to see the past and the future, I need to be the greatest two-way psychic the world has ever known. If I'm destined to destroy demons and their accompanying evil beasts, I might as well be the best damn demon slayer Vagabond's ever seen. If I'm on Earth to fall in love with a beautiful ghost and solve his murder, then I need to solve it and cherish every second I have left with William. As for the promised reunion with Mom, I'll have to force myself not to think about it until I actually earn it.

Wait. Maybe that's the message of the dream—that I can't see Mom until I embrace my true calling and commit to keeping the world safe from evil. Perhaps the invisible barrier between Mom and me represented my unwillingness to dedicate myself to the tasks that await me.

Yes. That's it. I can *feel* it. I'm still in the dream, but I'm stronger now and more energetic. It's as if somebody just plunged a needle into my heart and injected me with some sort of Perennial antidote. The powerful high of the drug disappears almost instantly. I scramble to my feet, screaming and cursing at the purple sky and experiencing a rage unlike any I've ever felt before. I feel inhuman, like a rabid wild animal ready to attack anything that threatens its existence.

The drug-laced dusty fog slowly fades, and the violent purple sky morphs to clear black. My dress is white again, my skin color back to normal. The air temperature cools. Darkness surrounds me. I breathe crisp, clean, and refreshing air deep into my lungs, feeling safe in the blackness and figuring I'm close to awakening in the comfort of my own bedroom.

But that's when something that feels like hot breath hits the back of my neck and prickles my skin. I turn quickly, reaching behind me for Blade, but then I remember what I'm wearing—a summer dress—and realize that Blade didn't make it into this dream.

I can't see him, but I know he's in front of me. I hear him breathing. Well, wheezing is more like it. It's awful—slow inhales and exhales through what sounds like a throat full of thick phlegm. He smells like spoiled garbage on a blisteringly hot summer day.

I can read his thoughts. He knows this and finds it funny, but what the leader demon known as Face doesn't find funny is that I'm the first person to ever break the hold of his precious Perennial. This worries him. This is why he crossed over into my dream. I'm an official threat to him now. The demon that murdered William Weed and most likely filled poor Marc Watkins with bullet holes has come to scout me.

No. Wait. I was wrong. Although Face knows I can read his thoughts, that's not what he finds funny. What he finds funny is that I don't have Blade with me. He's laughing at how easy I've made this for him.

My legs suddenly feel like rubber. Terror wipes away the rising confidence I had just moments ago.

Face is here to kill me in my dream.

That's my last thought as the same two powerful hands that killed William Weed two years ago grab hold of my neck and proceed to choke the life out of me.

CHAPTER 30

Friday, September 7

I'm jarred awake from my own hands pressing hard on my throat. I'm choking myself. My eyes bulge from the pain, and for a terrifying few moments I don't have control over my body. It's as if some unseen force is working me, like a puppet master controlling a marionette.

Face. He was there in the dream, but real. I'd fought off the Perennial high, and that angered him, but then he began laughing because he realized how easy it was going to be to kill me. And that's what he's doing right now. Killing me with my own hands. Suicide. He's making it seem like a suicide, just as he did in this same bedroom with William two years ago. He'll choke me to death and then somehow make it seem like I killed myself. Maybe he'll appear in my room after I'm dead and place one of those creepy suicide bags on my head. Then he'll use Dad's emergency gun on me in a way that makes it look like I shot myself to end the prolonged agony of suffocating to death.

I'm close to blacking out, but a loud slamming sound from downstairs shakes my bedroom and somehow allows me to regain control of my arms. It's as if the noise frightened off the invisible Face. Weird. Why would a slamming door scare off a powerful demon?

I roll out of bed and fall onto my hands and knees, coughing violently for several seconds before massaging my aching throat. I sit on my floor, slide on my glasses, and look around the room. It's 5:30 a.m. Friday morning. It's my day to destroy Oval City, and maybe—just maybe—see Mom again.

It's also my last day with William. I want him here now. My bed is much warmer with him in it. Although he's nowhere in sight, I feel him all over and deep inside me. I sense he'll escort me to Oval City earlier than expected, and I have absolutely no complaints about that.

Dad. I never heard him come home last night. Despite the horrific ending to my dream about Mom, that's how deeply I slept. Even with yesterday's demonic battles barely behind me, I feel refreshed this morning and full of energy, all of my senses operating at a level I've never experienced before. It's as if Vagabond or somebody from Light covertly slipped me some ultimate awareness drug while I slept.

I hear Dad downstairs talking to somebody on his phone and making sounds in the kitchen. I smell his fancy coffee beans wafting through the house, an aromatic blend of chocolate, subtle spices, and light floral notes that seems more intense than usual.

Dad was the one who slammed the door moments ago, I realize, inadvertently scaring off Face in the process. He has no idea I ditched school yesterday. Somehow I know this. Other knowledge spins through my mind, things I shouldn't know but do, like the fact that Face is now waiting patiently for me in Oval City and has some dangerous surprises planned.

Dad's voice is muffled but louder now. He's arguing with somebody. This is nothing unusual. I've heard him irate on the phone many times, but if this conversation has anything to do with his Perennial investigation, I need to learn as much as possible.

I open the bedroom door silently and tiptoe out of my room, hearing Dad's garbled shouting as I approach the stairs. He's clearly pissed at whomever he's speaking with, but all I catch are a few choice F-bombs and work-related obscenities I've heard countless times. It sounds like he's in full undercover mode and speaking with one of his street contacts, but I can't be sure, due to the poor acoustics. All I can think is that it must not be that important, because if it were, he'd finish the conversation in his office.

He ends the call with another loud F-bomb just as I'm passing through the living room and approaching the kitchen. I take a deep breath and tell myself to act as if this is just another school day.

"Sounds like you're having a great morning," I say as I enter the kitchen and sit at my usual spot at the table. He's facing the fridge and whispers something I can't hear. Then he shoves his phone into the front pocket of his jeans.

"You didn't happen to buy me more kimchi, did you?" I say.

"What?" he says, turning toward me. He looks exhausted.

"Nothing." I raise my eyebrows. "It's an attempt at a joke." I squint for a better look at him. "God, when was the last time you slept?"

"Let's just say I'm overdue." He sips coffee from a white mug, closing his eyes as he does so. The steam rising from the cup fogs his face and makes him look almost ghostlike behind his long, scraggly beard.

"What's wrong?"

He opens his eyes. "I'll give you one guess."

"The Watkins case?"

Dad nods and sets his mug on the counter, exhaling deeply and leaning his elbows on the granite. I've never seen him this tired.

"Alix, I have some news."

"About Mr. Watkins?" I wonder if he might actually tell me about Marc Watkins being the creator of Perennial.

"Sort of. Yes," he says, forcing a smile. "What the Watkins murder has shown me is that I can't do this job anymore. I can't stop thinking about his wife and kids and all the suffering they're going through. I've always been able to block things like that out and focus on catching the bad people, but for some reason I can't do it anymore." He pauses. "Alix, I'm retiring from law enforcement. I let my bosses know today. It'll take a few weeks before it's official, but I'm done with this, honey."

"Dad!" I smile and stand. Then I kick my chair out of the way, run to him, and give him the longest and strongest hug I've given him in a long time. He hugs me back and tells me how much he loves me and how he knows this is the right decision.

"It's totally the right decision," I say, ending the hug. "Think about all the work you can do on this house. And think about all the things we can do together, like go to Eastern Market. I'm so happy for you!" I pause. "And you know something? I bet Mom's happy too, especially knowing that beard will come off. You do plan on shaving it, right?" I scrunch my nose. "No offense, but you're starting to look like one of those guys on the Boston Red Sox."

"Really?" He runs a hand through the unkempt growth. "I was going for more of a Civil War Confederate soldier type of look."

"Whatever." As I head back to the table, I feel my phone vibrate in my pocket. "It's gross, okay? I suggest getting rid of it as soon as possible."

"Whatever you say." He laughs and finishes his coffee in one extended gulp.

I sit down and covertly check the text as soon as Dad turns his back to get something from the fridge.

It's a message from William:

ALIX, I LOVE U. WHATEVER HAPPENS TODAY I LOVE U AND ALWAYS WILL.

"Who's that?" Dad says.

I flinch and look up to see him watching me from behind the counter.

"William," I say without thinking.

"William? You told me about Lewis, but who's William?"

"Oh," I say, flustered and feeling my heart knock against my ribs. "Um . . . it's nothing. William is Lewis's middle name. That's all. People close to him call him William."

"So you're close to him?" Dad raises his eyebrows. "It's the fourth day of school and you're saying you're close to him."

"I like him," I say, pocketing my phone. "I already told you that. So would you if you ever met him."

"You say it like I never will."

That's because you won't, Dad. He's history at midnight.

"Really?" I say. "I didn't mean it like that. I'm sure you'll meet him soon."

He studies me for a few moments. Then he says, "I need your opinion. Do you think I should stay on until the Watkins case is solved, or should I walk away as soon as possible?"

"I just want you to be happy," I say, knowing that if I do my job today, I'll solve the Watkins case myself by midnight. "But from what you've said, it sounds like walking away now will make you happier."

"What if I regret it?"

"I don't know." I shrug. "Maybe open up a detective agency or something?"

"Funny," he says, scratching his beard. "I've actually thought about that."

"I guess great minds really do think alike."

He laughs but quickly falls silent when his annoying ringtone blares through the kitchen. He stares at his phone. Any sense of peace or happiness instantly drains from his face.

"I'm sorry," he says, rushing past me. "It's private. Have a good day at school, okay?"

"Are we still on for Eastern Market and a visit to Mom tomorrow?"

"I hope so."

My phone vibrates again. Another text from William:

MEET ME IN BEACONSFIELD LOT AT 7 – BUT NO SCHOOL 4 U 2DAY

I close my eyes and smile. Then I grab a protein bar from the pantry and rush back upstairs before Dad can ask me any more questions about my Dream Guy.

CHAPTER 31

I struggle to obey the speed limits on my drive to Beaconsfield High. It's a cold, overcast morning. Despite my sky-high energy levels, heightened senses, and manic excitement at the prospect of being with William, an underlying depression swims through me that matches the dreary weather. William disappears forever in seventeen hours, and there's a very real chance that I could die today.

I pull into the school just before seven. Blade rests on the passenger seat. I'm wearing jeans and black Chuck Taylors again, along with a black Detroit Tigers sweatshirt Dad gave me a couple of years ago. The strategic tears in the jeans seemed even larger this morning, so I slipped on a pair of tight-fitting black yoga pants from my nightmarish junior year fitness class to keep me warm. I even put on the matching black yoga tank beneath the sweatshirt.

The student lot is mostly empty this early, and I easily spot William's latest joyride backed into the last row nearest the tennis courts. It's a black Yukon Denali with custom wheels and fully tinted windows. I can't see William behind the darkened windshield, but

I know he's there. I park a few spots away and sheathe Blade before killing the Explorer's ignition and getting out.

The Yukon's powerful engine hums like a caged animal. The driver's-side window powers smoothly down as I approach, revealing William's gorgeous pale face, dark hair, and mesmerizing eyes.

"Good morning, beautiful," he says. "Need a ride?"

"A Yukon?" I shake my head. "Don't you think the owner has already reported it stolen?"

"Probably." He pauses. "Look, it's my last day and I wanted a nice ride, okay? And I don't *steal* cars. I borrow them without permission. Remember?"

"Right." I lean against the door and stand on my tiptoes to kiss his soft lips. "It's freezing out here."

"Hop in. It's warm." He nods toward the passenger seat. "And the backseat is the size of a bedroom, if you know what I mean."

I take a step back. "You really are dangerous, aren't you?"

Then I smile and walk around the front of the Yukon.

∞

It's impossible for us not to touch each other as William leaves Beaconsfield and heads for southbound I-75 en route to Oval City. We say little as darkness gives way to a clear sky and a brilliant sunrise. His right hand rests on my left thigh. My left hand caresses the side of his face and massages the back of his neck. His overall silence and intense gaze worry me. I keep hoping to get a reading on him. That doesn't happen, but Blade's lack of movement reassures me that all is well for now.

Rush hour traffic builds. We're barely moving by the time we reach Mack Avenue. What shocks me is how deserted the Friday morning Detroit landscape becomes once we leave I-75 and exit onto the service drive. We've gone from a busy commuter metropolis to a decaying ghost town in less than thirty seconds. It was dark the first time we came out here, which was creepy enough, but what I realize as William crosses Mack Avenue and passes the safety of Eastern Market is that daylight makes this place even scarier, especially on days like today when there isn't a market. Garbage lines the streets. Overgrown brush blankets the seemingly endless stretch of graffiti-tagged abandoned buildings. The smell of raw sewage penetrates the warm safety of the Yukon.

But it's the silence and lack of human activity I find most terrifying. There's *nobody* around. In fact, the closer William gets to the four gutted Oval City towers that glare at us like concrete demons, the lonelier and scarier our surroundings become. Though William says nothing, I sense that he feels the same way. His gaze constantly shifts from the eerie buildings to the pothole-riddled road in front of him.

He makes a right on Wilkins and travels farther down the street than he did the other night when we encountered the mysterious and evil homeless man. William eventually backs the Yukon into an ancient driveway flanked by sagging trees on both sides, giving us our own secluded view of Oval City across the street and the Detroit riverfront skyline beyond.

He takes a few deep breaths and stares at the vacant towers. His hand still rests on my thigh, and as he moves it higher I close my eyes and unsuccessfully try pushing away the thought that the Yukon's backseat is the size of a bedroom.

"It's so quiet right now," I say.

"Don't let the silence fool you." He stares straight ahead. "They're waiting for us."

I open my eyes. "When you left last night, you couldn't tell me where you were going or what you were doing. You came here, didn't you?" He nods. Barely. "This is where you've been staying since you crossed over on Tuesday. Am I right?"

"Are you reading me right now?" He finally looks at me.

"No. I'm putting pieces together. That creepy homeless man wasn't crazy. He really did see you the night before. That's why you looked away from him." He offers another slight nod. "Where exactly have you been staying down here?"

"I can't tell you."

"Why not?"

"Because you'll find out soon enough."

"You're afraid of something," I say, brushing my fingertips against his high cheekbone. "I can tell. It's like you're having second thoughts. What's wrong, William?"

He gives me a look. "Are you *sure* you aren't reading me right now?"

"I'm positive." I look out toward the haunting buildings. "What's wrong?"

William says, "What's wrong is that both the nightmare and the countdown begin the moment we turn onto Brewster Loop." He leans closer. Our mouths are inches apart. His proximity sends waves of warmth through me from head to toe. "I brought you here early because this is the last time we'll be alone together." He pauses. "Think about it. Nobody knows what will happen after this. I want us to last forever, but we both know it ends soon."

He kisses me softly and places his palms on either side of my face. I feel like warm putty in his hands. When he lowers his mouth and begins kissing my neck, I arch my head back and feel like a volcano that's about to erupt.

"How much time do you think we have?" I ask, breathless and leaning back against the passenger-side door as William positions himself gently on top of me and continues working his magic on my neck.

"You're the psychic demon slayer," he whispers without looking up. "You tell me."

I think about Blade still resting motionlessly in my back pocket and smile.

"We could have hours." I notice the windows fogging up. "Imagine that."

"I love you, Alix." His warm breath hits my skin. "You're absolutely beautiful."

"Oh my God, William. It's getting really hot in here."

"Yes." He presses his lips against my chest. "Yes, it is."

"Don't leave any marks on my neck." I pull him closer until his body presses firmly against mine. "My dad will kill you."

"Your dad can't kill me. I'm already dead." William emits a quick laugh. "But don't worry. I'm a ghost. Not a vampire."

He pulls me quickly but softly up toward him and begins removing my sweatshirt. I raise my arms to make things easier for him. William tosses my shirt into the backseat and runs a hand through my hair as his other hand lands on one of the rips in my jeans and presses against the black yoga pants beneath.

Eyeing my black tank top, he says, "Do the pants beneath the jeans match the tank?"

"Yes." I smile. "As a matter of fact they do."

"I bet they look great on you."

"Hmm. Would you like to see?"

William smiles. "I thought you'd never ask."

"It's a little cramped up here," I say, indicating the front seat and then nodding toward the backseat. "How about I meet you back there?"

"After you, my lady." He gestures with his hand for me to go first.

"William?"

"Yes."

There's a long silence.

Then I say, "I'm taking my glasses off for a few hours."

He watches in amazement as I slide my black chunky frames over the bridge of my nose and toss them into the glove compartment. Then I crawl toward the back of the Yukon with a wide smile on my face.

The next four hours change me forever.

CHAPTER 32

"It's time," William says.

"I know." I slide my glasses back on. "I feel it."

We're back in the front seat, fully clothed and ready to confront Oval City and all of its evil. William starts the engine and pulls out of the secluded driveway, turning left onto Wilkins before making a right onto the service drive.

"I don't know what to say right now other than I love you and always will," William says.

I reach for his hand, turn toward my window, and choke back tears.

"I love you too, William." I squeeze my eyes shut, knowing full well that we'll never be together like this again. "I love you too."

He makes the right onto Alfred Street and creeps toward Brewster Loop. We've yet to see another person or vehicle. The early morning sun hides behind ominous dark clouds. I turn and study the four empty towers to our left, hoping for either a vision or a word cloud but getting neither. It's as if the four old structures have blocked my powers and are mocking me. I imagine Face up there somewhere, watching our approach and loving every second of it.

The overwhelming nature of my task keeps hitting me: How do I destroy an entire city block and take down the demonic Perennial kingpin?

"I have no idea," I whisper.

"What was that?" William says, slowing for the left onto Brewster Loop.

"Nothing. I'm just thinking out loud."

London's voice in my head: *Trust your abilities, but don't trust anything or anybody else.*

Then Vagabond's voice: *My advice is to not trust anything or anybody except your abilities.*

I feel the two of them rooting for me from somewhere close by. They won't interfere with my test, though. Even if I'm about to die, they won't step in to save me. As with so many other things lately, that's just something I know and feel.

Making the turn, William says, "Hey, Alix?"

"I'm listening."

"Just be confident, stay strong, and kick some ass, okay?"

I smile for a moment, but the smile fades the moment he completes the turn onto Brewster Loop and Blade awakens in my back pocket. The knife vibrates with its strongest intensity yet. I sit up straight, head swiveling as I scan Oval City in all directions, seeing nothing but tall weeds, scattered garbage, walls of graffiti, and urban decay.

The word cloud finally hits, the crisp black letters resting against a welcome backdrop of white:

First tower—now.

"Stop!" I say.

William hits the brakes hard, jolting us forward and then back in our seats. Tower one is to my immediate right, but I'm staring straight ahead, breathing calmly and deeply as I prepare myself. I don't know what awaits me inside, so all I can do is keep telling myself that this is a test I can pass.

It's not impossible. Vagabond wouldn't do something like that to you.

"William," I say. "I know Face's portal is somewhere below-ground, but something's waiting for me in this tower. According to Vagabond's rules and the little deal you cut with Fire, you can't help me from here on out, correct?"

"That's correct."

"Then wait here," I say, furrowing my brow. "I'll be back as soon as possible."

"Wow. I've never seen you so intense. It's sexy as hell."

"I'm a demon slayer, William." I smile and stare at him as I open the door. "It's an intense line of work."

I hop out of the toasty Yukon and into the crisp September air. Then I remove my Tigers sweatshirt and jeans: I'm wearing a skin-tight black yoga outfit, a pair of black Chuck Taylors, and a magical silver knife sheathed at the small of my back. I toss the jeans and sweater onto the passenger seat and give William one last look.

"Damn, Alix," he says. "This is a total turn on. You really are a badass, aren't you?"

"You have no idea." I adjust my glasses and check that Blade is secure. "No idea at all."

William digs through the pockets of my jeans and holds up my phone. "You don't want this?"

"Keep it safe," I say. "Something tells me phones are useless in Oval City today."

He studies my phone screen for a few moments. "You're right." He shows me the screen. "The power's on but it's totally dead."

"Yours is probably the same. Take a look."

He retrieves his phone from his back pocket, inspects it, and nods.

"It's those damn demons," he says, shaking his head and giving me a concerned look. "Be careful in there. I look forward to kissing you again."

I flash one last smile before closing the door and walking toward the menacing tower with a confident look on my face but sheer terror charging through my cells.

∞

No boards cover the long-gone windows of the gutted brick towers, leaving countless evenly spaced, square-shaped dark openings all over the buildings. The main floor entrances are barricade-free as well. Although the absence of boarded-up windows will make for an easier escape from the tower (if necessary), the overall darkness and silence that greet me as I enter are unsettling.

Blade's frantic movements continue inside the sheath, so I remove the knife and hold it waist-high in front of me, moving the weapon in sweeping arcs as I venture into the ground-floor rubble. It's wide open in here, one giant, hollow brick and concrete room smothered in layers of graffiti and years of debris. The upper floors are mostly gone. Dim light slices through the blown-out windows. I see the top of the tower fourteen stories above. On the far wall in front of me, a dangerous-looking staircase leads to the jigsaw puzzle–like remains of the higher floors.

A childlike female voice from high above sings my name slowly, as if it's a lyric in a baby's lullaby: *"Al-ixxxxx . . . Oh, Al-ixxxxx!"*

Her high-pitched laughter echoes through the cavernous tower, making it difficult to pinpoint the voice's location. But I know the laugh.

"Hello, Aruna." I stop at the staircase and study the crumbling sections of the floors above. "What's on your mind today?"

"Oh, hello, special girl." She giggles. "It's so nice to see you again. Why don't you come up here and find out what's on my mind?"

Blade tugs me forward toward the stairs. This troubles me. Aruna isn't evil, and up until now Blade has only acted up when something demonic is near.

Which means Aruna's leading me into a trap.

I step over a disturbing pile of small drug pipes stained purple with Perennial and begin ascending a staircase that seems ready to collapse with every step I take. Aruna's idiotic laughter constantly carries throughout the tower. As I pass the remains of Floors 2 and 3, I realize that one false step will send me to the hard concrete of the debris-laden ground floor.

I pause on the fourth floor. Like the other levels, there isn't much to it, just a section of concrete about three feet wide that hugs half the perimeter of the tower. A copper taste fills my mouth again. My heart hammers away at my ribs. It occurs to me that I'm battling demons on their home turf for the first time. Blade urges me forward but I resist, knowing that I need a better sense of exactly where Aruna is.

"Aruna?" I say, my voice echoing. "You're sure quiet all of a sudden."

"You're getting warm, Alix." She continues to giggle. "Very warm."

I swallow hard and navigate the stairs to Level 5, which still has roughly half of its original floor remaining. Aruna's there when I enter. She's standing twenty feet away on a slab of jagged concrete that ends barely ten feet to my right and her left. If either of us falls off the edge, we're either dead or paralyzed for life.

I place my left palm on the cement wall next to me and stay close to it. Then I slowly approach Aruna, who now hums a tune I don't recognize. I'm holding Blade down by my right side, but the knife keeps thrusting forward, wanting me to attack. That's what I still don't get. I see no hint of a trap, just Aruna and me on a very dangerous piece of concrete. I can't possibly attack an actual human with Blade. That would be murder, not demon slaying.

Aruna looks even worse than she did behind Zeppelin Coffee. She's wearing the same old jeans and frayed black tank top. Her ribs push against the fabric of the shirt. Red needle punctures line her pasty, sticklike arms, and her long, matted dark hair fails to hide her gaunt, haunting face. She puts her hands behind her back and moves closer to the edge of the drop, smiling at me with rotten black teeth and bloodshot eyes.

"You sure picked a strange place to talk," I say, stopping ten feet away from her and leaning all of my weight against the wall.

"We're not here to talk, special girl," she says in her annoying adolescent voice. "We're here to watch you die." She laughs so loudly I have to cup my free hand over one ear. "Nice outfit, by the way. I never pegged you as the Lululemon type."

"I'm not," I say, my eyes glued to hers. "Aruna, where's Face? It's time to end this."

After a long silence, she says, "Like the Crawler told you in your daddy's special office, Face is everywhere."

I squint and feel my stomach flip. "How do you know about the—"

Blade's handle presses firmly into my right palm. White lights rips through my head. Aruna's face pops into my mind and flashes seven times. At first I don't know what to make of it, but the vision makes sense when I open my eyes and see *seven* Arunas connected at the hips like conjoined clones. There's a brief moment where I'm convinced my eyes are playing tricks on me. I blink several times but still see seven Arunas linked at the waist.

From less than ten feet away, fourteen thin arms and legs, along with seven smiling but ugly faces, begin advancing toward me, ready to wrap me up like a toy and throw me off the edge of the concrete, I imagine. I'm trapped with my back against the wall. The Arunas laugh in unison. One Aruna laughing is bad enough. Seven laughing

Arunas is like having sharp knives repeatedly jabbed into your ears. My only hope is the staircase to my right, but three Arunas already block it. As for the window to my left, falling five floors onto Brewster Loop isn't my idea of a safe trip.

The Aruna to my far left raises her outside arm. Something hard collides with the side of my head. A chunk of concrete the size of a baseball falls to the ground in front of me, and I scream from the pain of the impact and drop to one knee. Warm blood trickles down the left side of my face. I'm woozy but manage to squat against the wall as I try to regain my senses.

"Gee, I'm sorry," the seven Arunas say, followed by that awful laughter. "That must've really hurt."

The Aruna on the far right raises her outside arm, but this time I see the missile coming and raise Blade just in time to use the knife as a shield. A softball-sized lump of concrete explodes into white dust the moment it makes contact with Blade. The Arunas don't like it. Their screams rattle my bones.

Just as I'm ready to strike, the Aruna in the middle launches a soccer ball–size chunk of concrete straight at my head, but I manage to duck and roll to my left as it slams against the wall and disintegrates into a cloud of fine white dust.

"Enough already!" I yell, mustering the strength to spring to my feet and charge the Aruna on the far left, the one who scored the hit on me.

What I find odd is that she doesn't attempt to defend herself. That's what I'm thinking as I scream and launch myself airborne, raising Blade high over my shoulder and driving the weapon downward as fast as possible toward Aruna's left eye.

My eyes bulge with shock and surprise as I pass directly through her. It's as if she isn't there. She's an illusion, and the momentum of my stabbing motion nearly sends Blade straight into the meat of my right thigh. I stumble forward and fall to my knees three inches from the edge of the jagged floor. I scramble to my feet and turn.

The seven Arunas have turned as well. They face me and squeal with earsplitting laughter, all fourteen Aruna arms now holding chunks of concrete the size of bowling balls. They're laughing because they have me right where they want me—surrounded, on the edge of the precipice—and are ready to chuck their missiles from hell at me and watch with demonic delight as I fall to my death.

I have no chance.

Amidst the torturous laughter, I tighten my fist around Blade and take a final look at all seven Arunas, searching for any differences between them or any overall signs of weakness. This is obviously not the real Aruna, just another part of Face's test for me.

Three Arunas on the left. Three Arunas on the right.

One Aruna in the middle.

White light flashes in my head the moment I lock eyes with the center Aruna. And then it's gone, leaving me in a stare down with the middle Aruna.

She's the energy source. The light just confirmed it.

My lips curl into a smile. At the same time, identical looks of surprise cross the faces of the Arunas. As if trying to catch up to my white-light vision, they immediately cock their arms back and throw their concrete missiles at me. But they're too late. I'm already airborne again, screaming like mad as more than a dozen cement boulders whiz past me, a few of them grazing the sides of my face and body as I bring Blade down hard toward the left eye of the center Aruna.

Blade plunges deep into the eye socket like an arrow hitting wet sand, sending a geyser of yellow and red ooze skyward and onto my face and glasses. The middle Aruna shrieks like a wounded animal and falls onto her back, bringing her six phantom likenesses down with her.

I'm straddling her waist now, still screaming from fear and adrenaline as Aruna writhes in agony. Problem is I can't get Blade out of her eye. The knife is almost completely embedded into the demon's head. Only a few inches of handle sticks out.

That's when the floor begins crumbling and shaking from the impact of the Arunas' fall.

Great.

"Come on!" I yell, feeling increased heat coming from Aruna. I pull on Blade's handle with both hands. "Get out of there, Blade! Get out of Aruna's head!"

I pull with all of my strength. The knife finally gives with a loud sucking sound just as Aruna's pre-Fire heat seems to burn through the stretchy fabric of my yoga pants. I dive forward off her and roll until I hit the back wall. Then I sheathe Blade and look toward the Arunas. They're convulsing in unison and weakening the floor with every move.

They know what they're doing. They want the floor to collapse and take me with it.

Breathless, I stand and run toward the staircase. I'm three feet away when the seven Arunas explode into a massive fireball. Flames lick the back of my hair and seem to melt my skin. A loud snapping sound joins the roar of the fire. I feel the floor collapsing beneath me, so I scream and leap toward the stairs.

My hands grasp the weak base of the stair rail as the fifth floor crashes to the ground level with a deafening sound. I'm hanging on for my life to a loose vertical pole of the rail, my legs dangling in empty space beneath me. The whole section of rail is dangerously close to breaking away from the stairs, but I manage to pull myself up and wrap my arms around the pole long enough to raise my legs and roll to safety beneath the bottom opening of the rail.

Furious and in great pain, I stand and dust myself off, wiping demon ooze and my own blood from my face and hair. A massive cloud of dust rises from the crash that just occurred on the ground floor, but the silence is welcome after the demonic Arunas' wailing laughter.

That's when I hear William outside, yelling my name and asking if I'm okay.

"It's all good, William," I shout. "I'm coming out."

I cautiously navigate the fragile stairs down to the ground floor and make my way around a small mountain of fresh rubble. Approaching the main entrance, the smell of freshly burned demon energy taints the air, and I ask myself if I just earned one Fire or seven by eliminating the Arunas.

I guess I'll have to ask Roman and London about that the next time I see them.

CHAPTER 33

Despite the overcast early afternoon sky, I have to shield my eyes as I leave the tower and hit the natural light. William runs over to me from the Yukon. We share a long hug and even longer kiss.

"Are you okay?" He looks me over. "I was worried sick when I heard that sound. What happened?"

I tell him exactly what happened.

"You're bleeding and covered in dust." He runs his fingertips over the cut on the side of my head and shows me the blood. "That gash looks pretty nasty."

"I'll live." I turn toward the tower. The dust from the collapsed floor is just settling, but remnants of grayish-white material drifts out from openings on the first few floors like smoke from chimneys. "All traces of the battles in my house vanished the moment I won the fights, but it's different out here." Intense pain ripples through my head wound, and I'm sore all over from the jumping and falling. "I think it has something to do with the underground portal. I don't think I can heal when I'm on Fire ground."

William looks me over from head to toe like a worried parent inspecting a child for injuries. "How do you feel right now?"

"Not great," I confess. "I don't think I can stay here much longer." I scan Oval City. The whole place remains eerily silent and deserted. "People must have heard that floor collapse at least a half mile away." I shake my head and try to make sense of it all. "I don't think we have much time. Somebody might have already called the police." I cough and wince from a sharp pain in my ribs. "Where is he, William? Where's Face?"

"I wish I knew."

"Let's go." I head toward the Yukon. "Maybe we need to try the next tower."

We're stepping onto Brewster Loop and approaching the SUV when we hear distant crying. It's faint and barely audible, but it stops us in our tracks. William and I glance at each other, turn toward the tower, and see a sight nobody should see.

Aruna—the *real* Aruna—stands at the edge of the tower roof fourteen stories above, arms limp at her sides as she stares down at the hard ground she's about to end her sad life on. I see it in my head before it happens, and it all connects with the vision of her death I had when we first met behind Zeppelin Coffee.

"Aruna!" William says. "Oh my God. Aruna, no!"

"William!" I grab his arm and manage to prevent him from running toward the tower. "It's too late. Don't look!"

Aruna's distant and pained voice: "I've always loved you, William. I'm so sorry I lost it."

Aruna jumps. I turn away and move in front of William, who closes his eyes, drops to his knees, and screams as I wrap him in my arms. Moments later, a dull thump behind me confirms that it's over. Aruna is dead.

"Not yet," William says as if reading my mind. "She's not dead yet."

He gets to his feet and bolts. I follow him as he races toward her, Aruna a small, wrecked heap lying a short distance from the entrance to the tower.

It's hard to look at her. Aruna's frail body is twisted into impossible angles, arms and legs in places they shouldn't be, her pelvis pushed way too far to one side. Blood trickles from her mouth, ears, and nose. Her eyes are open and gazing skyward as if taking one final look at the roof she stood on seconds ago.

William kneels over her. I stand beside him and try not to look directly at Aruna as she takes her final breaths in this world.

"You . . . came . . . back," she whispers, shifting her eyes to William's. "How?"

"Shh," he says. "Why'd you jump, Aruna? Why?"

She closes her eyes and swallows. "Face," she says through a mouth full of liquid. I notice her right hand ball into a weak fist. Then she extends her index finger as if pointing at something out on Brewster Loop. "Face." She closes her eyes.

William and I exchange looks. Aruna opens her eyes again.

William says to her, "What did you lose? You said you lost something."

There's a silence during which the last smile of Aruna's life crosses her face. "Your . . . baby," she whispers, sending my stomach to my feet. "*Our* baby."

"Oh God." William rubs his eyes and looks at me. "I didn't know, Alix. I never knew." He lays a palm on Aruna's forehead. "How did you lose it? Our baby. What happened?"

She closes her eyes and swallows. "Right after you . . . died . . . Face . . . beat me . . . bad . . . lost . . . the baby."

Warm tears stream down my cheeks. I kneel and join William.

"We're here to stop him, Aruna. I'm so sorry. Do you know where Face is?"

Aruna struggles to whisper, "He's . . . every . . . where, Alix . . . everywhere . . . Face . . . is . . . Sometimes things . . . looking . . . for . . . in . . . front . . . of . . . you."

She manages one deep inhale, and then she's gone.

"No!" William says again, standing and turning away from Aruna's corpse. "I never knew. I *never knew!*" In tears, he bends forward, with his hands on his knees. "I can't do this anymore. I never should've made the deal. They tricked me, Alix. I need to get out of here."

I stand, thinking about Aruna's final words as William and I share a long hug and he cries into my shoulder. I feel awful for both of them, but her last fragmented sentence won't leave my mind.

". . . Sometimes things . . . looking . . . for . . . in . . . front . . . of . . . you."

Sometimes things you're looking for are right in front of you.

Was she warning me about William?

I squeeze him close and focus on getting another reading on him. It happens, but all I get are random images of white light and intense fire. Light. Fire. Light. Fire. On and on—a continuous loop of fire and light. William is a good person who died a wrongful death. That explains his light. He's good at heart. As for the fire, all I can do is write it off to the stupid deal he made with Fire that allowed him to cross over to be with me.

"I didn't expect this," he says, ending our embrace. "We need to take care of her, Alix. We need to cover her or hide her or something. We can't just leave her here for everybody to see. It's not right."

He brushes past me on his way to the Yukon. Part of me expects him to drive off and leave me on my own, but that's not what he does. Instead he hops into the backseat and comes out carrying the blanket we spent four memorable hours together on. I say nothing as William passes me and gently places the blanket over Aruna's body. He kneels beside her again and looks as if he's praying. I've experienced the awful emotional pain of losing somebody you love, and although William might have long ago lost the romantic love he had for Aruna, I realize that at this moment he's grieving for the mother of his unborn child and the unborn child itself, a child William never knew about until today.

Poor William! I'm surprised he's holding himself together at all. Gut-wrenching grief and anger overwhelm me as I watch the heart-breaking scene play out in front of me. Why does life have to involve such tragedy?

Face killed Mr. Watkins, William, Aruna, and Aruna's *baby*. The ultimate unfairness is that Face can't die. He's a demon. All I can do is destroy his portal and send his evil ass back to the Fire world, meaning Face needs to go back to hell before he kills more humans.

He needs to go back now.

"William, wait." I walk toward him and take a knee beside him, remembering something that didn't seem like anything at the time but might be important now. "Show me her right hand."

"What are you talking about? She's dead, Alix. Why do you need to see her hand?"

"You couldn't see it, but I did. She made a fist and pointed. I figured she was pointing at me, but maybe she was trying to tell us something." I pause. "Or show us something."

William gives me a reluctant nod and carefully slides the blanket back just enough to see Aruna's pale, bony hand, still balled into a fist, her frail index finger outstretched toward me.

"It was probably some involuntary action," William says, lowering the blanket back over her.

I reach under the blanket and grab Aruna's cold, lifeless hand.

"Stop!" William says. "What are you doing?"

"Just one second."

I close my eyes and squeeze her fingers. White light floods my field of vision. Then I see an image of an iron circle with the word "Detroit" arcing across the top of it. The white light flares and disappears, leaving me breathless and staring at the blanket.

"That doesn't make sense." I release Aruna's hand and stand, hands on my hips as I turn and study the Yukon.

"What did you see?"

"I don't know, but we're so close, William. It's like I can smell Face."

William lifts Aruna's blanket-covered body in his muscular arms, a distraught look on his face as he cradles her and walks toward Brewster Loop.

"I'm sorry." I lay a hand on his shoulder and walk beside him. "We'll put her in the back of the Yukon and get her to the hospital as soon as possible."

William nods. Then I hustle ahead to the SUV, open the unlocked hatch, and raise the lift.

"It's just not fair," William says, laying Aruna's body softly into the back of the vehicle and adjusting the blanket so that she's completely covered. "I never expected anything like this."

"I know."

He closes the lift door and turns toward me. We share another long hug. Then I turn and walk toward the middle of the street to think.

I see it the moment my eyes meet the road beneath me. It's an old iron manhole cover with the word "Detroit" arcing across the top, the exact one I saw in my head when I held Aruna's dead hand. This is what she was pointing at.

Sometimes things you're looking for are right in front of you.

"I'm glad you're strong, William." I turn to meet his gaze and place a foot firmly on the manhole cover. "Lock the Yukon. I just found the portal."

William spots the iron manhole cover and nods. Then he grabs the keys from the front seat and closes the door. The Yukon locks with a high-pitched chirp as he jogs over to help me.

It takes a couple of tries and several grunts, but we manage to team-lift the insanely heavy manhole cover and drop it onto the road. It makes a loud metal clang that vibrates through our feet. We kneel and stare down a narrow, dark shaft that looks like a gateway to hell.

For all I know, that might be what it is.

CHAPTER 34

Rats. I hate rats more than Indiana Jones hates snakes. After climbing at least fifty feet down an old, rusty iron ladder hugging the side of the dark shaft, I drop the five feet from the last rung to the concrete floor of a warm, stinky, hallway-like space, where no fewer than two dozen brown rats emit awful high-pitched screeches as they scatter down the hall before disappearing into blackness. My skin crawls at the sight of the filthy rodents.

William jumps down from the ladder right after me and surveys our new surroundings.

"It's dark," he says.

"And dank and dirty and pungent and hellishly hot and at least ten other adjectives I could throw in." I scrunch my nose and wipe sweat from my brow. "This doesn't look like a sewer." I inspect the cinder-block walls and the exposed, leaky pipes and old wiring above us. "It's like some sort of maintenance tunnel. Maybe it connects to all the towers."

I look in both directions, but it's too dark to see either end of the hallway.

"Working phones would come in handy right now," William says.

"Agreed," I say. "Listen, I know you can't help me down here, but if you see any rats, feel free to kill them, because I hate rats, William. I'll take a fight with a demon over one with a rat any day of the week."

"Deal."

Blade begins moving against the small of my back like a vibrating phone. I reach for the knife. The handle seals into my palm and urges me forward in the direction the rats went.

"This way," I say, moving quickly but groaning at the thought of more rats. "Stay close."

"How do you know the way?"

"I don't. The knife does."

Walking down the hallway, I hear countless rats heckling us with their disgusting sounds, but I don't actually see or feel any of the horrific animals. We travel maybe a hundred feet before coming across a pair of closed metal doors to our right. The darkness is nearly pitchblack, but a thin band of faint light shows in the narrow gap between the doors and the floor.

William hasn't said a word since asking me how I knew the way, so I reach back to make sure he's still with me. He is.

I place my palm on the door.

"Ouch!" I yank my hand away and rub my sizzling palm against my thigh. "These doors are boiling."

"Listen to me, Alix," William whispers, sounding scared and nervous. "You need to be very careful from this point forward. Do you understand me?"

"What are you talking about?" He doesn't answer. "Do you know this place?"

"Yes," he says. "I couldn't tell you about it, but now I can because you've found it on your own. Be careful, okay?"

"Is it the portal?" I ask. His nod confirms it. "Are you coming in?"

"I have to."

"Why?"

"You'll see." He stares at his feet. "Open the doors."

Something's not right with William. I sense a strong wave of regret coming from him, but maybe I'm simply picking up on how devastated he is about Aruna.

Despite the intense heat coming from behind the doors, Blade wants me to enter the room. When it comes down to it, I *have* to trust Blade, but it crosses my mind that Face originally had the knife, which means it's possible Blade is leading me right where Face wants me.

Face is everywhere.

Perennial is all around you.

Oh God. What if I've been Face's puppet all along?

After a few deep breaths, I pull open the double doors and enter a space the size of a high school classroom. The concrete floor is full of small lighted candles. Hundreds of yellowish blue flames dance several inches above the floor like a swarm of nighttime summer insects. A dark, narrow path leads down the center of the room and ends at the rear wall.

The doors close with two dull clicks. I turn to see William gazing over my shoulder.

"This is where I've been staying, Alix. I'm so sorry, but it was part of the deal. Please believe me that I love you. I never knew Face would do that to Aruna, and I never knew about my . . . child." His brilliant eyes widen with fear. "Here he comes."

I feel increased heat pounding against the back of my neck. When I turn around, a large circular section in the middle of the wall at the end of the path begins slowly moving in a clockwise direction. Blade retreats for the first time, forcing me to take a few steps backwards until I'm nearly pressing against William by the doors.

The rotating circle is the size of a merry-go-round. It spins faster by the second, until it becomes a blur of bright red violently shaking the floor beneath us. The sound is awful, like having one hundred jet engines blasting in your ears, but what scares me most is that I have little power down here. I felt my abilities weakening in the tower, and my energy level has suddenly diminished to almost zero.

At first I figure it's the power of the active portal pounding me down to nothing, but then, as the bright red fades to the same disturbing shade I saw in the demonic eyes of the Heater and Crawler, a realization sends my terror levels skyrocketing: Face *is* everywhere and has been since this began. Face *was* the cat-beast Brawler in my living room. Face *was* the Heater in my bedroom. Face *was* the Crawler in my father's office. And Face *was* the seven Arunas I just destroyed. It's not that Face was too afraid to battle me on his own, as I originally thought. No. He's been battling me on his own the entire time, shape-shifting and testing the extent of my abilities with each fight. Face knows my powers as well as I do, and I've been stupid enough to think I could simply waltz on down to Oval City and destroy a leader demon that's been at this game far longer than I have.

Orange fire bursts from the wide circle and nearly reaches my face. The flames quickly disappear. An eerie silence follows during which a tall, wide, hooded figure in a black robe emerges out of nowhere from the now blackened and charred circular hole in the wall. People can call him Face or any other name they want, but the only word that describes what I'm seeing and feeling is "evil." Pure evil. I have no choice but to play his game. Face knows this. He can read my thoughts just as I can sometimes read his.

The black hood conceals his actual face. His chin lowers toward his chest, Face inhaling and exhaling deeply, each rattling breath sounding like rocks slamming together inside his lungs. The smell of rotten flesh fills the air as he interlinks his gloved hands in front of his chest.

"Hello, Alix," he says in the same low, gravelly voice he used before shape-shifting into the Crawler—a voice that will never fail to turn my skin to gooseflesh. "Nice to see you still have my knife. And you've learned to use it quite well. In fact, you've proven yourself worthy of keeping it . . . under the right conditions, of course."

Blade continues pressing back at me, wanting me to get out of here. Even the knife is terrified of Face.

"If it's *your* knife," I say, trying but failing to sound confident, "then why is *my* name on it?"

"Ah, you deciphered the cuneiform." He takes a few loud, troubling breaths. Each exhale sends a wave of garbage fumes my way. "Alix, you know I can do anything I want to you down here, don't you?" I feel him reading me. "Good," he continues. "You do realize that. So the question is, why are you still alive? Think about it. Why didn't I simply finish choking you to death in your little Perennial mom dream last night? And why am I letting you live right now as opposed to breaking open your skull and sucking your brain right out of it?"

"Shut up, Face," William says from behind me. "She doesn't deserve that, and you know it."

"Indeed," Face says. "Perhaps you're right, William. By the way, how's Aruna?" His sinister laugh prickles my skin. "Look, I did you a favor, my boy. Can you imagine that poor, pathetic girl ever being a mother to anything?" He laughs again. "Get over here, you foolish idiot. I'm about through with you and our so-called deal."

I turn sideways to allow William to pass. He gives me a desperate look and offers me his hand as he approaches. It's nothing more than a brief, gentle squeeze, but the word cloud it delivers convinces me that no matter what happens, William really does love me, and he was somehow double-crossed by Face.

I glare at William, feigning anger and saying, "You told me you made a deal with Fire to be with me. You never said the deal was with Face."

"Alix, he's been lying to you for days," Face says, laughing. "William *led* you to me. That was my requirement for letting him cross over without Vagabond knowing. Think about it. Would you have *ever* come to Oval City without William?" He shakes his head. "No. He's been with you every step of the way. You let a ghost seduce you, and now here you are, powerless in my arena and about to give me what I want."

There's a silence during which I read his thoughts and realize how trapped I actually am.

"You want either me or the knife," I say, trying to suppress a growing and genuine rage. "You want me to join Fire as a warrior and use the knife against Light. That's why you've allowed me to live up until now. I've passed every one of your tests and never gave up the knife when you asked for it as the Brawler and the Crawler. I have no clue how the weapon came into your possession, but I'm committed to the knife because it was made for *me*. I'm even strong enough to fight off your precious little Perennial high." I force a smile. "That one surprised you, I know. So what it comes down to now is that if I refuse to join Fire but try to keep the knife, you'll kill me with ease. But you'll let me walk away if I simply give up the knife, knowing that Vagabond and Light will have nothing to do with me if I voluntarily surrender the weapon to you." I pause. "You've planned well, Face. It's a win-win situation for you."

"Precisely," he says, all business now. "But first, aren't you curious to know what William wanted as part of the crossing-over deal, because I assure you it had nothing to do with loving you." He pauses. "Oh, I'm sorry. Is your little heart breaking for the first time, Alix? That's so sad." He places a gloved hand on William's shoulder. "Tell her the truth for once, idiot."

It's at this point that Face's massive size truly hits me. The demon is twice as wide as William and at least a foot taller. William looks like an elementary school student standing next to a large father wearing an all-too-real Halloween costume.

"I'm sorry, Alix," William says. "Face is right. He let me cross over only if I agreed to lead you to him on his own Fire ground."

"And what did he promise you in return?" I ask.

William closes his eyes and tries to message me, but I feel Face block it.

Then William opens his eyes and says, "I *hate* Vagabond, Alix. You know that. He thinks he's better than everybody and everything." He clears his throat. "Vagabond has used me as a pawn to test your abilities. I'm nothing but a dead, weak drug addict to him. All I wanted was some sort of active role in finding my killer, but he wouldn't allow it. My murder is nothing more than an opportunity for him. He doesn't care who killed me. He just wants to know if you can figure it out and get rid of Perennial, Oval City, and a demon as powerful as Face."

"I'll ask again, William," I say, maintaining a hateful glare. "What did Face promise you in return?"

"He promised me . . ." He clears his throat again. "Face promised me that if I led you to him, he would accept me into the Army of Fire as a demon soldier so that I could help with its goal of destroying Vagabond. That's how much I hate Vagabond, Alix. He had no right to use me like this." William looks away, unable to hold my gaze. "Face never mentioned anything about killing my baby two years ago and making Aruna kill herself today, though. I would have never made the deal if I had known those things."

"No," I say, lowering my head and shaking it slowly. "There's just no way, William." I look up and meet his guilty eyes. "You don't understand. Deep down Vagabond *wants* to help you find peace. Besides, *nobody* can destroy Vagabond, just like *nobody* can destroy Face. Don't you at least understand that much about Fire and Light?"

"Oh come now, Alix," Face says. "If William was stupid enough to make a deal with a demon, what makes you think he can possibly even begin to understand Fire and Light?" His deafening laughter fills me with dread. "I have to go soon, my dear. Have you made your decision yet?"

"Just one more question for William," I say, staring hard at the beautiful ghost I refuse to give up on. "You *knew* Face murdered Mr. Watkins, and deep down you suspected Face murdered you because of the love you and Aruna shared at the time. So, William, how could you *possibly* make a deal with the demon who murdered you and Marc Watkins?"

Face unleashes his loudest laugh yet, his huge body hunching forward and shaking.

"Oh, Alix," Face says. "You might be smart, but I'm afraid you've missed some important things along the way. Marc Watkins created something I wanted and needed in order to possess as many souls as possible, so I did what I had to do to get full control of Perennial. I *ordered* his death because he turned into a weak, paranoid snitch, but I didn't do the deed. And yes, I did cause Aruna's miscarriage two years ago, but Aruna made her own decision to jump from the tower today. I guess I might have driven her to it in some ways, but it's not like I pushed her off or anything." He laughs. "Most importantly, I assure you I had absolutely *nothing* to do with William's murder. William Weed was my top dealer in Oval City for a long time."

"Top *dealer*?" I say, now genuinely furious at William. "You said you were *addicted* to Perennial and got clean. You never told you me you were the top *dealer*. Why, William?"

He has no answer. All William can do is look at me with those guilty eyes and then stare at the ground.

"You see," Face says. "More lies. But I respected William for getting clean. In fact, you and him are the only two people I'm aware of who have beaten Perennial after experiencing it. It never crossed my mind to eliminate William. The Perennial addiction and possession business stayed brisk after he left, and I knew he would never turn against me. He was too afraid of me to ever do anything that stupid." He pauses and finally raises his head, but I still can't see his face. "Somebody else killed William, Alix. It wasn't me. You have my word."

He's telling the truth. Despite all the evil he's committed over the years, Face is telling the truth, I realize.

Baffled, I shake my head and say, "If you merely *ordered* the hit on Mr. Watkins and had nothing to do with William's murder, then who's responsible for their deaths?"

Face groans as if he's frustrated with me. Then he says, "The same person."

"Who?"

I feel Face reading me. He knows the strength of my Light and that I'll never join Fire, even if it means dying in this hellish dungeon at the age of seventeen. I'm sickened by the next message he sends me—to the point that I actually consider dropping the knife and walking out. I can't do that, of course, not when Vagabond, London, William (even with his lies), and Mom are counting on me.

Alix, regardless of what happens here tonight, I will always be everywhere. As long as you work for Light, I will see to it that you and I do battle often, and you don't have the strength, courage, or abilities to defend yourself against the kind of pain I can and will inflict upon you. I will be your top demon, Alix Keener. I'll be watching everything you do. I'll track you like a hellhound day and night until you can't take it anymore and finally give up from agony and exhaustion. You can't handle me forever, Alix. Nobody can.

"That all may be true," I say, choking back fear. "But I need to know who killed William and Mr. Watkins." I swallow hard. "I'm not leaving here until I know."

"Then let the games begin," Face says, followed by a round of hacking laughter. "Give me the knife, and I'll give you the killer's name." He extends a long, glove-covered hand toward me. "The knife, please."

Blade pushes back against me with extreme force and nearly knocks me off balance. William is looking at me again and desperately trying to message me, but Face is too strong and easily blocks everything.

"How do I know I can trust you?" I say, considering the offer. "After all, look what you've done to William. You obviously have no plans of making him a Fire warrior."

"That's because William's an idiot," he says, growing impatient now. "You're not. I respect you, Alix. Therefore, you have my word. Give me the knife and I'll tell you who killed William and Marc Watkins. Then you can walk out of here unharmed and run to your big bad cop daddy."

"Okay," I say, wanting to trust Face and at least catch a killer. In the end, that's why I decide to surrender the knife. Even if Vagabond denies me acceptance as a demon slayer for Light and a member of the Group, I'll still catch a killer and help bring closure to the friends and family of William and Mr. Watkins.

"Here's the knife, Face," I say, bringing Blade up from my side in an underhand motion, ready to toss the weapon. "Catch."

That's when William spits out "Alix, no! It's a trick!"

"Idiot!" Face yells. He snaps a finger and turns his hooded head as a thick purple cloud of dust—Perennial—surrounds William and knocks him unconscious to the floor.

At the same time, the word cloud William sent me when we last touched returns:

DEMONS FEAR LOVE. I'M NOT PERFECT, BUT I LOVE YOU, ALIX.
USE THE LOVE.

Face screams with rage as I message him the word cloud while simultaneously putting all my strength into my right hand and releasing Blade in one swift and powerful motion. Distracted by the word cloud, Face wraps his hands around the sides of his hood as if he has a headache and never sees the brilliant silver knife rocketing toward his head.

Blade enters Face's left eye with the speed of a missile. The velocity of the blow jolts Face's head backwards, causing his hood to fall off. When he brings his head up, I get a momentary view of his actual face and understand why he's always concealed it. Behind the fountain of yellow demon ooze exploding from his left eye socket, I see a bloodred face and a hideously deformed, hairless head full of leaking blisters and grotesque purple lumps. His right eye is a dull shade of red that grows dimmer by the second, like an old lightbulb about to burn out. His pre-Fire heat builds, and I watch in horror as his awful red head begins melting like candle wax.

Between his angry screams, he manages to speak two final sentences: "Perennial is all around you, Alix. It always has been."

Blade rockets out of Face's destroyed eye, reversing its original path and landing securely in my right hand. White light suddenly explodes in my head and drops me to one knee. I see an image of the four Oval City towers burning uncontrollably and know the entire complex is about to explode. When I open my eyes, Face is stumbling toward the back wall, and William still lies motionless on the ground.

That's when the room begins shaking like there's a violent earthquake.

"William!" I stand and launch myself toward him. I smother him with my body as Face explodes into an orange, red, and blue fireball that flares brilliantly throughout the room before disappearing into the back wall. And through it all, Face manages to send me a final message—one that is so terrifyingly unbelievable, all I can do is scream as the entire Oval City complex begins to self-destruct.

CHAPTER 35

I'm kneeling beside William and shaking him, but he won't respond. He's lying on his side. The candles have all gone out, leaving us in a dark room trembling with great force. I'm not sure how much of Face's Perennial cloud William inhaled, but the thought that he's overdosed fills my mind.

Along with that unbelievable message Face sent me.

There's no way. It's just some sort of final cruel joke of his.

"William?" I say. "Wake up, William. Come on. We don't have much time."

Oval City shakes at its foundations, and I'm knocked sideways. Ancient dust starts falling from the ceiling. I figure we're goners if we're not aboveground and off Oval City soil in less than five minutes.

"William!" I shake him again. He groans and rolls onto his back. "Yes. That's it! Wake up. We need to get out of here. The place is self-destructing. You've beaten Perennial before, which means you can do it again."

"Alix?" He opens his eyes and looks at me. "Why? After everything I've done, why are you still helping me?"

"There's no time to talk." I take his hands and squeeze. "Can you move on your own?"

"I . . ." He closes his eyes and nods slowly. "I think so."

A violent tremor, followed by awful cracking sounds, brings William quickly to his feet.

"The walls," I say. "They're caving in."

"My head feels like it's caving in. Where's Face? Did he hurt you?"

"Face is gone, William. And so are we if we don't get out of here right now. Are you sure you're okay?"

"Yeah," he says. "Dizzy, but I think I'm good. Did Face tell you who killed me?"

"Just follow me," I say, ignoring the question. "It's almost over."

I take his hand and lead us out of a room that's moments away from sinking down to God knows where.

∞

, a stifling, hellish heat greets us the moment we climb out of the underground shaft and step back on Brewster Loop. The ground continues to shake. We hear the faint wail of sirens in the distance. William and I are exhausted and covered in dust, but we somehow manage to muster the strength needed to drag the manhole cover back over the opening, hiding any hint of us having been down there.

"The police will be here any minute," I say. "Can you drive?"

"Always."

Brewster Loop shakes angrily, forcing us both to keep a hand on the side of the Yukon for balance. Once inside, we slam our doors closed. Then William starts the engine, executes a tire-squawking U-turn, and heads straight for the exit.

"Hurry, William!"

"The road!" he yells. "It feels like it's sinking!"

"Just get out of here and we'll be fine!"

"Oh my God," he says, staring wide-eyed into the rearview mirror when we're one hundred feet from Alfred Street. "Alix, look."

What sounds like the world's loudest thunderclap makes me flinch and scream. I glance over my shoulder and see Aruna's tiny, blanket-covered body. Then I look above her and out the rear window. The four Oval City towers are collapsing, sending an enormous cloud of purple, gray, and black skyward that forms what looks like a multicolored dome-shaped smokescreen over the ruins of Oval City. What scares me even more is the sight of Brewster Loop caving in like a sinkhole twenty feet behind us. The cave-in snakes toward us as if hell-bent on taking the Yukon down with it.

"William, the road," I say. "It's collapsing and chasing us at the same time."

"I see it!" he yells. "Hold on tight, Alix."

Although the right side of my head bangs against the passenger-side window, William somehow manages to keep the Yukon under control and expertly completes a dangerous high-speed right turn onto Alfred Street. I feel all of my wounds heal instantly and my strength and abilities fully returning the moment we leave Brewster Loop. The evil road completely collapses behind us, sending a fresh cloud of purple, gray, and black into the afternoon sky.

The final explosion occurs as we cross over I-75 and turn left onto the northbound service drive. I watch in stunned silence as a fireball the size of a football stadium erupts over Oval City. On the opposite side of the service drive, the first wave of emergency vehicles approaches the fiery scene, but they're too late, and I know that's good. What I wonder is if anybody else sees the thin band of Perennial purple surrounding the fireball.

William is silent as he merges onto I-75. I watch the fire until we're too far away to see it. After one last look at poor Aruna, I turn to William and break into tears.

"Alix, what's wrong?" William says. "You did it. You destroyed Face, Perennial, and Oval City! It's obvious that Face was lying about not killing Mr. Watkins and me. He's the only one who had motives. I don't care what he said about respecting me for beating Perennial; the simple fact is that I was his top dealer and a huge threat to him once I walked away. He wanted me dead. Face killed me, Alix. You passed Vagabond's test."

I pull myself together and stare out the windshield. William is right. Oval City is gone. Face is gone . . . Well, for now anyway. Most importantly, I sense the entire Perennial operation is ruined. A dangerous factory that produced a sinister drug no longer exists. Yes, there's still Perennial out there, but the leader demon is history. No new Perennial will be produced, meaning Face can no longer pursue his goal of using Perennial to possess human souls. Somehow I know this.

But one troubling issue remains.

"It's all one big lie," I whisper.

"I know I've lied to you," William says. "But I love you, Alix, and in the end, I couldn't let Face trick you. His plan was to take the knife and kill you with it."

There's a long silence.

"Take me home, William," I say calmly. "There's something I need to know."

William nods and speeds toward Beaconsfield. Police and emergency vehicles speed past in the southbound lanes, their sirens screaming. I reach around to the small of my back and feel Blade securely inside the sheath. Then I put my face in my hands and think hard about my past, present, and future.

∞

Dad isn't home. William and I stand in my father's office. I'm back in my jeans and Detroit Tigers sweatshirt, staring at Dad's large safe and thinking back to my battle with Face as the Crawler. Face wanted something from this room besides Blade and my soul. He wanted something inside Dad's safe. I sensed it.

"I know the combination," I say. "I've never had to use it, but I know it. My mom told me when I was a little girl." I pause. "Dad has no idea."

William and I stare at each other. I know he loves me. And as crazy as it might sound, I love him and always will. Yes, he's told many lies, and I'm smart enough to realize I'll never fully trust him, but in the end he redeemed himself in the underground portal room. William more than likely saved my life. I was ready to give up Blade and trust a demon. Technically, William has about nine hours left before his energy disappears and he's gone from my life forever, but something tells me he'll have to vanish much earlier than midnight.

I take a deep breath, crouch in front of the safe, and spin the dial, stopping it on the six numbers that match the month, date, and last two digits of the year I was born. I turn the steel handle clockwise. The safe door opens toward me with a loud click.

Inside I find countless neatly arranged stacks of hundred-dollar bills in ten-thousand-dollar bundles.

Dad has millions in here.

I move a few bricks of cash aside and see numerous clear bags full of the evil purple powder that has changed my life forever. Perennial. The only other item in the safe is a sheet of yellow paper, folded in half. I unfold it and find myself staring at a list of ingredients. The recipe has no title. It doesn't need one.

Tears streaming down my face, I take out my phone and dial 911.

And that's when I hear Dad barge into the house, calling my name and demanding that I come see him immediately.

I wipe my face and stand. Blade is motionless and secure in the sheath. The demon slaying might be over for now, but the human danger hasn't passed yet.

"Stay in here, William," I say, giving his hand a squeeze as I pass him and head for the closet. "This is between my dad and me."

I grab the emergency gun in the top corner of the office closet, the one and only gun Dad has taught me how to clean and use. The irony, of course, is that I'm taking the weapon because I'm afraid of him.

∞

He's waiting for me in the middle of the living room, halfway between the foyer and the kitchen. Clint Keener looks pale and unstable. His eyes constantly dart around the room as if he senses a trap. There are some people you can never really know at all, no matter how well you think you do. My dad is one of them. That's what I'm thinking as I stare across the room at him, both hands behind my back, one gripping the gun, the other balled into a tight fist.

"Alix, why did you miss school today?" he asks quietly. "And whose Yukon is parked in our driveway?"

There's a long silence.

"I know about you, Dad." A warm tear trickles down my face. "I know everything."

He nods but doesn't say anything, just scratches his unsightly beard and stares hard at me.

Finally, he says, "And what is it that you think you know, honey?"

"Mom didn't know for sure, but she suspected, didn't she?" I pause. "It's been going on for years. That's why she gave me the combination to the safe."

He looks more distraught now. I tighten my grip on the gun.

"Did you look in my safe, Alix?"

"You killed William Weed and Mr. Watkins, didn't you?" I start crying but manage to stop. "You're a dirty cop, Dad. You work for Face, but you want the whole thing to yourself. There was never any insurance money, was there? It's all Perennial drug money."

"Alix, listen to me." He raises his arms in a calming gesture. "Everything in that safe is related to an undercover Perennial investigation. You're getting emotional and making up crazy stories. I'll explain everything, but you need to breathe and relax, honey. Be a master of your actions as opposed to a prisoner of your re—"

"I am a master of my actions!" I yell. "You have no idea what I can do. I'm different, okay? I can see things other people can't. I'm a two-way psychic, Dad. How do you like that? Even the government is interested in me. So don't lie to me, okay? I'm *sick* of people lying to me. Face is gone! Perennial is gone! It's over!" I choke back more tears. "How could you do this?"

"Alix, did you have anything to do with what just happened in Oval City?"

"Do you know who Face really is?"

"I'm not sure what you mean by that, Alix. And I'm not sure how and why you even know about Face. But I'll tell you who Face is. Face is a freak. He's a drug kingpin who likes wearing things over his head to hide his identity and intimidate people. Problem is I'm not somebody who's easily intimidated." He keeps glancing at my waist, surely wondering what my hands are doing behind my back. "You just said he's gone. What did you mean by that?"

Blade's lack of movement confirms that my father knows nothing about Fire and Light. To him, Face is exactly what he just said—a freaky drug dealer.

"I meant that Face is gone forever from your life," I say. "But he sent me a message before he left." I swallow hard. "Face asked me how well I really know my father." Dad doesn't respond. "Marc Watkins was the creator of Perennial and the main maker of the drug. You killed Mr. Watkins at Face's request because you were Face's partner in Perennial, and Mr. Watkins was in the process of exposing everything, especially *you*. You have the Perennial recipe in your safe. You know how to make the drug, so getting rid of its creator was no big loss." Dad closes his eyes for a few moments and then opens them.

His vacant stare chills my bones. "Two years ago you killed William Weed in this house because William was the top Perennial dealer and decided to quit the drug business. Face was okay with William leaving, but you weren't. You killed William and made it look like a suicide, and I'm guessing you snatched this house up once you had enough cash to move us here. I mean, no Beaconsfield cops would ever think to come sniffing around the house of the almighty Clint Keener. As long as you own the house, you own the crime scene of the murder you committed." I hear the faint sound of something clicking outside and pause, but my unstable father shows no sign of having heard it too. "I think what you ultimately wanted was to get rid of Face, but he always ended up being stronger and smarter than you, didn't he?"

"You shut up!" he yells, forcing me to take a step back. "Goddamn you, Alix. Everything was for you. Don't you get it? All of this is for you. I want you to have the future you deserve."

"Oh my God, it's all true." Tears stream down my face. "Why, Dad? Why? How could you do these things? It goes against everything you and Mom taught me about how to succeed in the world. You're like some kind of monster I don't even know."

"Alix, stop it," he says. "I need you to listen. If what you're saying is true and Face is gone, then we can keep all of this between us and get far away from Beaconsfield. Nobody needs to know. There's enough money in that safe to keep us comfortable for the rest of our lives."

"No," I say, shaking my head. "Don't even try that. Please. Just stop."

Dad is about to say something, but then he looks over my right shoulder, and his eyes bulge like basketballs.

"Hi, Mr. Keener," William says, entering from the hallway and standing near the entrance to the kitchen. "We never met officially, but I'm sure you remember me."

"What the . . . ?" Dad squints. "Who are you, and what are you doing in my house?"

"You know who I am," William says. "If not, maybe this will help." He rolls up his sleeves to show his dragon tattoos. "I was fond of baseball hats and sunglasses when you knew me." He gives me a look. "So tell me, Mr. Keener: What does it feel like to be a cold-blooded killer?"

"William?" Dad says, suddenly pale and confused as he stares at the tattoos. "No," he whispers, shaking his head. "It can't be. I killed you."

It happens too fast for me to stop it. Dad draws a gun from the small of his back. I scream as he fires two shots at William. The sound blasts through my ears, but what shocks me most is that William doesn't even flinch. The bullets pass right through him and lodge into the plaster wall.

William smiles. "You can't kill me again, Mr. Keener. I'm already dead."

"Stop it, Dad!" I bring my gun around and aim it at my father just as he's about to squeeze off another shot. "Drop the gun, Dad. Please, drop the gun."

My father looks at me for a moment, stunned. Then he lowers his gun and stares at William in disbelief.

"What's happening?" Dad says.

William turns to me and says, "Congratulations, Alix. You passed." Then he smiles at me with those perfect teeth and stares at me with those aqua-green eyes. "I love you. Good-bye."

He's leaving for good.

"William, no!" I say. "Not yet!"

The front door crashes inward and flies off its hinges into the living room. Four bodies enter the house in a blur. When I look back for William, he's gone—vanished without a trace.

Then chaos.

A female voice: "Alix, drop the gun!"

Dizzy and in shock, I look away from the kitchen and see London Steel staring at me from a few feet away. She has no weapon that I can see, but the government man and woman from the Group have their guns drawn and aimed at Dad, the two agents saying things about what Dad is being charged with. The fourth person surprises me. It's Mr. Dobbins, the big guy who took over for Mr. Watkins, but the sight of a gun in his hand convinces me he's not actually a substitute teacher at all.

I drop the gun and fall to my knees. My father drops to his knees but doesn't drop his weapon. We're staring at each other, father and daughter. Less than ten feet separates us. The room is silent.

"Why, Dad?" I ask one last time. "Why?"

"I'm sorry, Alix," he says. "I have nothing left."

He's bringing his gun up toward his open mouth when another loud blast fills my ears and makes me scream. Dad's gun flies out of his hand and lands on the other side of the room. Three people pile onto my father and subdue him.

I'm wailing and crying. The room is spinning. The last thing I see is London Steel opening her arms and wrapping them around me. The last thing I *hear* is her voice close against my ear. "Let it out. Let it *all* out. It's all over now, Alix. It's all over."

Then I drift into silent blackness.

CHAPTER 36

The next thing I know, I'm moving through an endless sea of cottony white nearly identical to the one that started all of this only four days ago. The only difference is the presence. William is gone, but Vagabond has kept his promise. My mother is here.

I come to a sudden stop. The cloudy white gives way to clear, crisp white light. I'm barefoot and wearing the same white summer dress I wore in the nightmare, but this time there isn't a speck of purple in sight. This is no nightmare. I know it the moment she appears in front of me. Martha Keener wears a white dress identical to my own. She's barefoot too, her long, dark hair combed straight back over her delicate shoulders.

Words aren't necessary. We simply smile and then cry as we embrace. I feel her cool skin for the first time in more than a year.

"I'm so sorry, baby," she says, kissing my cheek. "But I'm here right now and this is real. You need to stay strong for me, Alix. Can you do that, honey?"

"I think so." I dry my eyes and hold her hands. "It's just so awful, Mom. I've lost you, and now I've lost Dad. You knew he was doing bad things, didn't you? That's why you gave me the combination all those years ago."

"I suspected he was hiding things, but I never dreamed it was as serious as it was." She gives my hands a good squeeze. "You did the right thing, Alix. Never second-guess yourself."

"It's so hard," I say. "Knowing your own father could do such horrible things. I always thought of him as a perfect king."

"For a long time he was."

She gives me a look that makes it clear our time together is short.

"I don't know what to do now, Mom."

"That's part of the reason Vagabond allowed us to meet," she says. "Alix, you've been given rare gifts that can help keep people safe. By destroying Perennial, you've already saved countless lives. You're seventeen and have your whole life ahead of you. You're destined to slay demons and all the evil they bring for a long time to come." She smiles. "I mean, how cool is that?"

"I guess," I say, allowing myself a quick laugh.

"Join the Group, Alix." Mom pauses. "The Group needs you. We *all* need you. Your father's actions will haunt you for as long as you live. There's nothing I can do about that. My advice is to always use your Light to guide you."

I nod. "You're leaving now, aren't you?"

"I am."

"Will I see you again?"

"That depends on Vagabond." She smiles. "I think he has a thing for me. Maybe I can pull some strings for us."

We smile and then cry as we share a final hug.

"I love you, Mom."

"I love you too, Alix." Still hugging me, she says, "Actually, I've already pulled a string for you."

"Huh?"

"Look."

Mom is gone. Just like that. Vanished. I'm alone again, standing in the cottony version of the white light, expecting to awaken at any moment.

And that's when William Weed emerges from the cloudy white and stands directly in front of me. I can't help myself. The incredible hair, face, eyes, and body are too much for me. I should be pissed at him, but how can you be pissed at something so wonderful?

"Just one question," I say. "Did you know about my dad when you were alive?"

"No. I had no idea who he was. But he obviously knew all about me."

"Are you lying right now?" I say. "Because you've been known to tell a lie or two."

"I'm not lying."

"I know," I say, allowing a slight smile to cross my face.

We stare at each other.

"Vagabond's not so bad after all," William says. "I can't believe he allowed this."

"He likes my mom."

"I see." He pauses. "It's time for our last kiss, Alix."

"Then we better make it the best one ever."

"I love you, Alix Keener."

"I know you do." My smile widens as he places his palms on either side of my face and leans toward me. "I love you too, William Weed. I better get to see you again sometime soon."

The kiss we share makes me feel like a bomb ready to explode.

∞

The voice makes William disappear, leaving me alone again in the white light, but I feel it slipping away. Yes. The white is definitely fading to black.

"Alix? Alix, wake up. It's time."

I open my eyes. London Steel is standing beside my bed. She hands me my glasses. I slide them on, not knowing how I got here. At first I'm thrilled, thinking about my encounter with Mom and my surprise last kiss with William, but then I remember everything that happened with Dad.

"What time is it?" I ask, sitting up in bed and squinting from the brilliant sunlight slicing in through the window.

"It's seven o'clock," she says. "Saturday morning." She squeezes my hand. "Let's go. The car is waiting. Don't worry about a shower." She smiles. "You'll see what I mean when you get there. For now, I'll just say that demon slaying has its perks."

London leads me out of my bedroom and downstairs. I close my eyes as we pass through the living room, not wanting to relive anything that happened the night before.

Mr. Dobbins stands in front of the passenger-side door of the dark US government sedan. The windows are rolled up, but I know the same man and woman from last night are in the front seat.

"Where's the Yukon?" I ask. "Aruna's body was in the—"

"It's okay, Alix," London says. "Everything's been taken care of. Aruna is in a much better place now."

I nod. "Are you coming with me?"

"Of course." She puts an arm around me. "Remember the last thing I said to you when we first met?" She doesn't give me time to answer. "I said we'd see each other soon under very different circumstances." She shrugs. "Well, here we are. We're partners now, Alix."

"I'm glad," I say, stopping in front of Mr. Dobbins. "Give me your hand," I say to him.

He gives London a look.

"It's okay," she says. "You know Alix has the skills."

He gives me his large, meaty hand. White light floods my head. I welcome it and smile.

Moments later, I open my eyes and say, "Your real name is Harrison Foster. You were the guy who grabbed me and shoved me in that custodial closet on Tuesday. You also planned the car accident that gave me a killer case of whiplash. You told me to stay away from Perennial." I pause. "It didn't work, did it?"

"All part of the test, Alix," he says. "We had to see how far you were willing to go. Sorry if I was too rough. I was told to make it as difficult as possible."

"It's okay," I say. "No hard feelings."

The back door opens automatically. London motions for me to get in first. When I climb inside, I'm surprised to see Vagabond sitting on the opposite side, looking fresh and crisp in his perfect dark suit. His shaved head has a healthy glow, and his piercing blue eyes remind me of the fact that he knows far more about the world than I ever will.

"Hello, Alix," he says. "Before you even ask, the answer is yes, I knew all about William crossing over as Lewis. It was a clever move. I have to give him credit. The risk he took shows how much that boy truly loves you." He squeezes my shoulder in an almost fatherly way. "It's time to say good-bye to Beaconsfield and hello to the Group."

London sits beside me. Harrison "Frank Dobbins" Foster closes the door from the outside and walks toward the porch. The female agent gives me a slight nod from the driver's seat. The male agent does the same from the passenger seat. It's quiet as she backs the car out of the driveway and proceeds down Maple Grove.

The silence is welcome.

ABOUT THE AUTHOR

© Lisa Potter

Ryan Potter has had numerous stories and novels published since he began writing in 2003, including the young adult novels *Exit Strategy* and *Roman King and the Armies of Fire and Light*, the adult novel *The Cleaner*, and the story collection *Welcome to Detroit*. He lives in the Detroit area with his wife and enjoys baseball, yoga, and routinely suffering through Detroit Lions games.